6001

ICEWORLD

Invasion of the Torterats

Published in Australia by
South Head Press
ABN 75823432905
P.O. Box 7135
Bondi Beach
N.S.W. Australia 2026

The National Library of Australia Cataloguing-in-Publication entry:

Author: Widerberg, W.R.
Title: 6001 ice world: invasion of the torterats/W.R.Widerberg.
Edition: 1st ed.
ISBN: 9780980809602 (pbk.)
Dewey Number: A823.4

Cover design by Alli Spoor

Text typeset and designed by Mercier Typesetters Pty Ltd, Granville NSW

Printed in Australia by Ligare Pty Ltd, Riverwood NSW

6001

ICEWORLD

Invasion of the Torterats

Book 1 of The Camarilla Chronicle

W. R. Widerberg

To my granddaughters

Natasha

and

Charlotte

The Author

Bill Widerberg grew up in Clovelly in Sydney's eastern suburbs, attending Sydney Boys' High School and the University of Sydney.

6001 ICEWORLD Invasion of the Torterats is his second book. His first, *The Big End of Town*, is an adult thriller that was acclaimed in all media throughout Australia. Widerberg's short story, *Sunday Morning at the Bay*, recently won first prize at the Stroud Writers Festival.

Widerberg has researched extensively. Using his knowledge and his imagination, he has written an engaging, page turning novel. *6001 ICEWORLD Invasion of the Torterats* is Book 1 of a trilogy that shows the reader what life on Earth could become.

Acknowledgements

I am indebted to Cathy Symonds, Children's and Young Adult Librarian at Waverley Library, for her guidance in writing a book to appeal to the young and not so young. To Alan Davidson I express my gratitude for his wise counsel over a number of years. I wish to thank Elizabeth Finniecome and Haylee McGlashan of Ligare for the work they have done in producing the book and for introducing me to Rod Mercier, whom I thank for his advice and assistance in the presentation of 6001 ICEWORLD Invasion of the Torterats. My sincere thanks also go to Alli Spoor for the cover design and to Julee Gould for correcting the errors I failed to see.

Chapter 1

Mangrove tugged at the cords of his hood to tighten them, pulling the fur closer to his face. He slipped the ring made of bone higher, the toggle clamping the cords to prevent their slipping. The hood now almost covered his face. That is what he wanted. The warmth of his body was better retained and there would be no telltale steaming from his breath to give his position away. He lay still again and scanned the snow, looking for movement.

The day was unusually quiet, with little wind and broken cloud cover through which the sky was startlingly blue. Occasionally the parting of the cloud would let the sun flash and in those quick moments he felt the warmth that was so rare. Mangrove slowly moved his head through more than two hundred degrees of arc, examining the terrain. The bursts of sunlight gave sudden shadow to the hummocks of snow and ice that stretched into the distance, shattering the unending white into shards of dark that as quickly reformed into uniform white. Mangrove breathed deeply, blinking, widening his eyes so that he would miss nothing, but the clouds acted like shutters and the disrhythmic, jerking shadows were unsettling.

He turned to take a quick glance down to the river. Snotty was still hacking at the ice, shielding the site as best he could with his body, trying to reduce the noise of his work. Mangrove held the hood away from one ear and grimaced as he heard the sound of the stone axe smashing at the ice. Sound waves could advertise their presence, but there was no other way. He watched as Snotty knelt to place the warming pot inside the greased skin they had left on the last occasion they had fished. The skin stuffed into the hole was frozen, but it prevented the ice from totally closing, and once thawed a little it could be hauled out. In this way the ice hole could be used repeatedly. They were a long way from home and tempting fate, but they had reopened the hole many times, always with success.

Mangrove turned again to face the north, searching the snow for movement, for any sign of Torterats among the moguls of ice that stuttered from light to shadow.

Like the rats that brought the Black Death and the Great Plague of London in the distant past, the Torterats had multiplied, but food for the Torterats was no more abundant in the north than elsewhere. They were forced to move south and as they came they began to encroach on country that the Camarilla had always regarded as their own.

The Camarilla, the small trusted band, numbered a mere sixty souls. In the year 6001, they were the last remnant of humanity on earth. They lived in a frozen world, striving to survive in the era of ice that had gripped the planet following the global warming and the wars of the twenty-first century. For the Camarilla, finding food had never been easy. With the arrival of the Torterats the crisis became severe, because they came in numbers, eating what they could find, attacking the humans and driving them further south.

At the river, Snotty felt the tap-tap on the line as the fish tasted the bait. He jerked the line and smiled in satisfaction as it went taut, the hook home hard. The fish was big and fought, zigzagging below the ice, straining the line. Snotty pulled, leaning back from the ice-hole, the line slicing a groove into his gloves as he hauled the fish upward and finally lifted it from the hole. He dragged it clear and taking his flint knife from its scabbard slit the fish below the gills. The blood ran red on the snow. He let it run until it stopped and then gathered the bloodied snow and put it into the hole, watching it melt and swirl away.

"Good," he said. Blood in the water would attract more fish. He baited the hook and dropped the line into the ragged circle of water once more. Again he felt the tug and again he landed the fish.

Mangrove looked back at the fish lying silver in the snow and experienced the mix of feelings that always came. The fish were welcome, they would feed the clan, but even though Snotty had got rid of the reddened snow, the Torterats had an excellent sense of smell. The blood could betray them. Mangrove returned to his task, scanning the lumpy outcrops, looking for danger in the appearing, disappearing shadows. He was edgy. So far the breeze had blown from the north. If Torterats were about, he and Snotty would be down-wind of them, but he could feel the wind fading. What had been a fairly safe situation might not be so for long. The cloud was thickening and that would help. It put an end to the coming, going shadows, but the increasing cloud cover indicated a change in the weather.

Life is getting tougher, he thought. The challenge of overcoming hunger had always been difficult. Hunger and cold were bad, but now the thieving Torterats could leave them empty-handed after hours of hard, risky work.

Mangrove turned again. The expedition was progressing well. There were now four fish going solid as they froze in the snow. Perhaps they should go. As he looked, he felt the faint stirring of air as the fur on his hood brushed lightly at his cheeks. The new front was building from the south. If he and Snotty had to run, had to get out in a hurry, the fish would be a heavy burden. Worse, the wind would now be in their faces, slowing them even more. Mangrove slid the toggle on the cords of his hood, puckered his tongue and gave a short sharp whistle. Snotty looked up from the ice-hole and, as Mangrove gave the signal that they should head home, he raised his gloved hand and with a finger indicated just one more fish. Mangrove shook his head, but Snotty ignored the caution, once more concentrating on his line — five fish would be little enough for the Camarilla.

Mangrove peered into the distance. The sky had darkened to a foggy blanket that hung low over the snow and in the diminished light there were no outlines visible. He could see no ice humps, no distinguishing features of any sort. As he had feared, the wind was picking up and the smell of the fish and their own presence would travel north. He glanced toward the river and had to search to find Snotty, the light had become so bad.

Mangrove whistled again, two short, sharp blasts — get ready to go. He bent forward, straining to see movement, one last check that there was no enemy approaching. His head turned slowly, his eyes narrowed against the poor light, trying to find form in the white oblivion. "Nothing, nothing," he murmured, continuing his search. "No, we're sweet." Even as he was mouthing the words, the lunge of a body and then another triggered fear that flooded him with urgency. Mangrove tried to sharpen focus on the opaque area, finding it difficult to estimate the distance to the movement, trying to tell whether it was a random foray, or whether the scent of the fish was attracting attention. Of one thing he was absolutely certain. What he had seen was the characteristic movement of Torterats. They always travelled close, touching each other, sometimes one running over the back of another, all the time communicating in their high-pitched squeaking, their voices out of keeping with the size of their bodies and the rough fur of their coats.

"Yes," he spoke aloud. He could make them out. A sizeable phalanx, each Torterat the size of a small dog, jostling in excitement to get to the source of the scent, overrunning one another, always a new front-runner immediately replaced by one more eager. *Trats and they're onto us.*

He turned away to shout toward the river. "Snotty, Trats coming. We gotta go." As he spoke he was bending, forcing his leather boots hard on his skis, fixing the bindings. Still in a crouch, completing the ties, he shushed down the slope, the tracks of the skis streaming behind. He knew that the low-hanging cloud and the poor light would not be enough. The tracks of the skis would last until the wind or fresh snow wiped them away. He might as well leave arrows to point the way for the Trats.

"How far off?" Snotty was moving quickly, shoving the frozen fish into the backpacks that lay on the ice.

"Close, we haven't got long." Mangrove attempted to jam the skin into the hole in the ice. The skin had stiffened, making it hard to bend. Breathing hard he jack-knifed his body to fold the skin and worked with both hands to mould it roughly to the shape of the hole. It had to be done. They would be back. The site was too good to lose and to rework a hole took hours of effort. He plugged the hole and packed loose snow over it. It would do.

Snotty handed Mangrove one of the packs and humped the other on to his back before he stepped into his skis.

Mangrove frowned at him, waving his free hand at the ice. "Where's the diversion?"

It was foraging practice if attacked. Leave some of the catch, whatever it was. The Torterats would stop to eat. A fish would halt pursuit. If only for a short time, it could be enough to allow escape.

"Leave one, Snotty."

"We can't. We're all starving."

Each imagined the members of the Camarilla waiting for them to return, the pale, pinched faces, hungry, relying on the two most experienced Foragers to bring food.

Mangrove shook his head. They had no time to argue, but not to leave the lure could prevent them gaining time, the time that could mean their survival. If the Trats weren't diverted he and Snotty might not get back and the Camarilla would have nothing.

"They need the whole catch, Manny. We have to risk it."

There was no doubt that every skerrick of food was essential, Mangrove knew that very well. What troubled him was the way Snotty was always prepared to court danger, his double-or-nothing attitude.

Snotty saw the worry on Mangrove's face. "Do you want to feed Trats or the Camarilla?"

Mangrove shook his head in defeat. "You win."

Snotty grinned at him. "Then let's go."

They dug their poles into the snow. Homecave was two day's travel in good weather. In the poor light their progress would be slower.

Silently Mangrove weighed the factors that would assist and the counterweighing elements that could overwhelm them. They needed snow and they needed the night. Darkness would hamper the Torterats, their vision was not great. Snow and the night would hide the tracks of their skis and snow would dull and bury their scent. But nightfall was hours off and though the cloud was low and leaden, snow did not fall.

He did not speak of it, but he knew that the Torterats had the advantage. The dim light made it hard for the skiers. Shape did not exist and their skis rose over unexpected obstacles and dropped where the ground fell invisibly away. Mangrove and Snotty were experienced, but the going was hard and the loads on their backs exaggerated the difficulties of the uneven terrain.

Conversely, the Torterats, low to the ground and close to the tracks, had no difficulty and with the ability to pick up the smell of their quarry, had the upper hand.

Snotty signalled to Mangrove that they should stop. He lifted his head and turned, raising the flap of his hood, listening for the sound of their pursuers. All he heard was the rush of the air and the whistle of its complaint as it hit whatever lay in its path.

"Nothing," he said and they leaned forward into the wind and got going again.

For Snotty it was a good omen. Okay, the Trats would need to be very close before they were heard. If he could hear them, he and Manny were in real trouble, but so far so good. He looked up at the grey fog that hung low all over. "Come on," he murmured. "Give us a big dump."

He was not unhappy with their situation. They had five big fish. The Camarilla would benefit from the oily flesh — upwards of 18 kilograms of meat. *Manny worries too much*, but he knew that while Mangrove's attitude was totally different from his own, that was what made them a good team. Their mix of daring and caution let them pull off hunts that others would not contemplate. *And we'll do it again.*

They began to climb and the rising ground slowed them more. Snotty was not concerned. They had a head start and their skis had probably let them travel faster than the Trats. Now that he and Manny were in the range of hills, once at the crest they would have the further advantage of downhill skiing.

The Foragers were breathing hard. The slope and the weight of the fish and the need to keep moving were tiring them. They were young and accustomed to demands on their bodies, but Mangrove was aware that constant threat had its way of depleting strength. Fear found its way into muscles and their capability leaked away. He sucked cold air into his lungs and pushed down on his poles. He was treading in the herringbone tracks that Snotty was leaving and was thankful that he was not leading.

They reached the top of the ridge and paused, breathing heavily, gulping oxygen for their hearts to slow.

Mangrove twitched and raised a finger, totally alert as his chest heaved. "Snotty," he hissed and motioned toward the way they had just come. Snotty pulled his hood from his ear.

Chapter 2

The Camarilla gathered under the dome of the cave, the common dwelling of all. They were so few and warmth was hard to find. Living together under one roof retained heat.

Queen Avon had been carried to her dais. She raised her hand in greeting, attempting to inspire hope, and to give strength to those looking up at her, but her wave was feeble. Their Queen was dying and everyone knew it.

"I must take the decision," Avon said.

A murmur of dissent rose from the upturned faces, but it was inevitable. The Queen might live for some time yet, but her decision had to be made while she still had the ability to think clearly and to speak her mind. Few as they were, her people had to have a designated leader, one to take the place of the Queen when she was shrouded in the Endless Night.

"My mind is made up and you should hear my reasons."

She looked toward the group of Foragers on her right, the best of the youth, the group on which the Camarilla relied for food. "My successor will be one of the Foragers. That is the tradition and I will continue to follow the ways we have always known."

In case there should be any doubt, Avon stressed the advantages of taking the next leader from among the young. Only they were strong and agile enough to gather food. The young were quick in mind and body, they thought fast and acted fast and they could be presumed to live longer and so give stability and endurance to the leadership.

"I have selected one of our young, one whose maturity is advanced, whose judgement is always based on logic." As she spoke, Avon let her gaze rest on Dram.

The girl — the eldest of the Foragers — smiled and thought of the honour that would be her due as leader. She stood taller than all the other Foragers and her strength was unmatched. As if fate had marked her out, Dram was also the most beautiful. It was natural that she should be chosen.

Avon's eyes moved to Dumperty, the youngest and smallest. Little Dumperty would probably never grow to normal height. The pregnancy of his mother had occurred at a time of exceptional famine and Dumperty would always bear its scars.

The little boy was without the older friends that he revered, beside him a space where Manny and Snotty would normally be. Avon closed her eyes to think of Snotty and inwardly smiled, the boy was so able, so sharing and so committed to providing for them all. He and the brave and careful Mangrove were such a dependable team. Without them, the lives of the trusted band would be very different.

Avon imagined them on their hunt and silently offered a prayer that the two would return safely.

The gathering watched in silence, fearing that their Queen might not be able to go on.

Avon slowly opened her eyes. "When I am gone, the Camarilla will need a leader who questions alternatives, because, I regret to say, we cannot live the way we are for much longer. The difficulties that approach are greater than those we have ever known. To find answers to the pressures that you will suffer will require a very special leader."

The assembled crowd understood what those pressures were. The threat from encroaching Torterats was compounded by geography. Had it been possible for the Camarilla, they might have made their exodus, taken the decision to leave the land they had always known, abandon it to the Torterats and go. This could not happen. To the south was the land of Kaldor.

Avon continued to inspect the line of Foragers. She lingered on Biscetti, so blonde that her hair was almost white and never quite losing the lisp that she had had as a child, Biscetti, whose good nature was a delight to the whole clan, although it was true that when given good reason, she would lose her temper completely. Biscetti was a puzzle. Able to mimic and to mock the foibles of others with a smile on her face, rarely causing offence and yet at times she herself was easily offended. Perhaps one day she would come to lead, but this was not the time. She would serve as an able confidante, someone from whom the leader could seek opinion, certainly before long she would become a mature Forager, but as yet she was too young to wear the mantle of Queen.

Standing next to Biscetti was her sister Tasha.

"Yes," Avon's lips did not move and the word came almost soundlessly in a soft sibilance that only she could hear.

Avon had watched Tasha grow. A happy, inquiring infant who loved to amuse adults and older children with her dancing, Tasha had developed into a thoughtful girl. The intelligence she had shown as a toddler had grown with her stature, so that at fifteen she had the ability to solve problems that baffled most. Whether Tasha had recognised and nurtured her talents, or whether she had been born gifted — her parents' genes providing her with a congenital advantage — Avon could only guess. Whatever it was that gave Tasha her skills did not really matter. That she could compose tunes and keep them in her memory, recalling them to entertain their community gathered at night by the fire in Homecave, was a joy for them all. Tasha was not the only one to play the wooden flute, but she was the master composer. Her vocabulary was superior to any but Avon's and Tasha took care in using the right words to explain what she was thinking. Of all the Camarilla she could best visualise distance and space and understood that an untried journey or a new and difficult task needed thought and calculation and that it paid to consult those who could give advice. Tasha possessed the quality of calm, which gave her an untainted view of life and the people around her. She had an even, settled way of dealing with them.

Tired, feeling the pain and the great tiredness that like a tide rose in her body, Avon's lids drooped. A murmur of concern fluttered through the assembly, rose from them to echo on the rock dome of the cave and fill their hearts with despair. From among their number many rushed forward to assist their Queen.

Weakly she waved them away, wanting to give her attention to the Foragers, wanting to be sure that the choice she had to make could never be criticised. The future of them all hung on what she would finally say.

The twins Sola and Situ smiled as Avon looked at them. The look-alike boys were a happy-go-lucky pair who gave little thought to the morrow. Quick and with great athletic ability they were ever ready to use their speed. On the rare occasions when a snow hare or other game was seen, it was either Sola or Situ, sometimes the two together, who on skis would attempt to run down the escaping animal or drive it towards a concealed Dram or Snotty and Mangrove. Whether successful or not, the twins would laugh from the sheer exhilaration of movement. Life for them was a game, but they had no place in Avon's calculations; excluded because in their fun-loving natures, no room could be found for serious thinking. Sola and Situ would never have the patience to weigh the problems that would continue to face the clan. Avon answered their smiles and looked over the remaining Foragers, the lovely Dandle with her long red hair, Kalich and Ulan, boys who were destined to follow orders, never to give them. Although Kalich, with the ability no one could explain, was able to listen to a numerical problem and from his head draw an answer that was always correct. His explanation was that the numbers simply appeared, that he could see them as though they were before his eyes.

Avon's gaze travelled further. Had she known of ancient Rome, the four she examined would have been regarded as simple foot soldiers, ready to do as they were bidden by higher authority. Belle, the ringleader, Zita, Hock and Vellum enjoyed each other's company and usually worked as a group. They pulled their weight, but, like Kalich and Ulan, none had the qualities required for leadership.

Finally she looked at Cloud, the dreamy child, so spindly thin and terribly myopic that to see anything clearly she had to hold it close to her eyes. Strangely, Cloud could then see detail so fine it was invisible to others.

Cloud, on occasions, would appear to be distant, as though in a trance, and emerging from her reverie would speak of things which had happened in places she had not been and of which she should have no knowledge. At times she saw the future, revelations that had come to her as she gazed fixedly at nothing.

For Avon, neither Cloud or Dandle, nor Kalich and Ulan met the standards that the Camarilla would require. The foursome was entirely out of contention. She closed her eyes and wished for sleep, but there remained things that she had to say.

Once more Avon's eyes opened and with effort she tried to look into each of the faces before her. "My decision is made. In fairness, and in keeping with our tradition, all of the Camarilla must be present when I utter the name of my successor. You will learn of it when Snotty and Mangrove have returned."

Exhausted Avon fell back on her couch, but making a final effort before she slept she gave her instruction. "If the two have not returned by the day after tomorrow, we must search for them. Dram, you will take Biscetti and Tasha and find the boys."

Chapter 3

The excited squeaking of Torterats could be heard over the miserable crying of the wind. Snotty peered back the way he and Mangrove had come. Down the slope the herringbone pattern of their skis was visible for twenty metres before the whiteout made it impossible to see further, but the sound of the Trats was becoming increasingly loud.

Snotty turned and lunged forward, pushing hard at his poles, straining to get to speed on the downhill run. "We'd better be quick. They're closing the gap."

Anticipating the move, Mangrove was beside him. That was the way it had to be, skiing in parallel, close so as not to lose sight of the other, making no turns, knees bent with arms tucked to their sides to present the least possible resistance and stocks jutting behind like pennants in the wind. They travelled fast, unable to see what lay ahead in the white world that had no form, continuing to gather speed with the added weight of the fish they carried. The two Foragers were in a wild race, hurtling blind down a steeply canted wall of snow, relying on skill and the resilience of knees to take the shock of moguls that suddenly appeared in their path, rising and dropping, jarring their bodies and draining away their energy.

Behind them their pursuers had already gained the top of the ridge.

Four thousand years of cold had further evolved the Torterats. They did not attempt to use their legs when travelling down mountainsides of snow. They had developed ways and means to reach desired objectives more quickly.

Their fur, long and thick, protected them from the cold, a perfect layer of insulation against the radiation or convection of body heat, but the fur had other properties. As though hinged, when required it would fold sleek to allow the Torterats to make use of gravity and the almost frictionless snow. Like penguins, they lay on the snow with their limbs trailing and sledded down the slope.

The Torterats could not match the speed of the skiers, but the smell of the fish came to them on the wind and the straight tracks of two pairs of skis were under their noses. For them it was only a matter of time. When the fall line became valley and another mountain rose, their quarry would begin again a slow ascent. Then the Torterats knew that they would regain the advantage, letting them get closer and when close enough, to seize the prize.

The stratagems of a foe can never remain unknown. Foragers on earlier hunts had seen the smooth lines on the snow of hillsides that on the flat merged with and became the unmistakeable depressions made by the paws of Trats. It was a simple step of logic to deduce that the marks were made by the same animal.

As they raced in the gloom, Snotty and Mangrove knew that the grey bodies would be skidding in the snow behind them.

With his hand, Snotty signalled. Without speaking they veered to the left, a counter-stratagem designed to confuse.

For three hundred metres, with their speed barely diminished, they cut across the face of the mountain, a long traverse that took them out of the path of the Torterats.

So close to the snow, without advance notice of the change of direction, unable to stop quickly, the Trats overshot the ski tracks and with their prey no longer directly upwind, lost the scent. In bewilderment they swung legs to brake their progress and tumbled in flurries of snow and a jumble of furry bodies. From the throat of every Torterat, from open mouths that showed their long and pointed teeth, came a screech driven by hunger and sharpened by rage.

The frozen air filled with the high-pitched screams of frustration, but not for long. Fanning out, they used their numbers to search the slope, seeking to find which way the Foragers had gone. Ten minutes passed before the stripes engraved by the hurtling skis were rediscovered.

In that time Mangrove and Snotty had gained distance, but the terrain was now against them. They were climbing again, breathing heavily, their flight slowed to an arduous plodding in the snow.

Mangrove looked up at the cloud. It was thinning, the light improving. "We've got no hope of snowfall." His words came short and separated as he gasped for breath.

"No." Snotty looked back for a sight of Torterats. He could see them hurrying, the moving, ever-changing pattern of fur crossing the white mantle of snow, getting closer. "Sorry, Manny. I don't think we'll make it."

Mangrove shrugged. "It's too late to use the fish lure trick." The steam of his breath fogged the air as he struggled to speak. "The Trats will want the lot. They've found the scent again and in this light they can see us. They'll follow us until they get the whole catch."

He didn't say so, but in his mind was the thought that it would not only be the fish; he and Snotty would become part of the catch.

In all the skirmishes that had occurred in the past, as Camarilla and Torterats vied for the little food available, no direct contact had ever been made. Foragers had been able to outfox the Trats, adopting the tactics of caution, setting an advanced sentry to constantly observe the frozen land while a partner hunted, and running well before danger truly threatened. For survival, the Foragers had relied on fast reaction, a quick get in and get out. What might happen should one of them be caught had never been contemplated.

The slope steepened and the going became tougher. Both Foragers strained to keep climbing, heads down, grunting with the effort. From below they could hear the yipping of Torterats, the rising squeals of excitement as the distance closed.

His shoulders rolling as he planted his poles, legs lifting to stamp the mark of herringbones on the snow, Snotty raised his head to gauge how much further it was to the summit, how much further before they could again outdistance their pursuers by shushing downhill.

The sounds from behind gave him the answer. He and Mangrove would not make it to the top before they were overrun.

He held out his arm. There was no need to explain why they should stop. Snotty and Mangrove shucked off their packs and turned to face the Torterats now leaping at them through the snow.

"Use your poles, Manny. Use them as spears or as clubs. It's life or death. We won't be breaking the code."

Manny nodded. He and Snotty had sometimes talked about death, how they would feel when the time came. They were agreed. Dying did not trouble them, it was the Endless Night that would follow, the boredom of the eternity of black emptiness, of being alone, companionless with nothing to do and nothing to amuse. He sniffed, a quick, short sound that was not so much for the intake of air to his lungs, but to clear his mind, a sniff that came as a punctuation mark, a full-stop to the life he had known, a marker that separated the past from what was about to occur in the next few minutes. Gazing down the hill with eyes wide, Mangrove prepared for death. In his mind that time was now approaching.

At his side, Snotty stood defiant, holding a stock like a pikeman from mediaeval times. He knew nothing of ancient warfare and had no idea of the similarity, but the Camarilla — despite their superior intelligence and despite the tenets they held that harm should be done to none, with food the only reason for killing — were part of the animal kingdom, born with the instinct to defend themselves. Snotty, like Mangrove, knew that he would soon go down and would never rise, but he would go down fighting and those who would take his life would pay dearly for it. In a sudden flash he felt a thrill of satisfaction that some of his killers would also die, that he would enjoy this one last triumph. Inseparable with that thought was the realisation that as his life approached its end, this was the first time he had experienced such a feeling, an urge contrary to the teachings he had learned from birth. He dismissed the notion of remorse. If he and Manny were to enter the Endless Night, he would send as many of their enemy as possible to the same blank eternity.

They watched the Torterats coming at them up the slope, awkwardly jumping in the deep snow, but advancing surprisingly quickly.

A high-pitched chattering came across the frozen space. Sounds that varied, giving the impression that communication of tactics was occurring and, as if to give credence to this possibility, the undisciplined, scrambling phalanx of Torterats began to spread into a new formation.

"Snotty, the Trats are talking to each other."

"You can't call that racket talking."

But the Torterats did seem to be making an encircling manoeuvre, as though the actions they took were guided by a system of command and response. In the way that the Zulu, millennia in the past, had swarmed through Africa defeating their enemies, the Torterats, on either side of their main attacking body, were forming the horns of the buffalo, the pincers that would envelop the two Foragers.

"Talking or not, whatever you call it, they *are* working to a plan. Look." Manny pointed with his stock at the developing semi-circle. "They're enclosing us. They'll be able to attack us from the front and from behind."

Snotty watched the continuing manoeuvre and he knew that Mangrove was only half right. They would be vulnerable from all sides. The Torterats were preparing an attack against which defence was impossible. He and Manny would put up a fight, they might delay the final outcome, but their lives were drawing to an end.

He tried to estimate how long they might have before it was all over and reckoned on minutes, no longer.

Turning, he faced Mangrove. "I'm sorry, Manny. We should have left when you first saw sign of the Trats. I should have listened to you." He sighed. "It's been great knowing you."

Mangrove placed his arms around Snotty and hugged him. "You're the best friend I ever had."

They smiled at each other and took guard, back-to-back so that with a turn of the head, each could see one hundred and eighty degrees, an arc that covered the snowy slope above and below them. Together they had a complete view. There would be no surprises. When death came, they would watch its arrival.

"Let's give 'em hell before they take us down."

Even in the grimness of the situation, Mangrove had to grin. That was Snotty: full of fire. He gripped his stock with both hands. Whether he thrust or clubbed, two hands would make the blow stronger. The hope slipped like a shadow across his mind that his life would end before Snotty's. To have as his last conscious moment the sight of his friend dying was not what he wanted.

The Torterats were close now. The odour of their bodies — heated from the exertion of the chase and the excitement of being so close to their quarry — came strongly on the wind, a pungent, unpleasant smell. Involuntarily, the Foragers flinched and with faces distorted, tried to pull back in escape from the tainted air.

The Torterats saw the movement and interpreting it as a sign of weakness began a concerted squealing. The horns of the buffalo were now joined; the encirclement complete.

A single, loud cry pierced the chill of the air, hung like an icicle and then shattered as the Torterats, screeching in unison, rushed at Mangrove and Snotty.

The Foragers brandished their stocks, challenged the enemy as though the ski poles were muskets with bayonets attached. And as they made their threatening feints the cries of the Torterats rose in crescendo.

"Goodbye, Manny."

"See you," he replied, thinking as the words left his mouth how silly it was to make the normal, expected response. He would never see Snotty again.

The Torterats came at them, shrinking the space until those that the Foragers faced were just a metre distant. Close up the ugliness of the animals was frightening. Their bulky bodies stood higher than the Foragers' knees. With lips drawn back, the rat features were contorted with hate. Bared teeth foamed with spittle that fell to fleck thick Torterat fur. Snotty lunged at the nearest, grunting advice to Manny so that he too made the same jabs.

The Torterats moved back, luring the Foragers to follow up the advantage. Wanting to slay before he was slain, Snotty in anger took a step forward and made another thrust. As if expecting the move, as though they had been waiting for the pair to be parted, the Torterats from above charged in a flank attack that knocked the two from their feet. In a flurry of snow and ski poles and tumbling bodies, the avalanche gathered pace, rolling and sliding down the slope. The circle of Torterats below broke ranks, parting to allow the confused, smothering mass to pass and as it did, more threw themselves at what they believed were the Foragers, adding weight to the jumble of snow and Torterat and Forager and fish that slid from backpacks, all intermittently appearing in the huge snowball as it crashed down the mountain. Driven by the momentum and force of the avalanche, the snow in its path exploded into powder and rose in clouds to hover and mark the passage of the carnage.

It was all over for Mangrove and Snotty.

At the bottom of the mountain the rolling cascade slowly ceased to move and from the pile the Torterats, using their teeth, dragged the dazed Foragers, their hair, their eyes and ears, covered with snow.

Disarmed, their stocks probably snapped and hidden somewhere in the great, stilled hillock that had been the avalanche, Snotty and Manny expected the teeth to sink into their flesh, to die and to be eaten.

It did not happen.

The Torterats let the two get to their feet, but as the Foragers tried to rid themselves of snow, shaking flakes from their hair, wiping them from their faces and flicking lumps from their clothing, they felt a nipping at their heels and heard an angry yipping. Some of the Torterats were digging into the piled snow, searching for the fish, others making it plain that Mangrove and Snotty should do the work of retrieving the frozen carcasses and return them to the backpacks.

The hunters, who had become the hunted, were now prisoners, forced to obey the commands of the Torterats.

From the snow they hauled the food that had been intended for the clan. As the rigid bodies were jammed into the sacks, their fish eyes, still bright, seemed to catch the eyes of the Foragers with the message that they too were now like the fish, hooked and landed!

With the job done, the loaded packs again on their backs, the snapping became more vicious. Involuntarily Mangrove and Snotty lifted their feet and moved to get away from the teeth. At close range, the large incisors, the curved front teeth, were bigger than they had imagined, with an edge that could cut and tear.

Torterats followed, continuing to snap at their legs, while others took up the position of vanguard, leading the way back up the mountain.

All the while the Torterats kept up a re-echoing screeching. Cries of triumph mixed with snarls to keep the captives moving in the chosen direction.

The Foragers stumbled along in the midst of the angry animals, prisoners obedient to the demands of their captors, wondering what fate awaited them.

Mangrove shivered. The wild, erratic tumble had forced snow inside his furs. Against his skin it was now melting. Tentacles of fear gripped him. Every Forager knew that to sweat and be caught in the cold for the sweat to freeze was deadly. The snow — now held against his body, dribbling its way to wet him and his clothing — worse than sweat, would freeze again to lower his body heat. He would be *iced*. Even as he opened his jacket to rub at the damp inner layer of clothing, dark shadow was creeping ahead of him and Snotty. Night was falling and with it the temperature would plunge.

Stumbling upwards in the deep snow, trying to avoid the razor sharp incisors of the Torterats, Mangrove muttered through chattering teeth. "I'm icing, Snotty."

Snotty's face showed his concern. Whatever else lay ahead of them, iced, Manny had little hope of survival.

Chapter 4

The Queen, all her strength taken by the effort of speaking, had not moved from her couch. The audience she had given was at an end.

Dram smiled with pleasure. It might not be necessary to send an expedition to find Snotty and Mangrove, but all present had recognised the honour given to her. It was she who would lead, and this appointment would be the precursor to an even greater one.

The smile on Dram's face lingered as she looked at Tasha and Biscetti. Warmly they returned it, admiring the big girl who had such physical strength. They too shared Dram's faith in herself. If the hunters were in trouble, Dram was the best of the Foragers to lead the rescue party.

Still smiling, Tasha came to Dram. "The boys are probably just delayed by the weight of their catch. I'm not worried, but because of the cloud they'll be unable to navigate. I think we should light the beacon. In the dark it will guide them home."

Standing close by, Dumperty took Dram's hand and asked if he could help. Dram nodded. Dumperty made his way across the floor of the cave, the earth trodden hard to a smooth, even surface that in places glistened in the light. He stopped at the central fire that burned continually. The Camarilla were frugal with fuel and the fire was small, but its constant heat had a cumulative effect that took the sharp chill off the air in the cave. A clay pot stood close to the fire. Dumperty lifted the pot and, carefully taking burning coals and embers from the fire, filled it. That was the practice when the beacon had to be lit.

The three left the cave and climbed the ice steps cut into the rugged side of the mountain. At the summit, the steepled boughs and branches of the beacon were assembled in constant readiness. Dumperty approached the pyramid of timber and looked toward Dram.

"Yes."

And the tiny boy knelt to build below the thicker branches a criss-crossed arrangement of kindling that, had he known, resembled the defensive square of an old-time infantry regiment. He tipped the pot, letting the contents fall into the square and, criss-crossing more splinters of kindling upon it, began to blow at the glowing coals.

Dram and Tasha watched as the thin strips of wood began to burn, flames licking upward into the woven branches of the beacon until it too caught fire. The guiding light was ablaze, but in the contrary way of the elements the wind eased and the cloud began to break up as the though the fire had been the signal for the weather to clear.

Dram shook her head and made the comment that the climb had been unnecessary. But it was too late to change plans. The beacon was well alight. She beckoned Dumperty to sit between her and Tasha on the worn log that had served as a seat from a time well before they were born. The three sat close, the flames shining on their faces, the warmth seeping into their furs. Above them the cloud had cleared and a myriad stars dusted the sky and within the silvered dust glinted the brighter points of planets and far distant suns. In those parts of the sky to where their eyes turned from habit, constellations traced their patterns.

"There!" Dram raised an arm to point and they watched a meteor burn its life to nothing in a short, sharp, speeding trail.

In silence, they looked up at the bowl of night and Tasha marvelled that in those far off places of the universe, nothing had changed. The stars twinkled and followed their predestined tracks and among the stars that shone like gems, Earth continued with its chequerboard of nights and days, of darkness and light, as it had always done.

Tasha thought of the people in the past who had looked up, as she was doing now, and would have had a view no different. Far earlier generations — those who had lived in the Good Times — they too had looked up at the same night sky.

In the folklore of the Camarilla there were stories of the people of those earlier times, dreadful tales of an Earth so abused that Nature had rebelled and after years of drought and fierce storms, the seasons had disappeared entirely and been replaced with never-ending cold.

The stars above had never altered. It was only on Earth, their own tiny planet, that devastation had been brought about by the Camarilla's long dead forefathers. They had destroyed the beauty of their world and in doing so had condemned their descendants to a land of harshness and relentless famine.

The moon began to peep above the horizon and from the summit of Home Mountain, by its yellow light Tasha could see far across the waste of snow and ice and from out of the darker distance came the faint, haunting groan of rock being ground beneath the snail-like progress of a glacier.

What had it once looked like? How had it been here those thousands of years ago?

The thought came often to her when she sat upon the mountain, because she knew that it had been different.

But now there were more immediate matters to consider. Somewhere in the vast stretch of white on which moonlight shone, Mangrove and Snotty could be lying injured, or even worse.

She rose and checked the beacon. Perhaps they could see the glow of its flame, re-orient a course for home and by morning would be at the mouth of the cave. She prayed to the stars that this would be so.

Dram also stood. "There's nothing more we can do." She nudged Dumperty, who, snuggled into his furs, now dozed before the fire. "Come on, little one. We must go down now."

As they descended, light from the beacon distorted their shadows, long sinister figures that went before them, moving in odd, eccentric ways.

Chapter 5

Mangrove could feel his body chilling, the cold gradually taking over. His blood was losing the battle to keep him warm and as it circulated it too was cooled. The end would be as the eyes of the fish had predicted. He would die and stiffen as hard as frozen rock.

For the moment there was nothing Snotty could do. They were still struggling upwards through deep snow and without skis their legs plunged deep so that dragging them out took effort. The weight of the packs at times caused them to fall, so that their progress was a floundering, tiring business. The added torment was the chivvying of the Torterats, who seemed to delight in the misery of the Foragers.

When the ground at last levelled, Snotty un-slung his pack and handed it to Mangrove.

"Snotty, I can't."

"Just for a moment."

And as they continued to trudge through the snow, Mangrove watched Snotty slip the bone pins from the ties of his fur jacket and then remove it.

"What are you doing, Snotty?"

"Hold it." He handed his jacket to Mangrove and, gasping with the cold, removed another layer of his clothing. "Now take this."

"You'll die!"

"No I won't, but iced, you will. Now do as I say."

And under the pale light of the stars, with the Torterats snapping at them, keeping them moving, Mangrove and Snotty, in an intricate interchange of packs and jackets and inner layers, were successful in removing Mangrove's wet layer and replacing it with a dry one from Snotty.

Although each shuddered with cold during the transfer, fear of freezing gave them speed and Mangrove's wet inner layer was safely stuffed into the pocket of his jacket. The threat of icing was no more.

"You're risking your life for me, Snotty."

"I'm warm enough. One less inner won't hurt me. You needed to be dry and the way the Trats are hunting us along, we'll stay warm."

There was no stopping. Through the night, the cavalcade continued across the frozen waste, moonlight casting weak shadows from humps and ridges. The two Foragers, laden with the weight of their packs, contained like circus animals within the regiment of Torterats, stumbled through the snow to a never-ending yipping and snapping. In his usual fashion, Snotty was ahead, making it easier for Mangrove, who trod in the depressions of compacted snow that Snotty had made.

From time to time, at the prompting of one or the other, the Foragers would tilt their heads to look at the stars. Their purpose was not to marvel at the beauty of the night sky, but to plot the direction in which they were being forced to travel. With each observation, they conferred, confirming their position relative to Homecave and the distance as best they could approximate.

In the lulls between their conversations, Mangrove relived the moments when he had removed his final layer of clothing and the cold gripped with a pain that held him in its vice until he could pull on the inner that Snotty had freely given him. For a few moments they had both stood with torsos bare. Snotty had experienced the same pain and had given up one of his inner layers in order for Manny to be dry.

Yes. He's a truly great friend.

As Mangrove was thinking how fortunate he was, Snotty, his head bent, concentrating on where his next lumbering step would be, asked Manny what he thought the Torterats were up to.

"Snotty, they're taking us somewhere. Why, I don't know, but the Trats are smarter than we thought. I'm sure that they have a language. I can't understand it, but the big Trat seems to give orders and the others obey."

Snotty grunted his agreement. It looked that way. "Maybe we'll be part of their food supply. They're using us to carry home the fish and when it suits them they'll eat us as well."

The same thought had entered Mangrove's mind. For the time being he and Snotty were being used to tote the load the Trats were unable to carry. What might happen when they arrived at the destination, wherever it might be, was something they could only guess. About one thing he had no doubt. The Trats had intelligence and were capable of thinking ahead, the manner in which he and Snotty had been captured and now their use as porters was proof of the Trats' ability.

Mangrove saw Snotty raise his head, checking again on the stars. He too studied the sky for a few moments. They were heading due north, maintaining the course the Trats had followed from the outset, direct into the Trat heartland. The distance to Homecave was increasing, but the direction had not altered.

Around them, the Torterats maintained a rhythmic bounding as though they needed no rest, but for the Foragers, plodding onwards in a never-changing cycle of thrusting legs into snow and withdrawing them was tiring. The weight of the backpacks was becoming heavier with each dragging hour of darkness and as the sky lightened with the dawn, Mangrove dropped his pack and sat in the snow.

"Snotty, I have to rest." His chest was heaving, his words wavering, punctuated by the deep drawing of air into his lungs. He had reached his limit, his energy gone.

Snotty stopped and turned. Torterats were snarling at Manny, leaping towards him, screeching, nipping at him, wanting him to go on.

Slipping his pack loose, holding it by its straps, screaming his anger, Snotty swung it, aiming to drive the Trats from Manny. Above the mayhem of shouting and scrambling and the screeching of the Torterats, came a single, low-pitched bark. It was a sound that although different, reminded the Foragers of the lone cry they had heard on an earlier occasion: the sound that had been the call to attack when they had been surrounded on the mountain.

The Torterats fell silent, drew back from the Foragers and lay on the snow like dogs obedient to a master's order. The largest of them remained standing, looking at the Foragers. It was this Torterat that had given the battle command and now had brought the others to heel.

Snotty dropped his pack by Mangrove and sat on it. Shaking his head and with motions of his hand, he indicated that they had to rest. The largest of the Torterats, the one that Mangrove was now certain was their leader, called again, a number of different sounds and a Torterat rose from the snow and nudged Mangrove's pack, trying to open it with his teeth.

In the quiet of the plateau deep in snow, with the eastern sky aglow, now colouring from white to pink the icy drifts and frosted blanket of the land, Mangrove and Snotty followed the promptings of the Torterats and drew a fish from Mangrove's pack. As the rim of the sun rose above the horizon, the Torterats tore the fish to pieces, sawing at the frozen flesh with the blade-sharp edges of their teeth, eating the strips and chunks that separated from the carcase.

Another command came from the leader and a piece of fish was flicked to Snotty, another to Mangrove.

"They're feeding us, Manny."

Mangrove bowed his head, the realisation driven home by the actions of the Trats that he and Snotty were indeed in bondage. "There's a story in the folklore that in ancient times tribes would seize men from other tribes and make those men work. Those workers were called slaves."

"I remember hearing something like that, Manny."

"Well, slaves need to be fed."

"Then we'll eat. I'm hungry."

Mangrove gave a wry grin. Snotty just didn't seem to get it, or, regardless of the situation, could always manage a reason for optimism.

Snotty placed a piece of fish inside his glove to thaw it. When it had softened he ate and reached to get another piece. The Torterats permitted him to do so. Mangrove took a chunk of the white flesh and thawed it in the same way. Holding it to his mouth he nibbled at it and then tempted, took a sizeable bite. The raw fish was surprisingly tasty. Following Snotty's example Mangrove took more and ate with relish. As he chewed he recalled the words his long dead mother had used when food was scarce and he had complained that he could not eat the scant meals she had prepared.

"If you can't eat it, you can't be hungry."

It's true, he thought. Hunger gives flavour to almost anything. Just as well!

Resting, restoring their strength with the food, washing the fish down with melted snow, the Foragers for a brief period enjoyed the sight of the rising sun and in that short time forgot that they were captives. Another barked command ended the dream. The nipping and the yapping began again.

Lifting their feet, dancing from one foot deep in snow to the other so that they might avoid teeth that they had seen rip frozen fish to shreds, the pair shouldered their loads and began again the body-wrenching torment of the march.

Throughout the morning, contained within the phalanx of Torterats, the Foragers lifted one weary foot after the other, still heading north. Noon came and went and on they plodded until in mid-afternoon a low range of hills stood sharp in the sunlight.

A chattering rose from the Torterats, an excited squeaking as though a goal was in sight.

"Maybe the hills are home territory for them." Snotty said.

"I hope so." Mangrove was tired, ready to drop, past caring what might happen to him and as he spoke, from ahead an answering squealing rippled through the air and he and Snotty watched Torterats in the distance bounding through the snow toward them.

"Yes." Snotty narrowed his lids to slits, peering at the advance of the welcoming party, the familiar leaping and scrambling. Behind them he could see a dark hole in the hillside, an arched opening so symmetrical that he felt that it could not be the work of nature.

"Look, Manny, can you see where they've come from?"

"Yeah. What is that, a cave?"

Snotty shook his head. "I don't know."

Curiosity took their minds from the pain of their aching bodies until they were close enough to see in clear detail that the semi-circular arch seemed to be constructed from separate squares of stone, stone that bore the marks of being shaped from rock and laid to form the entrance to an opening in the mountainside.

Manny stared at the arch, wondering who could have made such a shape from blocks of rock and why. The greater puzzle was why the heavy pieces at the top of the arch did not fall. He examined the strange, unnatural structure, knowing that everything unsupported, fell. That was nature's way and yet the big stones did not. They were suspended above the gap in the hillside, bearing all the weight of earth and snow and ice of the hill above. In turn he looked at each stone, seeing a thickness of material between each block that must hold them together and then at the top of the arch he saw the tapered rock that was the keystone and it became clear to him how the rocks held together. They did not fall because the weight above and the weight of rocks around the keystone maintained a pressure on it, squeezing it but never moving it. Because of its taper it could not be popped out.

Yes. There is no magic. The stones are pushing at themselves and cannot fall because of the way they've been cut.

Manny marvelled at the arch and at the genius of the way it held together and knew that the Trats had brought him and Snotty to something that had been built in the Good Times. The Trats had found a home that had stood from the time the world had been warm.

Had books still existed, had some written record of history survived, Mangrove would have known that in the Good Times, in the rocky desert valleys of Egypt, archaeologists had discovered the tombs of kings lying within pyramids that also had stood for aeons. The archaeologists too had stood in admiration at the ancient work of engineers and stonemasons and the almost everlasting nature of stone.

The Torterats urged them on and when they had reached the arch, dragged the packs from their backs so that they lay in the snow. The Foragers sank down, resting against the packs, eyes closing in weariness only to be roused by the snarling of Torterats and the snapping of their teeth.

Rising, not knowing what lay ahead, Mangrove and Snotty were driven through the arched opening. They had never entered such a place before.

Light coming through the arch revealed a cavernous space cut from the rock of the mountain. Larger than Homecave, larger than any cave in which they had been, there was evidence nevertheless that the space had been cut from the raw rock of the mountain. Visible on the walls were marks that must have been made by tools used in its excavation.

"Look," Snotty pointed to the floor where metal rails ran in a number of directions. "What are they?"

Mangrove was also looking. The rails ran in parallel pairs from a central point to continue into dark openings that holed the wall. He counted them. From the spacious atrium four sets of tracks were laid, each set running into a separate opening. What lay beyond those four gaping mouths? To where did the rails run and for what purpose? Mangrove had no answer. He had never in his lifetime seen metal, none of the Camarilla knew of metal, nor that metal had been essential to the growth of the civilization that had been lost to the cold. Metal was not mentioned in folklore and rails could not even be imagined.

The metal rails were not the only puzzle.

Awed by the size of the inverted bowl in which they stood, Mangrove and Snotty stood at its centre and with heads tilted gazed about. That a space of such magnitude had been carved from the inside of the mountain was alone impressive, but other strange things caught their attention.

At one place on the curved surface of the wall, some three metres above the floor, a smooth, flat plate had been fixed. Rectangular in shape, it was held by a frame fashioned to be almost unnoticeable. The plate itself had a sheen that indicated it was made of some material other than metal.

"Manny, each side of that flat thing must be longer than Dram is tall. What is it, do you think?"

"I don't know." He pointed. "And look there."

High above, where the rock had been shaped in a hemisphere that was the roof of the atrium, they could see strips, or bars, many of them. These strips were aligned in pairs and appeared to be linked by a rigid rope.

In various parts of the atrium, placed close to the wall as if to be unobtrusive — as if to leave space for whoever had occupied the area to move about — were large wooden structures in which were square apertures.

While the Torterats busied themselves taking fish from the backpacks dropped in the snow, confident that while doing so they guarded the only way of escape for those inside, the Foragers took time to investigate their prison.

They approached the wooden structures, pushed at a door, recognising it as some type of closure, and watched it swing open. Entering, Snotty kicked at the dust on the floor. He crossed to one of the apertures and leant forward to look through the opening. His face crashed against a pane.

"Ow." He rubbed at his forehead and his nose and then gingerly touched the invisible barrier. His fingers ran across glass, a substance he had never come across.

Repeatedly he slid his hand over the strange barrier that, unseen, had prevented his further inspection of the cavern. Smooth and clear, it resembled ice, but ice it certainly was not.

"Hmm. Weird!"

He turned from the window and examined a table. Laying on it was a small round object. Through a lens of glass, he could see a face with markings around its circumference and at each quadrant a letter and a number. In the centre was a black needle shaped like an arrow. The point of the arrow was almost touching the number 180. Snotty picked up the thing and the needle swung wildly, only to come again to rest at 180. He moved his hand, watching the needle as it moved.

"Hey, Manny, come and look at this."

Mangrove watched as Snotty waved his hand back and forth.

"Wild eh, the way the arrow spins?"

Mangrove nodded and suggested it was some sort of toy.

"Yeah, it's neat." Snotty put the object in his pocket.

They came out from the structure, walked along the perimeter of the atrium and saw two identical metal boxes fixed to the wall. Attached to each box, at a height they could not reach, was a lever of the same metal. Running from the boxes were the same rigid ropes that joined the strips high above on the ceiling. In some unexplained way, the boxes with the levers were connected to the rectangle they had examined earlier.

Inquisitive, they felt the rails and, walking between the tracks, entered a tunnel for a short distance, unwilling to go further because they could not see beyond a vessel that stood on the rails.

Throwing questions and wild possibilities at each other, the Foragers attempted to fathom what sort of a place they were in. It was beyond them. Nothing had prepared them for the unnatural place to which the Torterats had brought them.

How could Manny and Snotty know what had happened so far back in time? But had there been a race of people on a planet in a distant galaxy, and had those people been far advanced in technology, they might have sent a satellite, or some exceptional remote-controlled vehicle, to observe planet Earth for an extended period. The pictures sent back to the far-off galaxy would have told the story of the human race. How for over a period of one hundred years the warnings of scientists had been dismissed as scaremongering, but that their predictions had been realised.

The Earth had warmed.

The scourge of drought had ravaged crops season after season. Fire had destroyed the forests of the great continents and the polluted atmosphere dimmed a darkening world. Melting icecaps caused the oceans to rise, to drown island nations and to inundate low-lying countries.

But the man-made disaster was not all. Co-incident with global warming, the ten million-year cycle of the cosmic tide had reached a turning point. The infinite forces of the galaxy in their ebb and flow altered the orbits of planets in the solar system. Earth wobbled, its magnetic field reversed and its orbit around the sun adopted another course. Ironically, darkened by smoke and haze that formed a barrier against the sun, the overheated planet began to cool. The new ice age had begun.

The cities of the world, built from materials designed to be light and strong, began to decay. Concrete and glass could not cope with the cold and the mounting weight of snow. Whole cities froze. Buildings split and warped and over time crashed to the ground or slowly disintegrated where they stood. Those places where people had worked and lived were eventually destroyed and buried under ice and snow.

The pictures relayed to the distant galaxy would show that attempts to grow food in glasshouses, or in specially constructed indoor gardens, were unable to yield the quantities required and so starvation caused the shrinking world population to decline further. With insufficient food and without shelter, the human race had begun the journey to extinction.

Had the satellite focused on the mountain which held the arched entrance, it would have revealed how an underground haven had been excavated and the arch built to withstand the ravages of cold and to take great pressure. Within the hollowed mountain electric cables had been laid, swathed in insulation that would protect the cables from penetration by cold and by water. The cables themselves ran through narrow passages drilled to the very peak of the mountain. There they were connected to solar panels made to last under conditions even more extreme than pessimistic forecasts predicted. Set into the vertical wall of an escarpment, the panels could never be buried under snow. Manufactured from the most efficient and most robust ceramic of the day, the panels had been built to last forever.

The construction of the haven, with its requirements for power provided by the sun, was a fine success, but climate change came too quickly for those who planned to survive within the mountain. They died before their dream had been completed.

No record of those events was ever transmitted, but had there been, the observers living on the distant planet would have seen that the huge atrium, with the individual huts and the tunnels with rails laid to allow more excavation as the community grew, had been built in vain. Like the pyramids of Egypt, the mountain retreat remained, but only as a monument to an ancient, devastated world.

Snotty and Mangrove were the first humans to enter the atrium since the beginning of the era of ice. Only with the recent invasion of the Torterats had animal life returned. For the Torterats it was a temporary convenience, somewhere to shelter from the elements, a base from which to hunt, until like locusts they had eaten everything available and were forced to continue south.

Still guessing what might have existed in the excavated mountain, the Foragers entered the three tunnels not yet explored. They followed the rails for as far as the light from the entrance would allow, but unable to see their way further, returned to the atrium and sat. All that they had discovered was that rails had been laid on the floor of each tunnel and the narrow strips they had seen in the atrium also appeared at intervals on the tunnel ceilings. Along the concave walls of the tunnels, the rigid ropes had been fixed in long straight lines like the sinews of an arm stretching into the darkness. To these things they could attach no meaning. It did not really matter. Tired and hungry, Snotty and Mangrove wanted food and sleep.

There was to be no further respite. With the threatening darting and snarling that the Foragers knew was a signal to move, a party of Torterats entered the cavern and drove the two from the shelter. A few pieces of fish lay on the snow.

"Manny, the Trats want us to eat."

Mangrove eyed the scattered lumps of fish and shook his head in disbelief. The rations provided were too meagre to satisfy the hunger of one, let alone two.

"It's better than nothing," Snotty said. And they stuffed the scraps into the pockets of their furs.

With the light fading, the Torterats gave them little time and like sheep dogs nipping and snarling, herded the Foragers back into the atrium and into one of the wooden structures.

Their captives now imprisoned, Torterats lay at the doorway, close-packed so that anyone attempting to get out would have no option but to tread on the guards. Others formed small groups and entered tunnels or prepared to settle for the night on the floor of the atrium.

For Snotty and Mangrove, their first day in slavery had drawn to an end. They ate the fish, then with their hands swept a space clean of the fur shed by Torterats, lay down on the floor of the decrepit wooden hut and slept.

Chapter 6

The identical twins, Sola and Situ, stirred, stretching, yawning, each movement enacted in unison, as though one brain controlled the movements of both bodies. They rose from their sleeping place in Homecave and took water from the pot by the fire. From cupped hands they washed their faces and then drank. Dawn was seeping into Homecave, giving outline to figures still sleeping under skins and furs.

The twins grinned at each other, glad to be up, ready for fun. But mischief had to be postponed. Their allotted task was to dig peat for the fire.

Each took his stone axe, polished and shaped at one end like an adze. Despite the keen edge of the adze, cutting and breaking slabs of peat from the frozen bog was hard physical work. The twins enjoyed it. To be out in the snow, giving their energy free rein, put a shine on whatever they were asked to do. There was also the chance that they might come across the tracks of a snow-hare or some other animal that could be put into the cooking pot or roasted over the fire.

Situ reached for his knife, its blade a wavy pattern of scalloped edges that made the sharpened flint a better cutting tool, one that could slice through skin and flesh should luck favour them with game.

Sola looked around the cave, at the mounds of furs each covering a warmed, sleeping body, except for one. Cloud sat at her sleeping place and appeared to be staring at him. Sola caught Situ's attention and pointed toward Cloud. Situ raised his brows and shrugged his answer to his brother's question. The girl might be looking in Sola's direction, but the twins knew that with her poor eyesight, Cloud would see only a blurred figure.

The boys approached her and in the weak light of daybreak the unblinking fixity of her stare told them that she was wandering in some other world. As they watched, Cloud's lips began to twitch and she rocked from side to side as though troubled. Her mouth opened. She did not speak, but made low, anguished sounds and one thin arm reached out as if to ward off some danger or to warn whoever figured in the scenes in her mind.

"Cloud," Situ touched her shoulder gently and patted. "Sweet Cloud, you are with us. You're quite safe."

Cloud's lashes closed and remained that way for a few moments, as if she needed time to return from a place far away, time to reassemble herself in the here and now of Homecave.

When she opened her eyes, she held them wide, still not totally convinced that she had come back. She took a long wavering breath and then, as though she had just become aware that the twins were by her side, Cloud peered at them through lids drawn close, lines radiating from her eyes as she tried to focus.

Recognising the twins she grasped Situ's hand that lay on her shoulder as he continued to calm her. "Torterats have Mangrove and Snotty."

"Tell us what you saw, Cloud," Sola said. "Where are they? What has happened?"

With detail at times well-defined, at times blurred in the way she normally saw her surroundings, Cloud pictured for them the events which had overtaken Mangrove and Snotty.

"I saw blood on the snow and a hole in the ice and then ski tracks." She went on to tell of Torterats chasing and catching the Foragers. "They're prisoners in a place that is strange to them."

"Where is that place, Cloud?"

She could not tell them.

As Cloud had been speaking, disturbed sleepers had risen and come to hear what she was saying.

Tasha placed her face very close to Cloud's, smiled and took her hand. "If we are to help Manny and Snotty, we must first be able to find them."

Cloud nodded. "Yes, but they have no understanding of the place in which they're held and nor do I." She looked directly into Tasha's eyes. "The stomach of a mountain."

Tasha squeezed Cloud's hand, reassuring her, trying to have her be more definite. "Do you mean like here, like Homecave?"

Cloud seemed not to hear, still seeing the things of her dream. "A mouth of stones that should fall down. A hollow mountain carved by ghosts."

With a crowd gathered around, Tasha tried to have Cloud give them clues on where they might find Mangrove and Snotty.

Again Cloud told of the hole in the ice and bloodied snow. "They tried to escape from the Trats." And again she spoke of ski tracks and herringbone and snow that hurtled down a mountain. "Then they were without skis, struggling through the snow."

Dram had joined Tasha and together they tried to have Cloud describe some landmark or be precise about direction. They were unsuccessful. Cloud could give them no more information.

"Then we must do as Avon instructed," said Dram. "I am the leader. We'll go now."

The decision had been made.

At the back of the crowding onlookers, Ingamo, the oldest of the Camarilla, muttered that they were cursed.

"Stones that should fall, stones that should fall." The old man was shaking his head, looking at Jemma, his wife. "A hollow mountain carved by ghosts. Ghosts," he repeated. "We'll never see the young ones again."

"Quiet," she said, fearing in her heart that Ingamo could be right.

He took no notice of her hushing. "Beyond the hills, beyond the river is bad ice, bad ice."

Dram, who had been standing near, gave him a quizzical look. The old man had once been a fine hunter, a Forager of note. In the weak light, the old man's white hair took on the appearance of a halo, giving his pronouncements credibility, as though he were the angel of darkness.

Seeing Dram's concern, Jemma put her finger to her lips and scolded Ingamo. "No more of that. Be quiet."

Ingamo said no more, but continued to shake his head. Standing alongside him, Janus and Tang, a couple almost as old as Ingamo, bent their heads to whisper in support that he could be right.

With all watching, Biscetti and Tasha gathered the items that they knew they would need. Dram called to them, running through a checklist. She needn't have bothered. Apart from snowshoes, which were a necessity, the sisters had little from which to choose, what little food the band could spare, an extra inner layer that could be worn should a blizzard hit them, a stone axe, a bow with four arrows, some bone fishhooks and line and a length of rope woven from the sinews of animals. The rope was old, but regular greasing with fat kept it in good condition. Pliable and strong, the rope had been added to over the years, its length increased as opportunity offered. Tasha coiled it carefully and placed it at the bottom of her backpack. With its many uses, the rope was one of the clan's most valued possessions.

Biscetti watched her sister stow the last of the necessities. "Bring your flute, Tasha. You can play to us sometimes."

"Okay." The flute was small and light, no burden to carry. Tasha slipped it into her pack.

As the rescue party left the relative warmth of Homecave, everyone followed, watching the girls bend to tie the bindings of their skis and assist each other with tightening the thongs of backpacks in last minute adjustments.

Situ handed his flint knife to Dram. "Take this. It's sharp. You may need it."

She thanked him and with the Camarilla's softly spoken wishes for success steaming the air in tiny puffballs, the search team pushed at the snow with their poles and skied away. Dram, in front, set course for a point on the horizon way beyond which was the ridge of hills and beyond the hills, the iced-over river.

With nothing more definite to guide them, Dram's decision was to look for blood on the snow and a place where the ice had been holed above the hidden river. If the weather remained favourable, and nothing went wrong, to cover the distance to the hills would take twelve or thirteen hours.

Dram's plan was to try to reach the hills before night fell, dig and shelter in ice-coffins for the night and move on again at first light. If by dusk bad weather had come, they would build a snow cave. Tasha and Biscetti agreed. With their territory continuing to shrink as the raids of the Torterats became more bold, the hills were close to the limits of safe travel. Beyond the highest ridge, and certainly beyond the river, the rescue party would be in constant danger. If they had to cross the river and extend their search, this would be better done during the hours of daylight.

Chapter 7

Mangrove stirred in his sleep, rolled his head from side to side and exhaled sharply through his nose. The pungent smell of Torterat was disturbing him. He opened his eyes and for a moment felt lost, unable to account for his surroundings. The feeling was fleeting, the realisation of where he was bursting upon him as he looked up from the floor at the planks of the walls and with the unpleasant smell sticking in his nostrils.

He turned to see Snotty still sleeping at his side. *I'll let him sleep.*

From other parts of the atrium the sounds of squeaking came to him. With dawn, the Torterats too were beginning to stir. Mangrove rose and looked out through the gap where a window had once been. Around the atrium and from other huts, Torterats were moving. From the tunnels two or three appeared, looked about and scurried back into the darkness only to reappear in greater number. At the arched entrance the sentries were also active.

I wonder what they plan to do with us?

Mangrove looked down at Snotty, questioning how he could continue to sleep with the smell, the growing noise and the increasing light. But that was Snotty. He could sleep wherever he laid his head.

Yes, Mangrove thought, he knows that for the time being he can do nothing, so his attitude is that he might as well sleep. Mangrove smiled at his sleeping friend, the boy prepared to go to the extreme, the risk-taking adventurer, never daunted by the odds or the dangers that he might face. Mangrove frowned and shook his head, recalling the way they had faced the Torterats the day before. *The trouble is I'm always with him.* He gave a long sigh. *Ah well, Snotty makes life interesting.*

The Torterats were now very active. The floor of the atrium was alive with furry bodies, a jumbled, moving kaleidoscope of pointed, twitching noses and bared teeth running hither and thither, screeching with hunger.

Snotty opened his eyes. "Hi, Manny. Sounds like the Trats aren't happy."

Before Mangrove could reply, a single, choking call rose loud and harsh above the peevish chattering. The atrium was instantly quiet.

Snotty rose from the floor and with Mangrove, looked at the mass of Torterats now lying flat, faces turned toward the biggest of them.

"That one is definitely the boss." Mangrove was whispering, watching the huge Trat dictate to those cowering before him.

"Yeah, you're right. Boss Trat gives the orders and the rest do as they're told."

"That sound was different from the cries he made yesterday. Just then he sounded like he was choking. It's dreadful to listen to, but the Trats do have a language. They do communicate."

"Okay," Snotty said. "I'm convinced."

As the Foragers watched and listened, the leader made more guttural noises, each sound separated from the other, as though meaning was contained within a single syllable. On hearing one particular command, the Torterats rose from their submissive position and, heads turned, looked toward the hut where Mangrove and Snotty were held. The leader gave one more rough bark and the sentries at the doorway of the hut rushed in, the claws of their paws skittering on the wooden floor as they nipped and snarled. The terrorising of the previous day had begun again.

Snotty pulled a leg from the jaws of a Torterat and cried out in pain. He bent to press his hand to the wound and felt the tear in his leggings. His glove had blood on it.

Trying to avoid the snapping teeth, the two were driven out through the stone arch into the snow. There they were made to strap on the backpacks, which had stiffened with the cold.

The yipping and nipping did not cease. With the horde of Torterats chivvying at their legs, Mangrove and Snotty were goaded around the mountain. In places, deep drifts had formed and the going was more difficult, but the moment they strayed from the Torterats' planned direction, sharp incisors tore at their clothing.

"Where do you reckon they're taking us, Manny?"

Mangrove shook his head. He had no idea where they were going, nor whether they would ever return.

Driven by the pack, the Foragers forged their way through the snow. They entered a valley and high above saw the bare rock of an escarpment, the vertical cliff face revealed when, at some time in the past, part of the mountain had split away, collapsed and slid into the valley. At places in the scree, the small rocks and stones that had been broken in the fall were now buried in snow, but huge boulders reared up, the reminder that all that lay in ruin had once been part of the mighty mountain. Wind had blown snow to pile against the boulders giving them an illusion of even greater size and on the tops of the boulders, snow draped in mantles of odd shape.

They skirted the fallen rocks and on the order of the Boss Trat, stopped. A number of Torterats began to dig at the snow, pushing it back through their hind legs until the Foragers could hear the scrape of ice.

"They've brought us to a river or a creek," Mangrove said. "It must run from the head of the valley."

"Why would the Trats do that?"

"There may be fish in the creek. The Trats can't get at them, but they know we can."

Snotty's face puckered in disbelief. "They want us to fish for them?"

"Yeah. That's what slaves do, Snotty. They work for their masters."

The Torterats shifting the snow moved back so that the Foragers could see the smooth sheet of ice.

Mangrove began to shuck his pack. "Get out your line before they start biting us again."

Snotty dropped his backpack to the snow and uncoiled the fishing line. The action satisfied the tormentors. The Torterats fell back and formed a circle, an audience to watch the workers and ready to drive them should they falter.

"Pass me the axe, Snotty, but do it slowly. I don't want the Trats to think we're threatening them."

Mangrove pointed to the pack and made motion as if he was using an axe. If they were to fish, the ice would need to be broken. Understanding his miming, the big Torterat grunted. Mangrove had been given permission to hammer through the ice.

Raising the axe high he slammed it down with all his might. The ice cracked in a starburst of opaque rays. Again he held the axe above his head and drove it at the same spot. Thin splits spread along the lines of the starburst. Smashing for a third time at the ice, Mangrove saw the splits widen and large chunks flew from where the axe had made its impact.

"Once more, Snotty and we'll have a fishing hole."

"I'm ready." Snotty had already taken a piece of fish from the snow and baited his hook.

Grunting, Mangrove hit again. The ice disintegrated and they were looking into the clear stream of the creek below.

Snotty fed loops of line into the hole, let it run a little and held fast, waiting for the telltale tapping. Encircling the Foragers, Torterats also waited and watched.

Mangrove kept his eyes on the line. Nothing was happening.

Snotty let out more line, jerking it in the hope that movement would attract fish to take the bait. Minutes passed slowly and the bait went untouched.

Around them Torterats edged closer, and from among them came the squealing of hunger sharpened by anger. Below their pointed snouts lips raised in snarls, baring teeth. Exhaled breath fouled the air as the Torterats crowded in on the Foragers. Instinctively Mangrove stepped back.

"C'mon, Snotty. Catch something."

Snotty plucked at the line, hoping that eccentric movement would lure an inquisitive fish. "I'm trying."

The noise from the Torterats rose in intensity.

"C'mon, Snotty make it work or we're finished."

Snotty played at the line, glancing at the encircling Torterats, nothing happening, and then it went taut and jigged about as the fish tried to throw the hook. Hand over hand, Snotty pulled in the line until the fish was visible, flashing this way and that in the cold waters of the creek. For a time the danger had passed, the fish hauled onto the ice with Mangrove slitting its throat and blood staining the snow.

He lifted the fish and threw it to the Torterats for them to rip it apart.

Snotty re-baited the hook and fed the line into the hole again.

Throughout the day the Foragers fished. When the Torterats had sated their hunger and could eat no more, the catch was laid on the snow for it to freeze solid. As the light began to fade, the big Torterat gave a command. The others rose from the snow. The day's fishing was at an end.

Mangrove and Snotty stashed the fish into their packs. The slaves would carry home the catch for the Torterat larder.

Chapter 8

For a time, the trio was able to use the fall of the land to ski with little effort. They travelled in line astern, Dram in front, followed by the smaller Biscetti, Tasha at the rear.

When the slope levelled and the terrain stretched flat and white as far as they could see, Dram looked back at the others. Using her poles she began to langlauf, her heels lifting from the skis as she thrust herself forward. Tasha and Biscetti followed suit. The going was more strenuous, but they were practised in the swaying rhythm, the shifting of weight from leg to leg, the alternate thrusting of stocks.

Above, clouds slowly crossed the sky, changing shape, sending shadows to drift over the skiers and wander on in moving patches of darkened snow.

Dram set a good pace. Years of experience in travelling over snow had developed in each of the girls a conservative use of energy. Efficiently they put distance behind them.

At noon Dram called a halt. They sat in the snow to rest and to eat. Dram opened her pack and took some food from it.

Tasha looked at the size of the portion. "We should eat only a twelfth of our rations now. Who knows how long it will take to find Manny and Snotty."

For a moment Dram looked at Tasha thoughtfully. "My plan is to catch fish at the ice hole to supplement what we've brought with us, but you may be right." Dram returned some of the food to her pack. "Why do you choose a twelfth?"

Tasha had been expecting the question. "We may be away for four days. If we eat twice each day, we'll have a little over for the boys. They may have no food."

Dram nodded that she understood, but repeated that it would be necessary to add to the rations they carried. "We're burning energy. The food we were allowed to bring won't replace it."

Tasha and Biscetti agreed. But the three knew that the clan had spared all that was possible to spare.

They resumed the lilting rhythm of movement across the snow. Two hours later the silhouette of the hills lifted above the plain, and with each passing hour their outline altered. Features became visible and then the detail of valleys and the shadows of hummocks where the snow had blown and gathered.

"Good," said Dram. "We're making good time. Let's press on. I'd like to be high in the hills before dusk."

A light breeze aided them, pushing from behind, increasing their speed until at the foot of the hills, Dram slowed and stopped. They would take off their skis and carry them. Snowshoes were more practical for the climb.

The three sat and slipped feet into the shoes, which looked like very short, fat skis, or even like the flat blades of paddles. Loaded with backpacks and skis on their shoulders, they began the climb to the ridge, shuffling, scarcely raising their feet, the broad shoes compressing the surface of the snow, never sinking into it.

Approaching the summit, Dram stopped and signalled Biscetti to crawl forward, a scout to scan the valley and the next hill. It was a precaution, a move to ensure that there were no Torterats on the blind side of the hill. All was clear.

"So far so good," said Dram. She pointed across the valley to the next ridge. "Let's keep going and camp for the night just below the top."

Tasha looked toward the west. A sliver of red gave her the last glimpse of the sun before it dropped below the horizon. They would need to hurry to reach their objective. The day was almost over.

They climbed the hill on the far side of the valley in the gloaming. Dram's wish for good weather had been granted. In still air, fifty metres below the ridge, each dug into the snow and made a hole just big enough for her own body to lie in, an ice coffin. The coffin was like a box without a lid, but with a depth to protect the girl lying in it should the wind increase.

Darkness came. Lying in the shallow pits, each could look up at the stars for the reassurance that all was well. Tasha held her flute to her lips and began to play a lullaby. Dram and Biscetti listened, caught the tune and sang the words of the song that their mothers had crooned to them as babies. They sang, thinking of Homecave and the Camarilla before weariness weighed them into sleep.

With dawn, the light breeze stiffened a little, enough to blow flakes from the parapet around each coffin and have them drop on the faces of the girls. One by one they stirred and climbed from the shelter of the pits where they had slept.

Dram looked at the sky, gauging what weather the day would bring. Neither stars nor sun could be seen. The cloud was high, a grey mass, slowly moving with an indication that it might thin and break up. She judged that as the day progressed the sky would clear.

"We'll go on to the river. We can eat there." An early start added hours to the day, valuable hours in which to find some trace of Snotty and Manny.

Without being asked, Biscetti made her way upward, using her elbows to inch the final few metres to reduce the chance of being seen. From the top of the ridge she scanned the way ahead. All appeared clear. Biscetti mimicked the call of the Snowy Owl, just the opening two notes, high and thin.

Tasha and Dram were already settling their packs on their backs, humping them to a comfortable position and tightening straps. They waved in recognition.

The rescuers were on their way again, the only sign of their temporary presence the ice coffins, and they would disappear with the first snowfall.

Adept at quickly changing one for the other, the girls skied down the slopes and used snowshoes for the climb. At the summit of each ridge they paused to check that no danger threatened.

From the top of the third hill they saw where the avalanche had been. It was as though for a distance the snow had been quarried from the slope, sent to slide and finally gather in a great mound on the valley floor. Even from the distance, the girls could see the tip of the ski that poked from the snow.

"And look there," Biscetti pointed to the ski tracks carved across the far slope. "The boys were coming this way. They must have been caught in a snowslide."

Dram cried out in despair. "Oh no. We're too late. Manny and Snotty have been buried."

Tasha was searching the area, fearing that Dram was right, hoping otherwise, straining to see some sign that the two had survived. The scene did not look normal to her. The snow had not slumped in the normal way of an avalanche, but she, Dram and Biscetti were too far off to be certain.

At close quarters they were able to gain an idea of what had happened.

The snow for some distance around had been trampled. The marks of pawprints and the deep depressions of footmarks were mingled haphazardly. In the hillock that had been the avalanche, ragged holes remained that were of varying size and shape and there were drag marks in the snow.

"Whatever happened here," Tasha said. "Manny and Snotty survived." She stood over the shafts where the Foragers' legs had sunk into the snow and around which it seemed hundreds of paws had left their imprint. "Cloud was right. The Trats have them. Mangrove and Snotty are prisoners."

Dram pulled at the ski whose tip jutted from the snow. Once freed, she could see that it belonged to Snotty. Further digging found his other ski and the two that Mangrove had worn. Only one broken stock was recovered. The rest remained buried somewhere in the hillock that had been the avalanche.

Dram tossed the skis aside.

Tasha watched with concern. Skis were valuable. So scarce was the wood or bone from which they could be made, that to replace a lost or broken ski might take months. "Dram, shouldn't we take the skis with us?"

"To carry them will weigh us down. We need speed if we are to find the boys quickly. We can pick up the skis on the way home."

"Yes," Tasha said, admitting that there was sense in Dram's reasoning. Delay in finding the boys could be fatal for them. "But when we find the boys, they'll need them. Without skis we'll never outrun Trats."

Biscetti was nodding. Each argument had merit. As she saw it, there were many difficulties to overcome. Since leaving Homecave the weather had been benevolent for the searchers. It may not have been the same for Manny and Snotty as they were led away as captives. If isolated snow showers had fallen and the tracks they could now see were covered, she, Dram and Tasha might spend days searching for them, and what then? "There is the chance we may never find them."

"Don't even think that, Biscetti," Tasha said, her voice raised. "We will find them. Look, you can see the way they've gone." She pointed at the trail of trampled snow that led from where they stood. "The Trats will be heading straight to wherever they have their base, their own Homecave. Even if snow has fallen, we'll simply continue in the same direction. We *will* find them and we *will* bring them back."

Tasha turned to Dram. "And for us to succeed, we must have the skis with us. We must! I'll use the rope to tie the skis and drag them behind. That way we'll be slowed very little."

"You're right. I hadn't thought of using the rope."

Tasha laid one of Mangrove's skis upon the other and used the bindings to lash them tight. She then did the same with Snotty's skis and placed them alongside Manny's. Shucking her pack, she used its thongs to tie the parallel sets of skis together and to keep the pack firmly lashed to them. Tasha had created a sled with the skis as its runners. With the weight of the pack, the sled would ride smoothly behind her, dragged by the rope in a figure eight looped around her shoulders.

Dram looked on, thinking how ingenious, yet how simple the solution was. Tasha was not only bringing the skis, she had freed herself of the burden of her backpack. Energy would be required to overcome the inertia of the sled, but once it was moving, Tasha's work effort would reduce.

Dram wished that she had given more thought to the matter of the skis. "Let's go," she said.

They moved off, Dram taking the lead, aiming for the river and the hole in the ice that Foragers habitually used. The high cloud had gone. In sunlight, the snow lay brilliant white.

Tasha's cleverness was evident at the next slope. Changing to her snowshoes, she bound her skis to the sled, another burden she did not have to shoulder.

Near the top of the hill, Dram dropped everything and crawled with caution to where she could observe the situation ahead. The tracks of Torterats and Foragers were easy to see, a wavering line of crumpled snow that led north. She moved her head from right to left, taking time to be satisfied that no danger remained. The course of the river was only identifiable by snow drifts that had built above the far bank. Cloud had spoken of blood upon the snow. If any remained, it could not be seen from where she lay.

Returning for her gear, Dram gave the signal that all was clear and beckoned the others to come on. "Tracks are clearly visible, for as far as I can see the Trats have been moving north."

Tasha and Biscetti nodded. It was to be expected, but it meant that the group would be heading into territory that was unknown to them.

Dram voiced their fears. "No Forager has explored the land north of the river."

Tasha looked straight into Dram's eyes. "One has."

And Dram remembered the words Ingamo had muttered as they were preparing to leave Homecave: *Bad ice.*

In his youth, Ingamo had gone deep into the country north of the river. Torterats were seldom seen in those years. Then, the

Trats had been only an occasional nuisance that had not deterred Ingamo. He had got to know the region well.

"Yes," Dram murmured. "A long while ago he was there." And in her mind Ingamo's words repeated: *Bad ice.*

As she stared at Tasha, a tremor of fear tingled within Dram's chest. She breathed deeply, settling herself. *I am the leader.* "Before we follow the tracks, we must look for blood upon the snow. We'll check the ice hole."

Tasha shook her head. "But, Dram, there will be no blood. Snotty wouldn't leave traces. He will have dumped the bloodied snow and blocked the hole with the skin. That's Forager practice and ..."

Dram raised a hand for her to stop speaking. "I want to check Cloud's story. We'll also try for a fish. We need more food."

Skis on again, Biscetti and Tasha obediently followed Dram.

Wind had blown away the snow that Snotty had hoped would hide the plug he had rammed into the hole. Frost had camouflaged the folds of the skin, but to the girls skiing along the edge of the depression in which the hidden river ran, the plug was easily seen. About to drop down the last few metres, the group stopped.

A small animal had hopped from the far side of the plug, a snow hare.

The girls sank quietly to the snow.

Dram hadn't taken her eyes from the hare. "Give me the bow, Tasha."

Low, dragging herself over the snow with her elbows, Tasha was already on her way to the sled. Unaware of them and curious, the hare was sniffing at the skin, at the lingering smell of blood that Snotty had been unable to remove.

Tasha handed the bow and an arrow to Dram. Lying flat on the snow, the bow held horizontal, Dram took aim and fired.

The arrow flew straight and true. It pierced the neck of the hare, which jumped high and fell to its side, quivering for a moment before dying.

The girls ran to the hare. Dram held it by its hind legs and with her knife quickly skinned away fur until the bare, pink body of the hare was steaming in the cold.

Tasha looked around at the uniform whiteness of the snow. The blood of Cloud's vision was no longer present. Snotty had done that part of his job well, but new blood was soon to make new stains.

Dram cut the throat of the hare and lifted it still quivering so that Biscetti, kneeling with her mouth open, could drink the dripping blood. Dram let Biscetti drink and then held the body above her own head, gulping down the blood until the flow had stopped.

Both wiped gloves across lips and chins.

"This will be enough for us and for the boys." She cut the hare into pieces, distributing the weight for each of them to carry. "Eat some now while it's hot and then we'll get going."

Hurriedly the girls tore at mouthfuls of raw flesh, each chewing quickly to eat her chunk of meat before it froze hard, at the same time wishing that they could linger over the meal to savour the flavour. For them and for all who dwelt in Homecave, the taste of fresh meat existed only in memory.

Biscetti laughed, pointing at Dram. "You have blood on your face."

"So do you."

Both laughing, they took handfuls of snow and wiped their faces clean.

Tasha smiled. *With food comes happiness.*

Working together, every bloodied flake was gathered and buried under clean, fresh snow. It was always better to leave no trace and there was now no need to fish.

With the speed that comes from a lifetime's practice, the three girls pushed feet into skis and fastened bindings.

"Ready?" Dram looked for confirmation. "Okay, let's go."

They crossed the ice and climbed the far side of the depression. The search for the hole in the ice had taken them some distance from the mish-mash of disturbed snow that would lead them to Snotty and Mangrove.

As they backtracked to pick up the trail, each was conscious that they were now north of the river. They were in unknown territory and it belonged to the Trats.

Tasha leaned into the rope that criss-crossed her chest. The wind had changed direction and was rising, bringing wisps of scud to fleck the sky.

Dram too, had noticed the filmy shreds of cloud that were blowing from the south. She raised an arm and shouted back that the weather was changing. The grey bits of scud that hurried overhead were the forerunners of a storm.

Dram altered course forty-five degrees to the right. The tracks were not yet in sight, but when last seen they had pointed north. To save time she aimed to cut across the long side of the triangle and pick them up. Biscetti and Tasha followed.

The sun still shone, but shadows sped over the snow and they were growing larger, merging as the wispy scud thickened to become real cloud.

"There. I can see the tracks." Dram shifted a degree or two further toward the north and soon they were langlaufing alongside the churned up surface.

Buoyed by the marks that Snotty and Mangrove had left, fresh with renewed energy from the food she had eaten, Biscetti drew level with Dram and laughed as Dram waved her on. Biscetti could take the lead.

In third place, the load of the sled riding easily against her chest and shoulders, Tasha looked ahead at Dram and her sister. Biscetti was setting a fine pace, the push of one leg quickly followed by the other as though she wished to impress upon the two following that although the smallest of the group, she would not fall short when needed.

The wind was behind them, assisting them and beginning to ripple the snow in a pattern of corduroy that gave beauty to the terrain.

Behind Biscetti, Dram moved easily. Tasha admired the economy of the way Dram shifted her weight, her long legs striding effortlessly as she made one step for every two of Biscetti's.

Yes, Tasha thought, we make a good team.

Maintaining the regular rhythm, the three put distance behind them until they were but dots on the featureless landscape.

Biscetti kept to the left of the tracks, occasionally turning her head to check that she had not strayed. Cloud had engulfed the sun and the tracks no longer stood out with the clarity of earlier in the day. She squinted, looking ahead for assurance that the Torterats had not deviated from the straight-line north, but the cloud was descending, visibility worsening. Automatically Dram reduced the gap between her and Biscetti. Tasha closed on Dram. They needed to remain in visual contact.

In minutes the whiteout had enveloped them.

Biscetti moved closer to the trail of broken snow, her skis travelling at its edge. She could see no further than two metres and the outlines left by paws had become indistinct, so that she had to constantly concentrate, blinking to clear her vision in an effort to be sure of where she should make her way. Her worry was that the group had to move fast in conditions that made speed difficult. She thought of calling to Dram, ask her what to do? But Dram might then doubt her ability. Biscetti kept on, straining to see.

They all heard the crack of splitting ice. It came like the drawn-out ripping of a knife through an animal skin. In the almost blind progress in the whiteout, the shock hit Biscetti's ears and eyes simultaneously, the sound of ice breaking as the chasm opened under her skis.

Dram and Tasha swung tightly, their skis throwing up snow with the sudden stop, Tasha screaming, "Biscetti, Biscetti!" as the dim figure of her sister fell from sight.

Then it was totally quiet, all sound swallowed by the mist.

Blind as moles, Dram and Tasha stepped out of their skis and crept on all fours to the edge of the crevasse. The parting ice had created a vacuum. Air was still rushing into the void, sucking with it the blinding draperies of cloud. For a moment Biscetti was visible, hanging inverted from skis that had wedged in the walls of ice. She swung like a pendulum, held by her bindings. That was all Tasha and Dram saw before the mist blotted out every outline.

"Biscetti!" Tasha leaned over the precipice of ice, shouting, wanting to hear her sister make some sound.

She waited, looking into Dram's face so close to her own, hoping, *willing* Biscetti to respond. No answering call came.

With the heels of her hands supporting her at the edge of the ice, Dram called Biscetti's name again. There was no echo, no sound in reply. She puckered her tongue and whistled, loud and penetrating, a sound that should have cut through the cloud. Only silence ensued.

"Hold my legs," Tasha said and with Dram holding tight to her ankles, Tasha lowered herself as far as she could, calling, waiting, calling again, a repetition of her sister's name.

She dangled like that, her ears straining and at last the faint response came.

"I'm okay, Tash, but I'm upside down."

Tasha sighed her thanks and relief tinkered with her lips, a brief smile that Biscetti was still alive.

Dram hauled Tasha back. They sat at the edge of the crevasse, knowing that the split in the ice might be hundreds of metres deep. There was no way of telling. In the few moments of clear air when Biscetti had been visible, the blue walls of ice had descended far below into darkness. Should the gap widen and the skis dislodge, Biscetti would plunge to her death.

"Dram, we have to get her out and quickly."

"Tasha?" Dram was shaking her head, Ingamo's words echoing in her brain, *bad ice, bad ice.* "It may be too dangerous. She's so far down and if the crevasse widens?"

"We saw her. You saw her. With the rope we can reach her and bring her up."

"How?"

In the single word Tasha recognised Dram's disbelief in the possibility, a reluctance to attempt a rescue because of the risks.

"We'll dig in our skis. Dig them in deep. Use them as a snub to take the weight while I lower you down to Biscetti."

"Why me?"

"You're taller than I am. Your reach is greater than mine. With you on the rope we extend its length more."

Dram was shaking her head. "But I'm stronger than you. I can support you and you may not be able to hold my weight."

"The snub will be assisting me. I won't let you fall."

"And if I do get hold of Biscetti, can you hold our combined weight?" Dram could seeing herself hanging in the mist of the crevasse, only the thin sinews of the rope keeping her from dropping into the abyss. She would be blind, groping for Biscetti and then holding her as Tasha tried to haul them up. If the rope was not strong enough or frayed where it dragged against the edge of the ice, the two of them would plummet into darkness, gone forever into Endless Night.

"Dram, we have to act quickly. If you won't do it, I'll go down. You lower me. I just hope I can reach her."

Tasha untied the rope, dismantling the makeshift sled. Working together, she and Dram dug a hole that angled away from the crevasse. They dug deep, lashed the four skis together with their bindings and drove them as one into the hole, jamming them tight, almost burying them, stamping the snow down hard, leaving only ten centimetres of the skis jutting into the mist. Dram would be the anchor, but she would not lower the line directly. She would face away from the crevasse and feed the rope back to make a u-turn around the skis. They would take most of the load, as the line, snubbed around them, lowered Tasha inch by inch.

Dram looped the rope around the skis, circled her waist and with three half-hitches, secured it. Taking the other end, Tasha used the same ties to tether herself. Dram stood beside her and as Tasha, with her back to the crevasse, stepped off the edge, Dram allowed the rope to feed around the snub they had created from the skis.

Tasha's descent had begun.

With her feet against the wall of ice, she abseiled. Tasha was a spider on a thread, hoping that her reckoning of Biscetti's position was correct: directly below.

Dram and Tasha were no longer able to see each other, to see anything. They worked by touch and by calling to one another in the smother of the cloud.

Dram made the most of her height and her strength, holding the rope tightly, watching the spools diminish as she repeatedly relaxed her grip, a momentary release to gradually lengthen the line as Tasha dropped down.

Between the walls of ice, Tasha could see nothing. She called to Biscetti and heard her voice.

"I'm here, Tasha. I think you're above me."

That at least was in their favour.

Slowly stepping down the face of the ice, gripping the lifeline, careful to place no sudden strain on Dram, Tasha peered downwards. In the eerie white mist, tinged with blue from the ice, she made out Biscetti's skis. They were inverted arches, stuck fast across the width of the crevasse where it had narrowed. An idiosyncrasy of the fracture had saved Biscetti.

Tasha dropped another metre. She could now see Biscetti looking up at her. "Hi."

"Hello, Tash."

On the surface, Dram watched the last loop straighten, held hard as the line nudged the last of its length around the skis. Tasha could expect no more. "Tasha," she shouted. "That's it. There's no more rope."

Her warning came muffled, a far away murmur, but it had meaning for Tasha. She tugged at the rope. It held solid, no more slack.

Another metre is all I need. Come on, Dram. Do something. Biscetti needs us.

The girl hanging from her skis saw the frustration on her sister's face. "The rope's too short, isn't it?"

Tasha stretched downwards, her arm extended. "Try to reach my hand."

Biscetti strained to raise her hanging body, the muscles of her stomach and thighs contracting. She held up both arms, reaching for Tasha.

Like trapeze artists hanging from high wires, the sisters grabbed for each other. Gloved fingers felt the breeze of other fingers flailing close. Hands closed, only to clutch empty air.

Tasha pulled at the rope, trying to get the length that would let her hold Biscetti. The rope, and Dram, would give no more.

Tasha stretched again. The hand she reached for brushed against hers, a touch, fingertip against fingertip.

Biscetti unfolded her body to hang vertical again. "It's no good Tash."

"Biscetti, it'll be okay. I'll have to go up, but I'll be back to get you," Tasha grinned encouragement. "Don't go away."

Biscetti raised her brows. She knew that Tasha was aiming to keep up her spirits, but she was hanging upside down in a split in the ice. Ice was not dependable. The fissure had appeared without warning and could widen. No longer held in the vice, she would fall and never be seen again. Or the crevasse might close, creak and grind as the walls came together, ice again meeting ice and she crushed between.

The alternatives were too horrible to think about. Biscetti gritted her teeth and watched Tasha begin her ascent, fading into the gloom.

Alone again, her hope was that her skis would continue to hold and that somehow Tasha and Dram would find a way to get her out. Tears filled her eyes. It didn't seem possible.

Chapter 9

Returned to the man-made cavern, Snotty and Mangrove were given fish to eat. The Torterats, more generous than on the previous day, increased the portion that each could have.

"Maybe the Trats are getting to like us," Snotty said.

"They'll like us for as long as the fish are biting." Mangrove chewed and wiped oil from his lips. "The day we fail to bring home food is the day our usefulness is over."

"Hmm," Snotty nodded. "Then, I suppose, *we'll* be on the menu."

"You could say that."

The two ate, thinking of what the future might hold.

Snotty broke the silence. "The search for us must've begun."

"Of course and it hasn't snowed. Our tracks won't be hard to follow. The question is, if we're found, what then?"

Both were quiet again, knowing that there would be two, maybe three Foragers looking for them. They would find the tracks and be led to the stone archway of the cavern. The answer to *what then* was easily given. The Trats were an overwhelming number. The rescuers would become captives too.

"We've gotta think of a way out of this, Manny."

"Oh really?" The sarcasm was undisguised. "I've been trying to do that ever since we got here." Mangrove's teeth tugged at the fish he held. "This would taste a lot better cooked."

Snotty looked at the wooden structures spread around the cavern. "If you like, I could start a fire."

The warming pot was gone, buried in the snow of the avalanche, but fire could be made. A spindle of wood rotated in a knothole would heat. Trat fur that lay like dust on the floor of the cavern or the lining from their own jackets could be ignited and fed with fish oil and shavings of wood. Each still had his knife. The idea was feasible.

"How do you get that across to the Trats?" But even as Mangrove asked the question, another came into his mind. *Why would we try to explain anything to them?*

Snotty watched the change in Mangrove's expression as ideas surfaced, each in turn considered like the turning pages of a book. "What are you thinking?"

"Animals are afraid of fire. Trats are animals." Mangrove spoke slowly, convincing himself as the plan developed in his mind. With his eyes he directed Snotty to check out the cavern.

Wherever they looked Torterats lay sleeping, some on their sides, mouths open, others flat on the floor, snouts forward and legs spreadeagled. Gorged with the feast of fish provided by Manny and Snotty, every Torterat had succumbed to the weight of food in his stomach, found a place to rest and to digest the meal.

"Can you get a fire going without waking them?"

Snotty considered the question. His fire-making spindle was probably still in his backpack. The pack lay by the stone archway and between it and where he stood, snoring Torterats lay like a creamy carpet on the floor. Stepping among them, even if he was lucky enough to find foot-room, would be certain to wake at least one. "I don't think so, unless ..."

He was looking at the door of the hut. It hung from ancient hinges, a thick sliver of wood splitting away from one of the planks. Shaping it with his flint blade would not be difficult. The operation would also provide shavings to boost the flame as soon as he had dust and fur smouldering.

"Manny, I'll need to shape a shaft. Once I have that, yeah, a fire would be no trouble."

"Hmm." Mangrove was nodding, still thinking.

"Do you want me to do it?"

"Make the spindle while we have the chance. We'll save the fire until the rescue party arrives. That's when we'll need some sort of distraction."

Snotty took his knife and drew it down the split in the timber of the door. A sliver came away, half a metre that he began to shape, thick in the middle, thinning as it tapered toward each end. He worked the wood quietly, shaving piece by piece and as they fell, Mangrove collected the wafer-thin slices, whispering that when they were aware the rescuers were close, that's when Snotty should get the fire going. That would be the time for action.

Completed, the thicker central section, smoothed to allow the shaft to spin easily in Snotty's hands, was placed back in the split from which he had taken it. Carefully forcing the spindle downward, he continued the pressure until it was held tight. The tool that would provide fire was again part of the door from which it had been fashioned.

Not a single Torterat had stirred.

Mangrove yawned. At this point there was no more that he and Snotty could do.

Chapter 10

"You have to do it." Tasha stood with her face close to Dram's. "There's no other way. We can't leave my sister to hang there until she freezes."

"I can't do it."

Tasha stepped back, her head tilted to one side as she looked at Dram. "Are you frightened to go down for her?" Disbelieving that Dram, her leader, would lack courage.

"Of course not! I told you. You won't be able to haul me and Biscetti out."

"Dram, whether you go down or I go down, coming up, Biscetti will pull herself out hand over hand. We'll put a double loop around the snub. The skis will bear almost all the load."

Dram looked away from Tasha. "I'm not going down. I have to stay as anchor."

"I'll never reach Biscetti." Tasha raised her hand and touching Dram's hood gently turned her face so that they could look into each other's eyes. "Please, Dram."

Dram shook her head.

There was no time for further argument. "Take the rope from your waist, Dram."

Dram did so and it seemed to Tasha that there was a look of shame on her face.

To give herself more rope, Tasha would do without the stanchion of the snub. Instead it would become the anchor, the line wrapped around the skis, hitched, wrapped and hitched again. Tasha pulled the hitches tight and leaned back with her whole weight to satisfy herself that the anchor would hold.

Dram stood aside, playing no part.

At the edge, Tasha let the line drop. Now knotted around her waist, the other end anchored to the skis, the loop fell into the mist.

Tasha watched it fall, turned to Dram and made a final plea. "Help me if I call for you, Dram."

With the rope as her lifeline, Tasha once again abseiled down the face of the ice.

When she could see Biscetti, she called to her. "I'm here. Are you okay?"

Biscetti's words came thick in reply, slow and sleepy. "I'm cold."

"Wake up. We're getting out of here."

Tasha lowered herself until her face was close to Biscetti's. Although their heads were now level, the body of the girl hanging upside down was now higher than Tasha's. "Put your arms around my neck and hold tight. I will pull myself up. When I'm a little higher I will undo the bindings of your skis. You must hang on, Biscetti. Once your bindings are loose, you must hold me tightly or you'll fall. Do you understand?"

"Hmm."

"Biscetti!" Tasha shouted, her face so close that her sister jerked in surprise. "Do you understand? Hold tight!"

"Okay, I will." And Biscetti, hanging like a bat, lifted her arms and draped them over her sister's shoulders. As Tasha, hand over hand, pulled herself to the point where she could free Biscetti from her skis, Biscetti tightened her grip and slowly, from being totally inverted, her body curled, feet still in the skis above, head and shoulders rising as she clung to Tasha.

"I'm at your skis," Tasha said. "I'll release your right foot first. Okay?"

"Yes." Biscetti was shaking. The skis were all that had held her in mid-air. For more than an hour they had kept her alive.

With the bindings undone, she would be clinging to Tasha. If her fingers cramped, if her strength failed, she would drop, until somewhere way, way down, her young life would come to an abrupt end.

Putting her faith in the knots she had tied, Tasha let go of the rope and dangling from it used both hands to get Biscetti's feet from her skis.

"Okay." But Biscetti was not prepared. With the bindings undone, her right leg dropped out of the ski. The jerk sent a shudder to swing the girls, bumping them against the ice wall of the crevasse. The sudden twisting movement dragged Biscetti's other foot from its ski. Her legs, from being above her and supporting her, fell and in an instant all her weight transferred to her arms and clutching fingers.

"Oh!" Biscetti feared that she would lose her hold. She wrapped her legs around Tasha, buried her face into her back and clung.

The sisters swung in the void, crashing into the ice, bouncing away, smacking hard again and again while above, the rope tugged at the anchor point, twisting, turning it, so that the packed snow began to give way.

Dram heard the rope sawing at the ice at the cliff edge, watched the anchor sway and enlarge the hole that held it. She ran to it, jumping to pack down the snow again and then, sitting, leaning back on the anchor to prevent it giving way, with her heels dug into the snow, she grasped the rope in her hands and took the strain.

Below, the wild swinging slowed, but Biscetti was a load that Tasha could not carry for long.

"Grab the rope, Biscetti. I can't do this alone."

"Sorry." Still gripping with her legs, Biscetti reached above Tasha's head and took hold of the line.

The four hands worked in harmony, always one of Tasha's and one of Biscetti's gripping the rope. With team work they lifted themselves to safety.

Biscetti was the first to roll onto the snow. She lay there as Tasha hauled herself over the edge and, exhausted, lay beside her.

"You got me out, Tasha. Thanks."

"That's okay. I'm glad. Now stand up and get yourself warm."

Tasha looked at Dram, still sitting with her back to the anchor point, the buried skis that belonged to Snotty and Mangrove. "Thanks, Dram."

Dram nodded. "I thought everything would give way. I thought I was going to lose you. What happened down there?"

Breathing deeply, still recovering her breath, Tasha took a few moments to explain what had happened. She got to her feet. "The skis are still down there. We can't leave without them. I'll need the axe. They're jammed into the ice wall."

Dram nodded. She knew that it was she who should go down to retrieve the skis, but the thought remained that the others might not have the strength to bring her up. Holding the skis, she would not be in control. She would be reliant on Tasha and Biscetti. Anxiety tightened the muscles of Dram's chest. What if something went wrong? She stared at Tasha. "Yes, you do that. Biscetti and I will pull you up. Signal when you're ready."

With Biscetti helping Dram to hold the rope, Tasha for the third time descended into the void. Suspended, she hacked at the ice, freeing first one ski and then the other. Already tired, the action tired her more. She held the skis with one arm and jerked at the rope. She saw it move, felt it tighten at her waist and then she was being raised. Slowly, she walked up the blue face of the vertical cliff of ice.

Again on the snow, Tasha lay down. "I must rest, Dram and I need to eat and drink."

"Well, for a little while. Remember that our mission is to rescue Snotty and Mangrove. Biscetti has cost us valuable time."

"Hey," Biscetti said. "It wasn't my fault *and I could have been killed.*" Angrily she stalked off to the backpacks, returning with part of the hare. She handed it to Tasha.

"We might as well all eat," Dram said.

"Puh!" Biscetti glared at her.

They sucked at snow.

Tasha carried the hare meat to her pack. "We must use the rations first. This fresh meat will keep for later." She brought portions for Dram and Biscetti and for herself. Dram frowned, but said nothing.

After an hour, the cloud thinned a little. With visibility improved, Dram suggested that they move on. Tasha would have gladly slept, but to argue with Dram would cause further upset. Success would only come if the group pulled together.

"Okay, what do you want to do? Do we bridge the crevasse or detour to try and find its end?"

Dram looked at the fissure, gauging its width. She grimaced. "We'll detour." The far side was at least two metres distant, probably more.

They skied close to the split in the ice, following its ragged southern edge. They travelled for thirty minutes before they saw the gap begin to narrow. In another five the blue walls came together. Beyond appeared unaffected, the snow windblown and ridged.

With Dram leading, the girls rounded the end, or the beginning, of the great split in the ice and followed it to where they could once more pick up the trail.

The cloud was lifting, a fresh breeze tearing gaps in the mist, blowing it away.

The girls were using their skis like skates, alternately pushing from leg to leg. Occasionally Dram looked back to check that the other two were keeping up, but she said nothing. The only sound was the rush of their skis over snow.

At the rear, Tasha watched Biscetti, the easy minimum movement as she transferred her weight from ski to ski, lifting each barely above the snow to conserve energy. *I could have lost her.* She looked ahead to Dram and through her mind ran the things Dram had said: her refusal to go into the crevasse, her initial attitude that they should leave Biscetti to her fate, that it was too dangerous to take a line to her. It was plain to Tasha that Dram should never have said the things she did and as leader it was Dram who should have gone down to make the rescue. *She's bigger, but with the snub I could have held her. She would have been able to reach Biscetti at the first attempt.*

It worried Tasha that Dram would soon be the new Queen. *She had me go down three times, even when she knew I was tired.*

For Tasha, Dram's actions were not those of a trusted leader and she wondered how the Camarilla would fare with Dram as Queen. The Camarilla looked to the Queen for strength in difficult times, looked to her for guidance, for decisions that could mean life or death for everyone. The Queen thought for them all, considering the safety of all others before her own well-being. That was the way it had to be.

Tasha thrust at the snow, following the two in front, hoping that Avon would not die.

"There." It was Dram shouting, pointing at the disturbed snow ahead. They had recovered the trail.

Tasha called to her to stop. Dram waited.

"What do you plan to do, Dram?" Tasha waved an arm at the tracks. "There must be dozens of Trats."

"More!" Biscetti said.

"Whatever. So many that they were able to capture Manny and Snotty. So how are we going to get them away from the Trats?"

"Fair question," Dram said. "But that decision can only be made when we catch up with them." She looked up at the sky, at the fleeting clouds. "The night will be clear and the moon is approaching full. We'll sleep now and get going again when the moon rises."

Dram looked at Tasha for agreement, knowing that weary as she must be, there would be no argument.

Tasha nodded. "You want to follow the tracks lit by moonlight?"

"Yes. I want to get close enough to the Trats to check them out. Night will give us some advantage. We'll see them without being seen."

"You hope," Biscetti said.

Chapter 11

Mangrove stirred. As the hours of night had progressed, the light of the moon had begun to enter the cavern, a pale shaft spearing obliquely through the archway. He opened his eyes and, lying still, watched the moonlight gradually expand to fill the entrance. Beyond the arch he could see the snow and, lying where they had been left, the fish he and Snotty had brought back. They had caught such an abundance of food that what could not be eaten had been left for another day.

Within the cavern, reflected light washed the dome and the walls, giving them a milky dimness. Mangrove let his eyes wander, staring at the shapes that, aeons before, someone had attached to the rock. Why, he wondered. Why did those people from ancient times make those objects and put them there? What's their purpose? He had no answer.

He looked around at the sleeping Torterats. Occasionally a grunt would rise from the carpet of bodies, or a series of sharp squeaks that came from a Torterat dream. It niggled at him that with their captors asleep, he and Snotty could not attempt escape. Even if they could make it through the archway, without skis, they would never outrun pursuing Torterats. The only hope lay with the rescue party.

Mangrove looked at the split in the door where Snotty had concealed the fire maker. In the dim light it was unidentifiable, but it *was* there and it *would* be used. He thought of the rescue party, the two or three Foragers given the task of getting him and Snotty to safety. If they came, when would they come? How could the two small groups combine to effect escape?

The moon continued its climb through the sky. The light entering the archway moved with it, slowly sliding from one side to the other, growing, diminishing, until it was gone and the cavern filled with darkness. All that time, Mangrove thought to devise some stratagem that would defeat the Torterats. Fire seemed to be the only way.

"Biscetti, Biscetti."

"What is it?"

"Wake Tasha."

Biscetti rubbed at her face with snow, the cold stinging her to wakefulness. She went to her sister and shook her. "Time to go, Tash."

The three of them sat and ate, using the provisions that they had brought from Homecave. It was a small meal. They kept to the fraction on which they had agreed, saving the hare for Mangrove and Snotty and for the time when the rest of the food had gone.

The full moon had long risen. Now overhead, the pattern of mountains and craters on its pale round face were the features of a familiar friend, distant, but reliable. In the moonlight, the snow crumpled by paws and the distinctive deeper impressions left by Snotty and Mangrove, stretched into the distance, a roughened trail, easy to follow. The night was still. Without cloud, without wind, the gelid air stung their cheeks and seeped into their clothing.

Dram licked her lips clean and stood. "Let's go before we freeze. And remember, on a night like this noise travels a long way."

Refreshed by sleep and the meal, they set off. Dram led and Biscetti followed, with Tasha hauling the sled. They skied without talking, each thinking that the end of the journey could not be far off, wondering where the trail would lead and what might lay in store for them. Occasionally a head would turn to the sky for reassurance that it remained free of cloud, glancing at the moon, confirming direction.

The quick checks gave them comfort. The tracks continued to point north and without wind to carry their scent, the Torterats would have no warning of their coming.

Dram raised an arm for the group to stop and come close to her. She pointed. The dim outline of another range showed dark on the horizon. The tracks aimed straight for the shadow of hills.

Tasha whispered. "A hollow mountain carved by ghosts is what Cloud said."

"Perhaps," said Biscetti, "that's where the Trats live. They must have a home somewhere."

Dram spent a few moments moving her eyes from the horizon to the moon and back, calculating whether it would set before they reached the hills. "If there is such a mountain and it lies in that range, we have another two, maybe three hours on our skis. The moon will still be up."

Biscetti and Tasha agreed. The moon would be low, but they would have its light for a short time after reaching the hills. When it set, they would be in total darkness and dawn would not lighten the sky for a further two hours.

"So what's the plan?" Biscetti was sceptical, still annoyed with Dram.

Dram explained that they would keep going until they had some idea of where Mangrove and Snotty might be held. "We use the moonlight while we can."

"Then?"

"Biscetti, stop it." Tasha admonished her sister. "Dram's responsibility is tough enough."

"Okay, but we think we've found them, then what? Do I whistle for them"— Biscetti blew the two high-pitched opening notes of the call made by the Giant Snowy Owl — "just like that? And they say, oh gee, that must be Biscetti and the rescue party. See you later Trats, we gotta go."

"Leave it."

Biscetti frowned, but said no more.

Dram looked to Tasha for support, for her opinion, but Tasha was staring at Biscetti.

"You imitate the Snowy Owl so well, like it was here, like you are the bird itself."

It was true. When Biscetti chose to mimic some sound, or the voice of someone she knew, everyone would be fooled. It was the same with the animals and birds whose sounds she copied. In the frozen land there were so few of them. For one to hear another was so rare that it brought immediate reaction, an urgent looking for the mate where none existed.

"I like doing it," Biscetti said. "It's fun."

"Perhaps more than fun, maybe the owl can be the way to rescue Snotty and Manny."

"We're wasting time, Tasha," Dram said. "You haven't heard what I have to say."

"Patience, Dram. Let me tell you what I'm thinking." And Tasha unfolded her idea. With the boys' prison, or wherever they were kept, located, the rescuers would wait for the moon to set. In the darkness, Biscetti would creep close and give the cry of the owl, the two notes followed by four throaty calls and then four more. The sound of the Giant Snowy Owl was unmistakeable, a menacing sound that small, and not so small, animals feared. "Sometimes we call her the 'The Terror', and you know why. The Snowy is a killer. Once her talons grip, her beak rips the victim to shreds."

"We know that, Tasha. No animal likes that owl." Dram had no patience, despite Tasha's plea. "What are you getting at?"

"If the Trats know the Snowy, if they've been attacked in the past, the sound of its cry will put the fear of death into them. The Trats will try to get away, fast."

"Hey," Biscetti had listened carefully. "You want *me* to get close to the Trats? What if they aren't scared of owls?"

"I think they will be. The Snowy is big and she's dangerous. What's more, the Snowy will enter caves when hunting. There's no place to hide from her." Tasha looked up at Dram. "Have you ever seen an animal that didn't fear that owl?"

"No."

"And, Biscetti, you won't be alone. Dram and I will be with you. We've come this far, what other way is there to rescue Manny and Snotty?"

"You're forgetting one thing, Tasha. We've always run from the Trats. No one has ever stood up to them. It's not in our nature." Biscetti's concern showed in her face. "Maybe Snotty and Manny tried, but the Trats have them."

"That's my point. We can't beat the Trats physically. There are far too many of them. *We have to make the Trats run.* We have to outsmart them." Tasha looked at Dram. "Don't you agree? We have a bow and four arrows, our knives and the axe. When we set out we didn't expect that the boys had been kidnapped. The weapons we have are no match for Trats. Force is not the way for us."

Dram weighed the argument. She had no wish to confront the teeth of Torterats, but she was the leader and somehow the three of them had to make an attempt at rescue. What worried her was that the subterfuge Tasha suggested might not work. The Trats would not be fooled, or had no fear of Snowy Owls. Either way, she, Tasha and Biscetti would fall to a tidal wave of Torterats and be killed. The Endless Night would claim them. The quandary for Dram was that in proving herself as leader, she might not survive. "Hmm," she said. "I'll make the decision when the time comes."

Again they propelled themselves across the snow, the silhouette of the range seeming to rise higher with their approach. As time passed and the distance decreased, the girls could make out individual peaks, clefts and valleys. The direction of the tracks never varied, due north toward the centre of the range.

Two and a half hours passed. The moon had dropped to within a few degrees of the western horizon. Dram raised her arm. The ground had begun to rise. The tracks had not deviated. Five hundred metres ahead, they seemed to stop at the face of the highest peak.

"Wait here," Dram said. She shucked her pack and bending low, skied for a further two hundred metres. There she dropped to the ground and gazed in astonishment. *A mouth of stones that should fall down.* With her lips she silently formed the words. The trail left by the Torterats disappeared into the arch that Cloud had seen in her trance. Dram shuddered. Snotty and Mangrove were with the Trats. *They're in the stomach of the mountain carved by ghosts.*

Dram rose, returned to Biscetti and Tasha and told them of what she had seen.

Tasha nodded slowly. "Cloud was right. The boys must be inside."

As she spoke, the moon began to slide from view. In minutes it was gone. The time for action had come.

"What do you want to do, Dram?" Tasha asked.

"It may be better if Biscetti *does* go alone. If there is a problem, I'll use the bow to drive off the Trats."

"Then we run and leave the boys to their fate."

Dram, tall, beautiful, looked down at the sisters. "I have to think of the clan. To lose two is better than losing five."

"How can you, Dram? Snotty and Manny are so close now."

"That's my decision."

"Dram, please reconsider. Listen to me. We came all this way to rescue the boys. We know where they are and ..."

Dram cut Tasha short. "Cloud may have been right, but we cannot be sure the boys are inside that mountain, or even alive. We must minimise the risks we take."

"I believe they *are* held by the Trats. And I believe Cloud really *did* see them in the belly of a mountain." Tasha pointed to where the tracks abruptly ended. "There, that's where they are! And another thing, you can't send Biscetti alone. We shouldn't split up. It weakens us. Dram, believe me, we should stick together."

Tasha had done her best to persuade Dram and knew that there was nothing more that she could do. The leader's judgement could be questioned and reasons for it sought. That was the custom of the Camarilla. A recommended course of action should be examined from every angle. It was the sensible way to achieve the best result in dangerous circumstances. Tradition also demanded that from the alternatives offered, the leader made the binding choice.

Tasha remained looking up at Dram, waiting for the answer. At her side, Biscetti imagined the situation, she alone in the dark, midway between the boys inside the mountain and Dram and Tasha hanging back at a safe distance. It was a frightening picture where, if Tasha's idea failed, her little sister would meet her end.

For Dram, the dilemma was now starkly highlighted. If the ties of sisterhood were too strong, if Tasha carried out her intention to go with Biscetti, she, Dram, would be the one left alone. Nagging at her too, was the need to come to a decision quickly. Rescue was best attempted when moon and sun were absent from the sky. Time was running away, the period of darkness in which they should make their move shortening minute by minute.

Dark as it was, Tasha could see doubt troubling Dram, how difficult it was for her to decide. "With only starlight, Dram, to aim with certainty, you need to be close to the Trats. Come with me and Biscetti. Let the three of us together win our way to the boys. And, Dram," she added words sweet to Dram's ears, "you are the leader. We are all relying on you."

Bigger than the others, older, Dram breathed deeply, conscious that she had to give direction. Among the worries of the present predicament, ambition was also nudging. She dearly wanted to be the next Queen. If she brought Manny and Snotty back to Homecave, Avon's choice would be made easy.

"*Remember that*! I *am* your leader! We'll all go together. Biscetti won't go alone."

Relieved, Biscetti exhaled a long sigh, her breath a streamer of steam in the cold air. "Thanks, Dram."

Her pack again on her back, Dram led the little group forward. What might develop would depend on how the Torterats reacted. They skied slowly and silently, eyes fixed on the stone arch.

No movement was obvious, the mountain, with its black opening, as still as the rock from which it was formed.

In the rear, hauling the sled, Tasha thought how uncanny it was. The only sounds that she could hear were her own breathing and the soft shush of skis on snow. Yet inside the mountain, now threateningly close, was the army of Trats and the two Foragers.

Dram pushed on until she was a mere hundred metres from the arch. There she signalled a stop and sought agreement. "Closer?"

Biscetti nodded and whispered that if they really wanted to spook the Trats, the cry of the owl would need to be near and loud.

"You take the lead," Dram said.

They edged their way on, each alert with an intensity fired by adrenalin.

Through her open mouth, Biscetti could hear her heart pumping, quick beats as she sucked in air.

As though skin was suddenly an organ sensitive to danger, Dram's whole body had lifted into goose bumps, yet from her armpits the sweat of anxiety dripped steadily.

The nerve endings around Tasha's eyes and ears seemed to be twitching, as though trying to force her to see the most minute things, and to hear sounds that could not be heard.

Biscetti did not make a direct approach. The plan had dangers enough. To amplify them by marching straight at the entrance was not, she thought, a great idea. Instead she took a course that angled them away from the arch and away from the line of sight of any Torterat that might peer into the night from the den. Once against the rock wall of the mountain, she would stay close to it as she led the group along it to take up position.

The detour took time, but soundlessly, like shadows, they made their way. Finally, the party that had come to rescue Snotty and Mangrove stood at the side of the open mouth.

The girls were so close that the odour of Torterats filled the air. Every breath the girls took let them know that they were but metres from the animal pack they feared. With the push of a ski Biscetti slid to the opening. For a moment she had the thought that if she were to stretch out an arm she could reach around the stones of the arch and wave to Snotty and Manny. If they were looking they would realise that an attempt to rescue them was about to occur.

How comforting that would be for them. She dismissed the idea. If the boys could see her, so could the Trats.

With one last look at Dram and Tasha, Biscetti gave the hunting cry of the owl, two high-pitched piercing whistles and then the series of deep, throaty calls.

The sound was as real as if the The Terror was on wing and about to enter the cavern, so real that Tasha could imagine talons and beak ripping flesh and shivers shook her body. Dram flinched, The Terror inflicted terrible wounds as it killed its prey.

Chapter 12

The first screeching whistles sent a ripple of alarm through the sleeping Torterats. Roused, the carpet of bodies rose and sniffed at the air and from many throats came a repeated yipping.

Also wakened by Biscetti's call, Mangrove and Snotty crouched by the window of the hut. Starlight coming through the archway barely diluted the darkness, just enough for them to see the Torterats' agitation.

"Did you hear that?" Mangrove asked.

"Yeah, a giant snowy, and very close. The Trats don't like it."

Some of the Torterats were standing on hind legs, noses twitching. Others were looking upward, turning their heads to find where the owl might be. Noise filled the cavern, but the initial yipping of alarm had turned to the angry squealing that the boys had come to know.

A bark of command bellowed to quell the din. The Torterats straining on hind legs, dropped to the ground. All looked in one direction.

Snotty glanced toward Mangrove. "King Trat has something to say."

The cry of the owl came again, but the Torterats remained still and as the twin bars of throaty calls ended, two sharp barks mobilised the Torterats. They rose from their positions of submission and squealing, climbing over each other in haste, ran in one unruly mob to the entrance and were gone.

"Now, Snotty, now. Start the fire. Something's going on."

Snotty removed the spindle from its hiding place and ripped a plank from the door. Digging into the timber with his knife he enlarged a knothole. "Okay, let's make this baby burn."

Rotating the spindle with his palms he looked for the first wisp of smoke, the signal that he was creating heat. He could neither see nor smell smoke. The spinning shaft began to wobble. "Manny, something's wrong. I'm not getting friction."

Mangrove put down the fluff and shavings that he held ready. In the scarcely existent light it was difficult to see what was happening. He bent low, his eyes close to the point of action.

The spindle was revolving fast and the wood should have been smouldering, but as Mangrove watched he saw the knothole enlarging and the shaft disintegrating. The ancient timber was turning to dust as one piece ground against the other.

"Give up, Snotty." Mangrove put his hand on Snotty's arm. "The wood's too old. It's just crumbling under the pressure."

Snotty pitched the shortened shaft at the wall. "Then let's run while the Trats are gone."

"Yeah."

Unsaid was the thought that this was their last chance to escape, an all or nothing throw of the dice.

As the horde of Torterats spilled from the cavern, Biscetti grinned. Her deception had worked. The girls pressed themselves to the rock face of the mountain and watched the fleeing Torterats.

"Yay." Tasha balled her fist and punched the air, happy that through Biscetti's skill, they had pulled off the stratagem.

Her joy was short-lived. Less than fifty metres distant, the Torterats' headlong flight had come to a stop. From the seeming melee, cohorts split and, fanning from the central group, wheeled to either side. The Torterats had about-turned and now faced the arch from which they had just run. Difficult as it was to make out detail, the girls could see the dim outline of Torterats manoeuvring. They were adopting the head and spreading horns of the fighting bull, the attack formation that had served the Zulus so well.

Dram's hand went to her mouth. "Oh no!" And Tasha realised that her brilliant idea had fallen apart. The Torterats had not run in fear of the giant owl. The sound of The Terror had no effect on them at all. The Torterats had picked up the scent of humans. The wild rush from the cavern was to enable them to identify where the Foragers were and then to eliminate them.

In alarm, both Biscetti and Tasha turned to Dram. The horns of the bull were now fully extended. The Torterats were ready to attack.

"We must defend ourselves." Tasha said.

Dram looked at her. "We have no chance against ..."

She stopped speaking, her eyes wide as Mangrove and Snotty shot from the interior of the cavern. "Manny, Snotty!" she shouted their names.

Taken by surprise, never expecting that their rescuers had arrived, the boys ran to them. Words of joy, of relief, of utter amazement, tumbled from five mouths as, all talking at once, they hugged one another.

The moment of happiness was brief. A single, shrill howl cut through the stillness of the night. Before the mountain had ceased to repeat the echoes of that cry, the screeching chant of the Torterats had begun. They were on the move.

Hugging abruptly ended, and the Foragers, in a single line, placed their backs to the wall of rock. In their minds was the thought that Endless Night was approaching, that each would be dispatched to eternity by the jaws of a Torterat.

Dram dropped her pack and with shaking hands drew the bow and the four arrows from it.

"Do you have axes?" Snotty asked.

"We brought only one." Tasha dragged the sled closer. "I'll get it."

Mangrove watched in disbelief as the sled appeared out of the darkness. "Are they my skis?"

"Yours and Snotty's. How else would you get to Homecave?" Tasha had slipped the harness from her shoulders and was wildly rummaging in the pack for the axe. As she pulled it free, her flute flipped onto the snow. She handed the axe to Mangrove and bending again, held the flute to her cheek before poking it inside her jacket.

Snotty was appraising the situation. Between them, they had five flint knives. *Useful only at close quarters. By then it's too late.* He counted the arrows. *Too few to drive the Trats away.* "What other weapons do you have?"

"A fishing line and some hooks," Biscetti said. "And we've got the rope."

Mangrove nodded and looked toward the advancing formation of Torterats. They were thirty metres distant, their concerted squeals a rhythmic repetition with which their paws trod in time. *The Trats are marching to the beat of the chant. They know exactly what their purpose is.* To Mangrove their position was hopeless. "Snotty, we can't stay here."

"Into the cavern?" The question was thrown urgently as the only possibility.

"Yes, yes." Dram looked at Snotty, pleading with him.

Tasha took her eyes off the Torterats for a swift glance at Mangrove. "Is there another way out of there?"

"We didn't find one."

"Never mind," Dram pushed him, "anything's better than staying here."

"Yeah, get out of your skis and let's go."

Like strung beads, one after the other the five slipped under the curve of the arch, the sled and its leash, skis and packs abandoned.

In the open, starlight had given some shape to the uneven surface of the snow and to the movement of the Torterats. Entering the cavern, the Foragers were swallowed by darkness.

"I can't see!" Dram's anxiety lifted her tone to a higher pitch.

"Me neither," said Biscetti.

Snotty felt for her. "Here, take my hand. All link hands. In a moment, when our eyes are more used to the darkness, we'll be able to see a little."

With the outlay of the cavern in his memory, he led them from the archway into the depths of the atrium. The chanting of the Torterats faded.

"Listen, the Trats are going." Dram was beginning to make out the figures of the others and her confidence was returning.

"I wish," Manny said. "It's simply that we're in the cavern. Outside sound is muffled."

"Oh." A glum, downbeat response. "Then we *must* find a way out of here. We *must!*"

"There are tunnels, but when Snotty and I had gone just a short way into them there was no light at all and where they lead is impossible to tell."

"Yeah." Snotty went on to say that they had tried to find for what purpose the tunnels had been made, but were forced to turn back.

The chanting grew louder. A boiling mass could be seen through the arch. Here and there spasmodic movement identified individuals in the advancing horde.

Snotty looked out at them. "They won't attack until the king Trat barks his order. That's when they'll be squealing and jumping over themselves to get to us." He spoke calmly, as though announcing some notable characteristic of the Torterat species.

"What are these?" Tasha was feeling the wall of one of the wooden structures.

"Some sort of dwelling, maybe." Mangrove said. "They offer no protection."

"Nothing in this place does," added Snotty. "What looks like stiffened rope is strung along the walls and the roof of the cavern. There are box-like things as well ..."

Whatever else he might have said could not be heard. The largest of the Torterats cried his order and screeching answered.

The archway filled with scrambling bodies, the wild stampede to be the first to maul the Foragers had begun.

Dram screamed and ran, searching for the ropes that Snotty had mentioned. *Where are they?* She tripped on the rails she had not seen, screamed again and stumbled toward the wall of the cavern. She could just discern the darker line that ran high along its length. *It's so high.*

Dram tracked it with her eyes. *Where can I grab it, where?* If she could get a hold on the rope, or whatever it was, she would be able to lift herself above the snapping jaws.

The pandemonium of the Torterats rose in crescendo, so loud that the air of the atrium seemed to solidify with noise, so loud that it was difficult to breathe, so loud that painful pressure buffeted her ears. Dram was crying, running with her hands touching the rock wall, looking upward, hoping to find a place where the line came lower.

"Yes." The box with the lever was there above her head. If she jumped and stretched, she might just get hold of it. That was her hope. Then she could pull herself out of reach of the Trats.

Dram leapt. The fingers of one hand wrapped around the protruding metal shank. Twisting, she swung her other arm so that both hands grasped it. She grunted with relief. Hanging there, she could now see that what Snotty had described as a rope, was in fact rigid and made of the same metal as the rails on the floor of the cavern. Better still, it had been laid in a channel gouged out of the wall.

With my feet in there, I'll be out of reach of the Trats.

It was a short term solution, Dram knew that, but delaying death was preferable to the alternative.

Concentrating on lifting her body, Dram felt the lever move. From its obliquely raised angle, it shifted a few degrees. Frozen in that attitude for aeons, the grease of lubrication a long-dried residue, metal ground on metal and screeched in protest. Dram's weight overcame the inertia of millennia. The lever, with Dram hanging from it, completed its downward arc and in so doing closed the points of the switch within the box. In one stroke, the energy collected by solar panels was let loose.

The result was immediate.

The cavern exploded with dazzling light. It was as though a dozen suns at their zenith had burst forth. The brilliance of the light momentarily blinded the Foragers. Only Snotty, his lids narrowed to slits, maintained watch on the Torterats.

With the flooding light a startled cry of fear came from every Torterat throat, instinct sending its sharp message to flee to the safety of darkness. In a tumbling mass, Torterats poured from the atrium and like water running from a basin down a drain they disappeared into the tunnels.

Before they had reached these hiding places, the sound of a human voice filled the great space of the atrium. The Foragers raised their heads and gazed in wonder. On the large, flat, rectangular plate that Snotty had noticed when he and Mangrove had first been brought to the cavern, a face had appeared. Big eyes were looking down at them and from the lips words were being spoken, words that the Foragers could not understand.

The face faded and on the screen, for that is what it was, came moving pictures of rivers flowing through green fields. Scenes of crops being harvested followed with the sound of machinery and people laughing as yellow grain poured into silos. From leafy orchards, cherries and plums, peaches and pears were being picked. Those scenes were replaced by pictures of city streets bustling with busy crowds, of schoolrooms where children sat with books or moved around asking questions as part of the learning process. For fifteen minutes the Foragers were shown life as they had never known it.

Then the scenes changed.

Time-lapse photography — a device, which although unknown to the Foragers, gave a message clearly understood — was used to show the passage of time. The rivers transformed from running streams to dry, lifeless ditches. Fields browned, and hands, outstretched from people no longer smiling, held a few pitiful grains to show the poverty of the land. In the cities great chimney stacks belched smoke into the air and a haze of pollution stained the horizon. Scene after scene filled the screen: of sea water being converted to fresh, of film taken from the air with all below a dead and desiccated land. The polar ice-caps were shown melting, broad sheets of ice breaking away to slowly shrink to nothing. All the while a voice was talking as islands were drowned by the sea.

Oceans were unknown to the Foragers, but they watched the sea invade continents, creeping into low-lying areas, spreading wide to inundate whatever lay before it. They were astonished by what they saw.

As the picture changed, humans could be seen involved in their daily activities and words were constantly spoken. The Foragers had no way of understanding what was said. Their own words and grammar had in fact evolved from the language they were hearing, but language is a living thing and over the millennia it had, like many living things, developed differences, so much so that to the Foragers it was a strange and foreign tongue. Nevertheless, the intonation of the voices and the facial expressions and gestures were familiar to the Foragers. Over time those human characteristics had remained the same and were instantly recognisable, reinforcing the message conveyed by the pictures.

The five stood silent, watching battles fought with weapons of great power. They saw rockets launched and cities destroyed as mankind was involved in wars for water, for food and for dry land on which families could live.

The technology of the twenty-first century ensured the eternal record of its errors. The Foragers looked on, sickened by what they saw, but this portrayal of the ancient world was but the overture.

On the screen snow began to fall on rural areas and on cities, those that lay in ruins and those that had survived destruction. A voice gave running commentary and if the words were not understood, once more the pictures told the story.

From the filming of reality, the camera switched to diagrams and animated cartoons. The globe of the world, then known as the *Blue Planet,* was shown in its orbit around the sun. To ensure that whoever saw the film on some future occasion understood that it was Earth he was depicting, the film maker had taken great care. The planet Earth was shown as it related to other visible planets and to recognisable constellations and heavenly bodies.

"Look," said Tasha. "That's our Earth."

"Yes." Mangrove too had realised that they were looking at the planet on which they lived.

As they stared at the screen, the image of a child's toy, a

spinning top, materialised beside the globe of the Earth. The top gradually lost momentum and, as its spinning slowed, it began to wobble, leaning outward, no longer upright.

The picture of the top faded from the screen. Engrossed, the Foragers saw the cartoon planet wobble in the same way as the top. When the motion stopped, planet Earth had a new axis. It had tilted a few degrees away from the sun.

The cartoon continued and in minutes showed how the tilt caused less sun to shine on the polar ice caps. Winters became longer and colder so that ice and snow crept over more of the Earth.

"Wow," Biscetti said. "Look at that!"

The others hushed her. More drawings had come to the screen.

Lines flowed to show that from that time, Earth took a slightly different path in its annual journey around the sun. An accompanying cartoon conveyed the message that the new orbit exaggerated the effect of the tilt, hastening the cooling of the world.

Had the Foragers been able to understand the voice accompanying the pictures, they would have learned that the tilt of the Earth in its relation to the sun varied every forty thousand years. Scientists had been able to measure the extent to which the axis wavered. The change was small, a mere two degrees, but enough to reduce solar radiation entering the atmosphere and so chill the planet. By cruel coincidence these orbital dynamics had come at the worst possible time, adding to the woes already being experienced by humanity.

The voice warned that the cooling of the planet would be cumulative, that the ice gradually extending from the poles would finally blot out the seasons. The world was doomed to freeze.

Flashing arrows appeared at either side of the cartoon world, one pointing upward, the other down. The arrows were indicating movement. A blue dot at the top of the globe was highlighted and then it too began to flash. As the Foragers watched, the dot shifted position. No longer at the top, it flashed from the bottom of the globe. To give further sense to the diagram, to ensure understanding, a navigational compass was shown. The camera panned in on the needle so that the group, huddled in the brilliantly lit arena of the cavern, could clearly see it swing one hundred and eighty degrees.

Snotty touched the pocket of his jacket. The thing he had found in the hut was the thing shown in the film. *The swinging needle must mean something.*

He had little to time to think about the compass. Its picture was replaced by people. They were working with machines and echoes of explosions sounded as rock and soil were hurled into the air.

Mangrove moved closer to the screen. "Look, that's this mountain."

Soon the Foragers were watching the excavation of the cavern in which they stood. They saw the steel rails laid and broken rock riding in skips wheeled along the rails. The archway was formed stone by stone and in the atrium they saw conduit — which Mangrove had thought was rope — set into its channel. Intrigued, they stood silent as lights were installed on the cavern roof and most astounding of all, they saw the screen from which the information was coming to them, carefully attached to the rock wall. The power source for all the magic before them was explained once again by the use of cartoons.

"They used the sun," Mangrove cried out aloud. "Somehow they captured the light of the sun on those flat and shiny panels and used it to light this cavern."

The others did not reply. The images of people had returned to the screen, emaciated figures of adults and children who held out empty bowls to show that they no longer had food. Sad scenes continued, of burials in the snow and weeping mourners who knew that they too would soon die.

Hands filled the screen holding a video camera. A finger pointed to a disc. With words and gestures, in elaborate charade, the film maker indicated that he had recorded the history of the twenty-first century and left it for whoever might one day view it. A woman, gaunt, black circles under her eyes, held a sickly child. Taking his hand, she waved it at the camera, a final symbolic farewell.

With those last poignant scenes, the images faded from the screen.

"That's what happened," Tasha whispered. "That's how the world once was and how those ancients ruined it."

"Why did the Earth change its place among the stars?" Biscetti looked to Tasha for an answer.

"I don't know, but all of it, everything we saw, was a story, the story of the ending of the Good Times."

"There's no more to see." Snotty glanced upward. "And if the light goes, the Trats will come for us. We have to get out of here. *Now!*"

Dram moved so that she stood in front of the others, facing them. "The Trats are gone." She pointed to the tunnels. The myriad eyes that might reflect light out of the darkness were not there. "They're gone. I frightened them away."

"Oh yeah?" Biscetti looked to the others for support.

"Listen," Snotty said. "If the Trats are gone, they must know of other ways that lead out of the mountain. They won't give up on us. We have to run."

"Snotty's right," Mangrove was already moving to the archway. "Let's grab our gear and go."

Anxiety spurred them. In seconds the sled was taken apart and all again wore skis.

Snotty glanced at the frozen fish that, stuffed with feasting, the Torterats had been unable to eat the previous day. "Everyone take a fish."

For a moment Dram thought of asserting her authority, forbidding any delay. She chewed at her lip. Biscetti made the decision for her, ramming the iron hard body of a fish into Dram's pack and then one into her own.

"Ready?" Snotty checked the group. "Okay." The best skier, he had assumed control. Taking his bearings from the stars, he fixed a course for Homecave.

They had travelled for thirty minutes, keeping just wide of the old Torterat tracks, when the sky in the east began to pale.

"We've done it!" Dram shouted to the others.

"Don't bet on it yet." Mangrove looked once again over his shoulder. The hollow mountain with the stone archway was far behind them and his quick searches had seen nothing following, but there were days of skiing ahead before they were safe. Even then, he thought, will we be really safe?

Dram raised her brows and pushed on to overtake Snotty. "I'll take the lead."

He shrugged and fell in behind her.

They skied on, strung out in a line, Tasha next, then Biscetti, Mangrove at the rear. The three girls used their stocks. The boys, with theirs still buried in the aftermath of the avalanche, were untroubled, skating freely over the flat terrain.

The sun nudged its rim above the horizon, splaying light across the sky before it came fully from hiding. The day had begun, an unusual day without cloud, bright with the hope of freedom and the expectancy of homecoming.

Every two or three hundred metres, Mangrove turned to ski backwards, scanning the snow for any sight of pursuers. Ski tracks ran beside the pock-marked trail, both a dead giveaway. Logically, Dram was taking the most direct route, putting distance as quickly as possible between the group and the hollow mountain. Mangrove shook his head in concern. Attempts at deception would have been useless. *The Trats know the way we must go. But we couldn't be more obvious.*

Chapter 13

Six hours after they had left the cavern, Dram called a halt. They would eat and rest.

The Foragers sank to the snow. Lack of sleep and the hard travel was taking its toll. Tasha opened her pack, handed some shoulder meat from the hare to Mangrove. He sniffed it before tucking it inside his jacket. "Thanks, Tasha."

Dram and Biscetti shared food with Snotty, all relying on the heat of their bodies to soften the flesh.

Uneasy about their situation, believing that he would be unable to sleep, Mangrove volunteered to keep watch. The others lay flat out on the snow and closed their eyes. When they woke they would eat.

Warmed by the sun, Mangrove sat thinking of the things they had seen on the screen, strange, unimaginable machines and happenings. Carving out the inside of a mountain to create a living space seemed incredible, but he had seen how it was done. With his own eyes he had actually seen it happen.

He chewed, relishing the flavour of the hare and as he ate, his eyes roved over the snow looking for movement. All was still. He yawned, rubbed at his eyes and once more searched the horizon for some sign. Around him the others slept.

The sun, so seldom seen, caressed them all. Mangrove's eyelids drooped. He straightened his back and inhaled deeply, fighting the weariness that begged him to lie down. His chin kept dropping to his chest, then jerking upright as he blinked and forced himself to open his eyes wide to stare into the distance. Four or five times his head fell forward and he recovered, but sleep was overpowering him. Mangrove slowly heeled to one side until he too lay sleeping in the snow.

The sun climbed high to noon and began its downward journey. For two hours the Foragers slept and while they did, the weather changed.

A suggestion of cloud appeared in the north-west, drifted higher, gathered size and darkened. Thunder rumbled, far off, barely to be heard, as yet not threatening but with the hint that more might be on the way. Taking time, gathering strength, the cloud towered into the anvil shape of thunderheads that merged and in boiling masses of grey and purple, rolled across the sky to snuff out the sun.

The warmth that had lulled Mangrove vanished. He stirred and sat up. *Oh no. How could I?*

"Hey, c'mon. We have to go."

Dram opened her eyes. "You worry too much, Manny."

"Maybe." He got to his feet. "I fell asleep and look what's coming."

Roused, the others had packs on their backs and were tightening bindings. Snotty glanced at the sky. "Any sign of Trats?"

"No, but I'm telling you, they'll be after us."

Dram was looking at the cloud. "We'll have snow soon. Our tracks will be buried."

"That won't matter to the Trats. They know where we're heading." Mangrove, angry that he had slept, apologised again.

Snotty waved the apology away. "Forget it Manny, if I'd taken notice of you when we were at the river, none of this would have happened. And Dram, we leave now. Okay?"

Tasha took one last look around to see that nothing had been left. A movement distracted her. In the periphery of her vision, something was out of place in the vast, white wasteland. She turned, squinting into the distance, already fearing that what she would identify would be Torterats. Seconds ticked by. The light had deteriorated badly, but there was no mistake. Trats, hundreds of them, were on the move, a scrambling patch of colour a shade darker than the snow. Tasha pushed hard at her stocks, angling her skis for power in her hurry to catch the others.

"Trats," she yelled. "They're onto us."

Snotty slowed until Tasha was alongside. "How far off?"

"Half an hour, perhaps less."

A gust of wind, forerunner of the approaching storm, struck them, raising a flurry of fine snow.

"Hmm. Well at least the wind isn't against us."

Dram, Biscetti and Mangrove hadn't slackened speed. Sleeping had cost them dearly. The advantage of the start was lost. Only speed would save them.

Tasha and Snotty caught up and, like a racing team, in single file, the Foragers skied south. The air on the naked skin of their faces grew colder and each tugged at toggles to tighten hoods.

Above them, tangled, angry masses of cloud were erupting, lightning flickering. In a shattering burst of thunder the blizzard began.

Dram led, skiing beside the old tracks, using them as a guide until falling snow covered them. In their stead, she let the nor-wester be her reference, unerringly heading south. In her mind was the single thought that if she skied hard, she would outpace the Trats, leave them behind in the blizzard, leave them floundering in new, soft snow.

Last in the line, Tasha increased speed until she was abreast of Snotty. "This is no good. We're heading straight for home." She had to shout, wind and snow punishing her with stinging force.

Puzzlement showed on his face, as though he thought that she had lost her reason. She told him of the crevasse. Dram was leading them to it. Their escape would be blocked because it was too wide to cross. He questioned Tasha. How far did the split in the ice extend? How long would it take to make the detour around it? She gave him her estimates and his face showed his disappointment.

"It may have closed again. Ice is like that." In hope, he put the proposition to her, knowing that if they had to deviate, the Trats would probably overtake them.

The problem dangled, waiting for solution.

"We'll talk to the others," Tasha said.

The skiers bunched up, shouting to be heard in the pelting, wind-driven snow. They weighed the alternatives, every minute diminishing the opportunity to make a run for the end of the crevasse.

Snotty gave his opinion: they had to continue on the present course. Somehow they would cross the gap.

The area of Biscetti's milk-white face not hidden by fur turned a paler shade. "Please no." Memories of hanging in space, fearing to fall, too vivid.

Mangrove considered the pros and cons. There was danger in whatever they decided. He worked the muscles of his face. The cold was paralysing his lips. "Sorry, Biscetti, we have no choice. Snotty's right."

She looked at him for a moment longer and turned her face away. She would fall, she knew it.

Dram listened to the argument. "What do you think, Tasha?"

Tasha had the picture in her mind. Ahead was the broken line of the gaping crack in the ice, far to the left it came to an end, but to traverse all that way would take time and she didn't really know whether there was enough time. The Trats were travelling fast, terribly fast. She shouted her answer, snow stuck in an icy fringe on the hood around her face. "Whatever we do, the risks are great, but," she tried to catch her sister's eye, to have her understand. "I agree with Snotty and Manny."

Dram nodded that she had heard. In her mind she could see Trats snarling, almost feel teeth puncturing her skin, tearing her apart. The experience in the cavern had been terrifying. She would take her chance that Snotty could find a way to cross the chasm that had opened in the ice.

In their chase, the Torterats had changed tactics. The blizzard was laying new snow, a fresh powder that made it hard for them to move at speed. To overcome the problem they adapted the characteristic disordered scrambling to give it a purpose. Like a tank or a tracked vehicle, they laid a firm base on which to run. Those in front lay down for the following ranks to tread upon them, the new front rank doing likewise. The phalanx of Torterats became an endless belt of living bodies racing over the deepening layer of powder.

Thick flakes of snow continued to be driven by the wind. Through the storm the Foragers held course. Twenty minutes behind them, the formation of Torterats rolled inexorably onward.

Dram searched ahead for the crack in the ice. It was difficult to see through the thickly falling snow. She slowed, and again the Foragers were presented with harsh alternatives. Rushing blindly could have them drop into the void, proceeding carefully allowed the Trats to close on them.

Snotty skied past Dram, led from the front and picked up the pace. He would rely on keen eyes to spot danger. In any case, he thought, there is no option.

Faces numb with cold, snow icing on eyelashes and blackening lips, the Foragers skied on, the gale howling around them, giving them extra speed.

All Biscetti could think of was that she was racing to reach the place where Endless Night awaited her.

The blizzard, the fresh snow, assisted Snotty. The blue of the ice showed up as a wavering line drawn across the white sheet of the land ahead. He turned, yelling into the wind that they were almost upon it.

They stopped at the brink, all five looking into the void, its sapphire walls dropping down to inky blackness.

Snotty asked Dram to take off her skis. He took tight hold of one and held it across the chasm. The tip of the ski was well short of the far side. Tasha watched as he ground his teeth and the muscles of his jaw tensed. Dram's skis were the longest, but not long enough.

"We'll need to lash two skis together." Snotty kicked out of his bindings and motioned for the others to do the same. He took the fishing line from his pack and asked Dram for the other.

Biscetti had begun to shake. She understood what he was about to do and what that would mean. Mangrove saw her trembling.

"It'll be okay. Just don't look down."

She shook her head in disbelief. To balance on the narrow ski, use it as a plank on which she would cross the crevasse was insane. "I'll never do it. I'll fall for sure."

"You'll be safe," he said and tried to wink at her, but the ice on his lashes made it an ugly gesture, mocking the assurance he intended.

Snotty placed Dram's ski on the snow and laid one of his own to overlap one end by half a metre. Smooth face to smooth face the skis were first bound together with one of the gut lines. There could be no error, knots and hitches were painstakingly tugged and tightened, but certainty took time.

Tasha watched the work progress. It seemed to be happening so slowly and the Trats would be moving fast. She turned to face the fury of the wind, pulling her hood even closer to her head, shielding her eyes with one hand. The driving snow cut visibility to a few hundred metres. She strained for some sign of Torterats. Snow was all that could be seen. *When they come, we'll have no warning.* The thought chilled her more than the flakes smacking into her face.

Snotty repeated the operation with his and Dram's second ski before binding them with rope tight against the first set. He had created a bridge two skis wide and, if his judgement was right, long enough to span the gap.

He lifted the makeshift walkway and carried it to the edge of the ice-cliff, the tail-end of the rope wildly flailing ahead of him. "Manny, grab the rope."

With difficulty, as Mangrove clutched at the whipping rope, Snotty stood the bound skis upright, fighting the gale that would blow them into the crevasse. "Okay, got it?" Manny nodded. "Right, lower away."

Slowly, and with great care, Mangrove let the rope run through his gloves until the awkward-looking bridge had come to rest, one end at Snotty's feet, the other resting on the far side of the great split in the ice. "Good." He tossed the length of rope into the air. It twisted like some maddened snake and caught by the gale fell to the snow on the far side. The rope would play its part again when they had all crossed.

Tasha glanced back, spent a moment examining the contrived and puny means of their escape. Snotty was expecting them to trust their lives to it, and like tightrope walkers, balance their way across this bottomless gulf with the wind howling. So much was against success, yet not to make the attempt ... She closed her mind to what might happen and peered again into the blizzard.

"I'm going over," Snotty said. "If it holds my weight, Biscetti, you come next, then Tasha. Dram, you're the biggest and heaviest. You follow Tasha."

There was no need to explain further what was in his mind. They all understood that his crossing was a test of the bridge. If it held together for him, Biscetti and Tasha would not send it crashing. Dram's weight might be a problem, but she was not much heavier than Snotty. Manny would be the last to cross. He knew what his role would be: the rearguard should the Trats arrive.

Snotty picked up his pack, preparing to place it on his back.

"Wait. Not that way." Mangrove took the pack from him. "Dram, can you throw this? Can you chuck it to the other side?"

All the packs were heavy, frosted solid with ice and weighted with gear and food.

Dram hefted the pack, her movement slow and jerky, limbs stiff with cold. She shook her head. "No."

Tasha shifted her eyes briefly from the distance. "Take the fish out. Throw it and then throw the pack."

With difficulty Dram broke ice from the ties and forced open the pack. She yanked at the rock-hard fish to free it and then like an Olympian hammer thrower, with her arms extended, both gloved hands holding the fish at its tail, she swung in a circle and hurled the fish. Spinning in the air it arced across the chasm and plopped into the snow.

Snotty patted her back. "Good one, Dram."

She smiled and in similar style threw the pack. It could be done. When Snotty had crossed, she would fling over the remaining packs.

Like Tasha, Mangrove was thinking of Torterats, measuring time and distance, computing how long the group might have. His skis and those belonging to Biscetti and Tasha would have to be carried. It would be terribly difficult, perhaps they all would die. "No," he muttered to himself. "Not if I can help it. We've come too far to fail now."

Snotty also understood that the skis could not be left, knew that he was the one to prove that his improvised bridge would do the job. He laid Mangrove's skis on one shoulder and breathed deeply, settling himself. He had confidence in his handiwork and no fear of the chasm below — getting across would depend on how he handled the buffeting of the gale.

Snotty filled his lungs and stepped on to the narrow walkway. He looked at where it rested on the opposite edge of ice, more than two metres, not so far. Keeping balance was hard. The wind was blasting at him, not with a constant pressure, but gusting with erratic extra violence. *I'm gunna run. It's the only way.*

Dram and Mangrove were watching him. Biscetti had shut her eyes. *Endless Night was about to take them all.*

Snotty took a last deep breath, waited for a gust and ran with it. The lashed skis under his feet sagged, rebounded, bounced like some narrow springboard, but held together. He was on the other side.

"Biscetti, your turn." Mangrove took her arm.

She pulled her arm free and backed away. "No."

"C'mon. You have to. I'll take your skis. You just run across."

Biscetti shook her head. She couldn't.

Time was wasting.

"Biscetti, please?"

Tasha's scream silenced him. "Trats, Trats!"

Through the thick curtain of falling snow they could all see the dim outline, the approaching throng, moving en masse, giving the appearance of a single living organism. The Torterats were minutes away, four, five at most.

Mangrove grabbed Biscetti. Said nothing, just grabbed her, swept her up and laid her on his shoulder, holding her legs. He stared at Snotty and called to him that he was coming over. He lumbered toward the bridge, Biscetti flopping at his shoulder, clinging to his jacket. Ignoring his advice to her, Mangrove looked down. He had to, the weight of two bodies was putting great strain on the lashed skis. They gave under his feet, took up an exaggerated harmonic motion so that Mangrove was forced to slow his run, time his stepping so that he rode up with the rising plank and sank with it. Through the strange, bobbing horror, Biscetti made no sound, her eyes shut tight.

Mangrove took one last step and at the edge, Snotty grasped an arm and pulled him on to the snow. Biscetti tumbled free. They had made it after all.

The Torterats could now be heard, their yipping blended with the howling of the wind. One hundred metres separated them from the Foragers.

"Go, Dram, go!" Tasha yelled, her voice cracking with fear.

Dram took one quick look at the skis lying where Biscetti and Tasha had left them. They seemed to stare at her, begging to be carried, silently saying that Tasha could not carry four skis. The shrill cries of Torterats came louder on the wind. Dram looked toward them. They were so close. She could smell their stink. *There's no time.* Dram ran. *Escape, get away from them,* the only thought in her mind.

Once more the bridge proved its worth and she fell terrified at the feet of Snotty.

Alone, Tasha turned to make the crossing. She bent to collect the skis, seizing one after the other, tucking them under her arm like sticks gathered for the fire. The noise of the Torterats was filling her ears. A ski dropped from her arm. Tasha fumbled in haste. The Trats were forty metres from her.

"Tasha!" Biscetti screamed for her sister to come.

Snotty glanced at Mangrove. Without the skis, Biscetti and Tasha were lost. "I'm going for them."

In three quick strides he bounded back over the gorge and swept up the fallen ski. "Give me another," he was wild-eyed, roaring the command at Tasha, "and go."

She fled. He followed, barely allowing her to gain the far side before he too was riding the springing planks to where Dram, Mangrove and Biscetti waited.

Torterats had seen how the Foragers crossed. They had no need to break off the chase. They would use the same bridge. In moments the humans would be theirs.

The Foragers grabbed the tail-end of the rope. The final, essential part of the escape plan had to be executed. Their only hope was to pull hard, treat Snotty's contraption like some mediaeval draw-bridge and raise it.

Taut, the rope began to sing with the wind, but the lashed skis did not shift.

"The tips must be stuck in the ice. We'll have to jerk them free." Mangrove ran toward the chasm. "Dram, all of you, come with me."

With the line shortened, they tugged with all their might urging the bridge to break free from the ice. It was happening, they could see the ice crazing, beginning to give. The bridge began to lift, but the Torterats had arrived. The frontrunner jumped, clawed his way on. Another followed.

Mangrove took command. "We have to shake them off. Slacken the line and when I say 'pull', run with it."

The narrow walkway sank back to rest. A great screech of triumph rose from the ranks of the Torterats, a momentary cry that turned to anger as the bridge suddenly whiplashed. Those clinging to it cart-wheeled into the air and then were falling, falling, bodies tumbling between the azure walls of ice until the blue darkened to ebony and they could be seen no more.

The Foragers collapsed on to the snow, chests heaving, sucking in air, looking at the army of Torterats slavering to get at them. The Foragers were safe. Trats could not walk on air.

"Let's go," Snotty said and they sorted out skis, retrieved packs and filled them with lines and rope and the fish that had once been intended for the Trats. As the Foragers went about the preparation for departure, the bark of the Torterat king came clearly to them. They stopped what they were doing and watched the army turn about and head northward.

Dram shouted for joy. "The Trats are going home."

"Ah, Dram," Tasha spoke quietly. "We haven't seen the last of the Trats."

"What do you mean?"

Mangrove answered for Tasha. "Don't you see, Dram, that it's us or the Trats. There's no room any more for both the Camarilla and Torterats."

Dram pushed the hood from her head and tossed her mane of hair. "We outsmarted them, didn't we, Snotty?"

"Yeah, we did," he grinned.

The others exchanged glances, turned south and with the blizzard howling around them, headed for Homecave.

Chapter 14

As he had done every day since the departure of Dram and the rescue party, Dumperty climbed to the mountain top above Homecave. He sat on the log beside the newly prepared beacon and looked across the broad snow-covered plain, grateful that the blizzard that had lashed the earth for two days had passed.

"I wish they'd come back," he spoke aloud. "I wish ..."

He broke off. There was a speck in the distance. Dumperty stood on the log, his eyes screwed up, trying to focus. There were more dark dots in the snow. He counted slowly, making sure, but yes, there were five and the tiny figures were moving, gradually increasing in size.

"Dram found them," he shouted and began his descent, hurrying down the steps cut in the mountain ice, yelling repeatedly, excitedly, that Dram had found Snotty and Manny. He had seen them, they were all coming back.

The word spread and the clan gathered at the entrance to Homecave.

"I'm going to meet them." Dumperty tightened bindings and sped away.

Long before he was in earshot, Dumperty was shouting his joy, cries of delight radiating from him, rising to the open sky, streaming behind.

As the distance between him and the Foragers narrowed, they heard him calling their names. When he was almost upon them, the five stopped, waiting, laughing, as happy as he that they were all together again.

Dumperty slipped out of his skis and put his arms out to Dram. She lifted him, kissed him and they hugged.

"You found them, Dram. You found them."

He squeezed her again and scrambled down to run to the boys. "Snotty, Manny, you're back."

Snotty held Dumperty high, looked up at the happy face. "Yeah, we're back." And tossed the laughing child to Mangrove.

"Hi, little one." Manny kissed his cheek and put him down for him to welcome Tasha and Biscetti, who each in turn was hugged and kissed.

The tiny boy's world was complete. His friends were back. They had all come home.

At Homecave the crowd watched the distant figures approaching, their skis laying parallels in the snow.

At her request, Avon was carried on her divan, her people in a semi-circle behind her. She saw the advancing Foragers with eyes different from those around her. They were welcoming home the best of their young, grateful that Dram's expedition had found the boys and all had returned safely. Avon shared those feelings, but uppermost in her mind was the question of her successor. She had to make the decision and that moment was approaching with the group coming across the plain.

Avon ground her teeth as pain drove through her chest and into her left arm. She stifled a groan and forced a smile. This should be a time of great happiness. Those around her should not see her agony, nor be reminded that the time when Endless Night would claim her was not far off. Perhaps I have a day or two before that happens, she thought, but certainly no longer.

The returning Foragers were now quite close, Sola and Situ giving to Cloud a running commentary on their progress, how easily they skied and how well they looked. Cloud's eyes were screwed to slits, but Dram and the others were an indistinguishable blur to the myopic girl. It didn't matter. Cloud was happy. The Foragers had survived the horrors she had seen in her trance.

Quiet until now, the Camarilla had begun to wave, calling out the names of those approaching. A murmur of appreciation replaced the greeting, tails of fish were visible.

Jemma grabbed Ingamo's arm. "They've brought food." She counted. A tail jutted from every backpack. "Enough for all of us."

Dram led the party to stand before Avon.

"Welcome home," the Queen smiled at Dram and sought each face so that all received her blessing. "And I see that you have brought food. That is especially welcome."

Avon called to Sola and Situ to stoke up the fire. A feast would mark the doubly-happy occasion. Once we have eaten, she thought, and after the recounting of the adventure, then I will announce my decision.

The smell of roasting fish filled Homecave, lingered after bowls had been filled and refilled and wiped clean with fingers licked repeatedly. With full bellies, all found places to sit and relax. It was time to hear what had befallen Snotty and Mangrove and how they had been rescued.

Avon called the boys to stand before the sated crowd. In detail they described how they had fled before the onslaught of the Torterats and how they had been captured.

"Snotty saved my life." Mangrove held his audience. Everyone present knew the mortal danger of icing. That Snotty had stripped to give Manny an inner vest was a brave and selfless act. The clan stood and clapped, sat and waited to hear more.

They were told of the things that Cloud had seen and of more which the boys experienced. Those listening shook their heads in wonder. "And most important, we learned that Trats can communicate. They have a language."

"Is that true?" Avon asked.

"Yes." Snotty said. "And they have a leader, a king perhaps, at least that's what we called him." Snotty pictured for them how, on the big Trat's command, the others formed the horns of the bull. "They know what they're doing and why. They made us their slaves."

The thought of slavery revolted Avon. She asked for detail. When given it, she sighed. There could be no doubt.

The Trats were more vicious and more sophisticated than she had believed.

Avon called Dram to come forward. "Tell us what happened to you and to Tasha and Biscetti?"

Dram described how they had found the hole in the ice and how she had shot a snow hare. "Some we ate, but we agreed that it was best to save most of the hare for Manny and Snotty."

She told of pulling the boys' skis from the aftermath of the avalanche and her decision, after some thought, that they should be taken with them, the skis would be needed when the time came.

The story of the sudden sundering of the ice brought a cry from Ingamo that he had warned them all.

"You didn't tell *me*," Biscetti muttered quietly. "I wish I'd known about bad ice."

Avon raised an arm for quiet and asked Dram to continue.

"The only way to get Biscetti out was for one of us to go down and get her." Looking into Avon's eyes, occasionally turning to the listeners seated around Homecave, Dram told how she was the only one strong enough to act as anchor while she lowered Tasha to Biscetti. "I let her down and hauled them both out. Once, when the rope was swinging wildly and the snub almost came out of the snow, I had to run to it, force it back into place and with my body keep the rope from failing. It was their lifeline."

Whispers rippled through the cave and voices could be heard saying how clever, how quick-thinking Dram was.

She went on, telling of the tracks that led them to the hollowed mountain. "It was here, with the Trats attacking us that I turned darkness to light and we were able to escape. The Trats followed and might have caught us at the crack in the ice, but Snotty used my skis to make a bridge. After I had thrown the fish and our packs to the far side, we ran across." Dram paused, and pointed toward Biscetti. "She was frightened, but Manny carried her on his shoulder."

"What about you?" Biscetti's anger flared. "It wasn't like you said at all. Tasha got me out of the crevasse. You were too scared.

You made her go down three times. And you were screaming in the Trat cave and ran from us."

"Snotty and I beat the Trats, didn't we Snotty?"

Tired and ill, Avon raised her hand, asked for quiet and beckoned Tasha and Mangrove to stand by her. "I'd like to hear from you, Tasha. Then Manny will have his turn. There seems to be some disagreement as to what happened."

As truthfully as she could remember, Tasha recounted for Avon, and the others listening, the events from the time the rescue party left Homecave until they had all returned. She avoided criticism, made no mention of Dram's willingness to leave Biscetti to her fate, nor that Dram would have abandoned the boys' skis at the avalanche. Tasha gave a simple account of all that had occurred. She admitted that it was her idea for Biscetti to imitate The Terror, honestly believing that it was the only workable stratagem.

"When we had run under the stones that should fall down, it was so dark that I could not see, but it was Dram who turned the darkness to light. It was then that we saw the most extraordinary things, things that were intended for us to see so that we would know what happened in the past." Tasha described the history that had been recorded on disc and shown on the screen.

Astonished, Avon asked Manny if this had really happened. He assured her that Tasha was speaking the truth.

Tasha completed the story to the point when Dumperty met the group. Avon was about to ask Mangrove for his version, but Tasha had not finished.

"Avon, we were successful. Snotty and Manny are back with us, but none of us are safe. We saw the ghosts who hollowed out that mountain. They left a grim message for us. They destroyed the Good Times until, fighting for the little food there was, they finally starved." Tears filled Tasha's eyes as she saw again the dying baby waving to her. "We must go, Avon. The Camarilla will either be killed by Trats *or we will starve*. We cannot stay. Food is so hard to find and the Trats are so many. We can't beat them, we'll never beat them. We must run before the Trats find us, escape to another, better place."

Avon sat silent and motioned Mangrove to speak.

"Tasha's right. We were lucky to get away from the Trats. We were almost caught again, but Snotty had the idea of a making a bridge. That was brilliant and he showed his courage when he went back to help Tasha bring over the skis. Dram was scared, she should have picked up a pair of skis, but she ran. She left it all to Tasha."

"I see," Avon said.

Manny had more to say. "On this expedition we have learned many lessons. Dram and Tasha and Biscetti achieved the goal you set them, they brought us back. But we came back with knowledge of the past and unless we run away, the past will be repeated. We must make the decision and leave. If we stay, Endless Night will take us all."

An agitated mumbling rolled around the assembly. To leave Homecave, to leave familiar surroundings, was an unwelcome thought. And run where? Kaldor lay to the south. No one had ever returned from Kaldor.

Avon called for quiet and asked that the meeting break up so that all could resume their normal tasks. Her wish was to speak again with the returned Foragers.

When the crowd had dispersed, Avon indicated that her conversations would be held in private with each individual. She chose Dram to be first. The others moved to sit by the fire, Avon first counselling them that until they had spoken with her, they were not to discuss anything that had happened while they had been away.

With Dram at her side, Avon asked for a full account of the events as they had unfolded. She listened carefully, looking into Dram's eyes, trying to see within the girl so that she might match truth with the words coming from Dram's mouth.

Purposely, Avon cleared her mind of any preconceptions. It was essential that her judgement be untarnished by opinion. She regarded all the Foragers with fondness, but the choice of her successor must rest on the cold facts of merit. Dram was physically strong, tall, capable and beautiful, loved by many, perhaps by all of the Camarilla. Avon listened and looked into the soul of Dram.

When the girl had finished, Avon thanked her and called Mangrove. Again, the Queen sought to find the truth, to separate personal viewpoint from actual event. What had really happened in the stomach of the mountain? How had the Foragers accomplished the crossing of the fracture in the ice? Who had done what? How had each acted and reacted?

Mangrove described the sequence of events as he remembered them and gave straightforward answers to Avon's many questions. She saw goodness in him. He was as she believed, an honest, thoughtful boy.

Avon thanked him and beckoned Snotty. The same questions were put to him and Avon could see the courage that fired his heart and his disregard for danger. She listened as he admitted his error in not leaving a fish to distract the Trats, listened as without self-consciousness he told of using his stocks to fight them and of giving Manny an inner vest. To Snotty bravery was natural, a part of his character that he did not question. His action at the crevasse, in running back to help Tasha, was simply explained: someone had to do it.

"And Dram, couldn't she have taken part?"

Snotty assured her that only Dram could have hurled the fish and the packs across the gap in the ice. "As for the skis, we were all rushing. Manny was meant to be last to cross, but Biscetti was terrified. He lumped her on his shoulder, the Trats were closing on us, Dram ran across, the skis had been forgotten. Tasha tried to gather them up. I ran to help her and we pulled up the bridge. Trats were already on it and it was iced over and stuck, but Manny jerked the rope and Dram is so strong, we got it up and the Trats were flung off. We watched them fall until they disappeared."

Avon nodded, smiling. They had almost lost their lives, but to Snotty it was such a matter-of-fact affair.

"I knew the Trats would come after us. They did, but our tactics were better than theirs."

"Will they come again? Is it their aim to wipe out the Camarilla?"

"Oh yes, but we proved that we are smarter than Trats. With luck we can beat them."

Biscetti was next. She did not mince words. Dram had let them down repeatedly. Avon reminded her of what had been said, that if Biscetti was to be rescued, Dram's argument was logical. *She* was the leader and the final decision *was* hers.

"It wasn't like that, Avon. Dram wanted to leave me!"

"But you were pulled out, Biscetti. Now please go on."

The blonde girl took up the story in the hollow mountain. "It was luck. She didn't know that lever could turn darkness to light. None of us could see anything, but I heard Dram screaming. She was really yelling. Dram only took over when the Trats had gone."

"I see. Tell me of what you saw from the past." And sadness enveloped Avon. The parallel was there. The Trats, so many Trats, would eat the land bare. What would become of the Camarilla?

Avon did not press Biscetti for details about her part in crossing the bridge. The Queen understood how her previous experience would have its effect. She thanked Biscetti. Tasha could tell her tale.

Now alone with her Queen, Tasha began with her own questions. Avon's worsening health was obvious, but Tasha wished to have that denied, to hear from Avon that she was recovering.

The Queen thanked Tasha for her concern. "But we all know that I have little time left."

"Don't say that, Avon. Please don't say that. You mustn't go now. It's such a difficult time for the clan. Without you, without your wisdom, what will we do?"

"Tasha, you will find that people die at the most inconvenient times." A calm, unemotional statement with the implication that nothing was permanent, that whoever took her place would need to rely on her own resourcefulness. "All of you must face the fact that tomorrow, perhaps the day after, I will be no more. Time for me is short. I must use the remaining hours in a way that will best ensure the future for those I am leaving. Now tell me, Tasha. From start to finish, what really happened?"

Tasha protested that she had given Avon a complete account. "Nevertheless, I would like to hear from you again."

During the retelling, Avon often broke in to clarify a point or to confirm the correctness of her understanding. Finally she thanked Tasha and lay back with her eyes closed. The exhaustive interrogation of the Foragers was complete. Avon needed to think.

She lay that way for most of the day. At intervals Jemma and Tang took turns to bring her warm broth, raised her and held her as she sipped. The nourishment was welcome, but Avon was slipping away.

With dusk her condition worsened. Torches were lit around her sleeping place and the Camarilla gathered.

For a time Avon slept. On awakening, as if calling on her last reserves of strength, she sat up. Furs were piled behind her and leaning back on them for support, Avon addressed her people.

"I will not speak for long. It is important that you hear what I have to say, so listen carefully." She paused, her breathing shallow, and with a raised hand indicated the confines of Homecave. "We must leave here before the Torterats invade and wipe us out. I have set tomorrow as the day of our departure."

An intake of breath was like a sudden rustle of leaves disturbing Homecave. To leave so soon, with so little warning, it was unthinkable.

"I know it is hard, but we cannot delay. We leave tomorrow." Avon's eyes closed. The clan waited.

Tiredly, her lids rose. "I will not be coming with you." She waited for the protests to subside and smiled at those with weeping eyes. "No, I will take my separate departure, and when I go you will have a new Queen."

Heads in the crowd turned toward the tall figure of Dram, many nodding that they knew Dram would be chosen, in their minds the thought that the Camarilla would need Dram's strength. Dangers lay in the way ahead, Torterats and Kaldor. Tall and strong, Dram as Queen would lead them all to safety.

Avon lifted her hand and beckoned Dram. "Come, stand by me, Dram."

Smiling, confident, Dram moved through the crowd, hands patting her shoulder in congratulation, until she stood by her Queen.

"Dram is the biggest and physically the most powerful of the Foragers and of you all. She has done much for all of us. It was she who led the expedition to rescue Manny and Snotty."

Voices murmured agreement.

"Dram has many fine qualities and is well liked." Avon waited for the whispering currents of approval to diminish and raised her hand again.

"Listen, all of you. From the beginning I have done my best to honour the trust you placed in me. My duty, to guide you and to guard you, does not end with my passing. The greatest responsibility a Queen has always had is to name her successor. It is her final act, one which guides the Camarilla into the future. The girl I choose to take my place must be the best of the Foragers. She may not shine in hunting, in climbing. She may not be the fastest across the snow. Her ability should lie in thinking, in wise counsel when the clan is faced with difficulty. This is the true test of her courage, faith in the correctness of her decision. Oh, there is no doubt that your Queen must be willing to risk her life to protect others, but it is the courage of her conviction that will preserve the group. In this way and through example she will gain your loyalty."

A chorus of agreement echoed around Homecave and Dram smiled at the assembly.

Avon sought quiet. "Tasha, come here please."

Tasha stood by Dram and looked up at her, admiring how tall and well made she was.

Avon coughed and Jemma brought more broth. The Queen sipped, taking time to get her breath.

"The Camarilla stands in harm's way. It will take an exceptional leader to ensure that you survive. Dram has many fine qualities, but my crown will not pass to her."

Avon took Tasha's hand. "For the reasons I have given, Tasha is your next Queen."

Resentment, fury, shadowed Dram's face. She stared at Tasha, not believing that she could be preferred. "But, Avon, I ..."

Avon stopped the rush of words. "You are disappointed, Dram, but in time you will find that I am right. Use your fine qualities to support Tasha. You must work together. The Camarilla cannot afford disharmony."

Dram frowned, but nodded her agreement.

Many were surprised at Avon's choice. Nevertheless, the ritual of acceptance of her successor was observed. All in turn came to Tasha to kiss her on both cheeks. The simple ceremony anointed her as Queen.

Attended by Jemma and by Tang, Avon was covered with her fur and made comfortable. She lay on her back, flames from the torches at the four corners of her sleeping place flickering red and yellow. The colours danced on Avon's face and as the torches burnt low and went out, the assembled crowd heard her draw her last breath, and watched the shroud of Endless Night wrap around her.

At that moment, with tears staining her cheeks, Tasha became Queen. Every face in Homecave looked at her. The baton had passed from Avon to Tasha. From now, for as long as she lived, Tasha's word would govern them. For better or worse, the stratagems she selected would determine their fate.

Tasha read the question on the faces, the doubt that she could hold secure the lives they put in her hands. She had to say something. "In the morning we will say goodbye to Avon. Then we go."

Wanting to soothe Dram, Tasha suggested to her that she should have the honour of lighting the funeral fire.

The plans for the immediate future had been announced. It was enough. Tasha's first act of leadership was accomplished. Calling Sola and Situ aside, she gave further instruction. At first light they were to commence preparation of Avon's funeral pyre. The twins would add fuel to the beacon at the top of Home Mountain. The beacon would burn for the last time. It would be Avon's final resting place.

Mangrove was troubled. There was no doubt in his mind that the Trats would come looking for the tiny colony of humans.

For this reason departure was the sound course of action and the sooner the better because for the moment the advantage lay with the humans. The blizzard had wiped the countryside clean with a deep layer of snow. The returning Foragers had left no tell-tale tracks. The Trats had no knowledge of the direction he, Snotty and the girls had taken, let alone any idea that Homecave existed. Mangrove's concern lay in the cremation ceremony.

He waited until the twins had left Tasha before he approached her and presented the problem: as things were, the entire group could make its way south unnoticed, to advertise their presence with the flames and smoke of cremation would remove the advantage created by the blizzard. "Is it wise, Tasha?"

She had no immediate answer. The sense of what Manny was saying was obvious, but ...

Tasha gave her head a shake as if that might clear her mind. The problem had no clear-cut solution, the correctness of each action pulling her in opposite directions.

"The fire is Avon's right."

"It will betray our presence, Tasha."

"Perhaps it will. Perhaps the Trats aren't yet coming this way and won't see the smoke." She looked at Mangrove for understanding. "We don't know *where* they are. What is certain is that Avon will have her burning. That's our way. I won't change it."

"Okay," he said and walked away.

Tasha sat alone. Would she always be presented with problems for which there was no single answer, or where two were possible and one conflicted with the other? As she thought about her new role, she came to the conclusion that simplicity would never require the attention of a Queen. Her people would look to her to resolve complexity, to guide them through a tangled web of never-ending dangers.

Conscious that her life had changed, Tasha thought for a long time before she slept. Around her many final acts began.

For just one more time, would Homecave provide shelter during sleep; after this night, never again would Avon rest in the midst of those who had loved her; in the morning the last meal would be eaten beside the friendly hearth. With these thoughts, the Camarilla closed their eyes and wondered what the future would hold.

Morning came and with it the farewell to the dead Queen, but whatever the cave dwellers did, or wherever they looked, they were reminded that they were not only saying goodbye to her.

Years before, Foragers, with time consuming labour, had cut the steps into the ice. As Avon's cortege made its way to the mountain top, each person was conscious that he or she would not mount the steps again. Every act had finality stamped upon it.

At his request, Dumperty carried the clay pot with its glowing coals and embers and solemnly led the procession up the mountain.

With all looking on, the old Queen's body was laid on the bed of interlaced boughs and more wood and peat heaped over her. Dram took the pot from Dumperty and, kneeling, emptied the hot coals into the kindling. She blew gently until the first flames flickered and took hold.

The fire spread quickly. Tongues of flame leapt high and in the heat Avon's body was consumed.

Chapter 15

Ten hours later the exodus of the Camarilla had continued without incident. Furs were worn and hunting weapons carried. Bedding and cooking utensils were piled onto sleds and dragged. A sled carried the store of rations, the leftovers from the meal of fish and the reserve of dried game. Another held fuel for fires, timber and sods of peat that Sola and Situ had recently cut. The very young were strapped onto the skins of bedding. They mainly slept, lulled by the motion.

Foragers hauled the loads, relieved briefly at times by older members of the group. It was the way to go. Distance increasingly stretched behind them.

Tasha walked beside Mangrove. Together they pulled the sled loaded with food. Behind them, way in the distance, a thin spiral of smoke still rose into the sky. Mangrove looked back. The smoke was a symbol of the past, a monument that would grow dim and fade to nothing as the embers of the funeral pyre went cold. Until that happened the smoke remained a signal to Torterats, a marker to attract, a starting point from which to follow the fleeing Camarilla.

The smoke worried him. The day was still and the smoke rose on the column of heated air generated by the fire. For three or four hundred metres it was carried upward. At that height some quirk of the atmosphere had formed a thermocline, a layer of air that acted as a ceiling for the quiet air below, but above which blew a gentle breeze. The vertical plume of smoke bent like a twig and drifted horizontally, high, but parallel to the ground and toward the north. Mangrove spent a few moments looking. What was done, was done.

An hour before sunset Tasha called an end to the day's march. While some got ready the evening meal, others would make preparations for the night.

Without being asked, Sola and Situ went off to hunt. To maximise the area searched, Snotty and Dram, each with bow, arrows and axe, went in a different direction. The communal larder held little enough, any addition would be welcome.

A fire was lit at the centre of a ring of sleds. Ice coffins were dug with axes and furs unbundled and laid in them. Tasha was determined that the first meal eaten away from their former home would be a happy one and that when they lay down to sleep, there would be no longing for the past, but hope for the future, a determination to make a new life in a new land.

Shadows were lengthening as the twins returned. They had found no game, but from a stand of low lying brush had picked a good quantity of edible nuts. Dram and Snotty had been more fortunate, flourishing a pair of ptarmigan, snow chickens, a rarity and so a favourite with the Camarilla.

"They were settling for the night," Snotty said. "Dram spotted them and we were able to get close. She only shot once. One arrow got them both. It was great shooting!"

With the pair surrounded by smiles and eager eyes, the birds were plucked and readied for the fire. Ingamo hefted them, gauging their weight. The birds were big, perhaps a kilo and half of tasty meat in each. Mouths were watering.

Sparingly, further makings of the meal were taken from the sled. There were no complaints. All were aware that their journey could be long and difficult, the flavour of snow chicken and nuts turned the small portions into a feast.

Content, old and young sat by the fire soaking in its warmth. Tasha took her flute. "Dance for us, Dram."

With the notes sounding by the light of the fire and fading into the darkness that surrounded the circle of sleds, Dram began to dance and soon Dandle had joined her with Dumperty. Snotty took Cloud's hand and they danced. Attracted, thinking of when they were young, Jemma and Ingamo, Janus and Tang, were swaying with the music, calling to others to take part. Biscetti skipped about, pulling people to their feet until the firelight shone on everyone dancing. Tune followed tune, until tired but happy, the dancers left the warmth of the fire for the warmth of furs in sleeping places carved into the snow.

Tasha gazed at the stars. The emigration had begun well.

With daybreak, the journey resumed and for five days the travellers headed south, but for the hunters, luck, or skill, deserted them. Game was almost impossible to find. In those five days, Snotty brought back one snow hare and Dram was able to snare two more. The twins found more nuts, but the store of food on the sled was diminishing.

For the next ten days the pattern was much the same. From early morning until near sundown the caravan of travellers filed across snowfields that most had not seen before. Skiing had become sluggish. Dragging the laden sleds was a chore and there seemed to be no end to the labour. At the end of the day sleds were circled into a protective wall and a fire lit. Occasionally good hunting brought jollity and full bellies, but on most nights the Camarilla slept fitfully. Hunger had a way of disturbing, a protest of pains and odd noises that rumbled through the gut.

At noon on yet another similar day, a smudge began to darken the horizon. Throughout the afternoon the procession trudged toward the black line. With every passing kilometre the line grew in height and what had appeared black became dark green.

Tasha raised her arm and the sleds stopped. She walked to where Ingamo was taking the chance to rest. "What *is* that, Ingamo?"

"Kaldor."

"Are you sure?"

"Oh yes. I've been this way before." And he told Tasha how fifty years earlier as a Forager he had accompanied Mali on safari. "In those days, hunting was usually good, but we were having no luck. It was Mali's idea that we enter the forests of Kaldor, that perhaps the game we sought was hidden amongst the trees. Mali was like Dram, tall, able and, like Snotty, Mali knew no fear." The old man tut-tutted at the thought of the girl from so long ago, at the foolhardiness of youth. "We got right to the edge of the forest, but Tasha, it was like nothing I'd ever seen. Oh no, oh no. Such a dark, forbidding place." Ingamo was shaking his head, memories of the day crowding him.

"What happened, Ingamo?"

He recalled events quite clearly. "I refused to go on. She chided me, tried to coax me, called me names, but no, I said no. I told her that if she went, she'd go alone. I said I'd wait for her and she promised to be back by nightfall. I waited. Mali didn't return. Tasha, I stayed looking at the trees, calling her name for two more days. She didn't come out of the forest. She never returned. We never saw her again."

Together they stared at the dark green tinge on the horizon.

"No one has ever come back from Kaldor, no one ever will."

As they talked, others had watched and strained to hear. Ingamo's story was known to Jemma and to the older members of the clan, but Mali was a name unmentioned for many years. To the young, to the Foragers, to hear that one of their own, a Forager herself, had disappeared in the distant dark green belt, was an uncomfortable thought.

Biscetti listened and felt little wings beating in her chest. *No one ever will.* Ingamo's predictions had come true for her already. And it was a fact that many had gone into Kaldor. None had come out.

Dram stood with Snotty and Mangrove. With heads close together they went over what Ingamo had said. It was Snotty's opinion that Kaldor would not present a problem.

"Those that were lost went into Kaldor alone. Okay, sometimes there were two, but look at us, we're many. The whole clan couldn't just disappear. We have weapons. Don't worry, we'll be okay."

Dram agreed. Safety did lie in numbers.

Mangrove said nothing, but there was a question in his mind. What if bows, arrows and axes had no effect against the unknown dangers?

Tasha continued to look at their objective. She estimated that there was at least another day's travel before they reached the tree line. What then lay ahead? How long might it take to pass through the forest? How good would the hunting be? She could not guess. One thing was for sure. The group would fare better if it were well prepared. The new Queen called the band together and announced her plan.

All Foragers, and she included herself, would scour far and wide for food. As a precaution, being so near to Kaldor, no one was to hunt alone. The main body of travellers would continue with the sleds until close, but clear of the forest and there set up camp for the night. Foragers returning from the hunt would make their way to the new rendezvous. Tasha wished the hunters good fortune. The meagre weight of provisions on the food sled stressed the need for success.

At sunrise, sleds were harnessed to the very young and the old. In file, like the shaft of an arrow, they made for Kaldor.

Separating from this central spine, the Foragers, like an opening fan, skied away, their aim to cover as much territory as possible before nightfall.

Snotty and Dram were quick over the snow, their ambition to make the greatest contribution to the communal larder. They would go furthest, giving themselves more opportunity in the tough hunt for game.

Tasha and Mangrove, Biscetti, who had joined Dandle, Sola and Situ, Ulan and Kadich, the foursome led by Belle, had all had similar ideas. With the sun hardly risen, the cavalcade of sleds and those who hauled them, were crawling alone over the snow.

By mid-afternoon, Dram and Snotty were far from anyone, moving over terrain that had gradually changed to rolling hills. They had come across the tracks of animals and from afar sighted a bird or two, but had added nothing to their backpacks. On a rise they paused to check out where they might go next.

"There," said Snotty. "That's different. Let's have a look."

He was pointing to a cliff face. A feature shaped from some long ago geological movement that had caused half a hillside to fall away and left bare rock. Among the rise and fall of snow covered hills, the ribbon of rock was unique.

"Wait. *You look*, Snotty. That cliff is alive."

Dram was right. From where they stood, they saw at different places on the cliff tiny movements, as if the stone itself was reacting to nervous impulses.

"Weird." But Snotty was already putting his weight on his stocks. He wanted a close up view.

They skied an undulating course toward the cliff and stood before it, looking up at crags and ledges that jutted from the rock face. Unusual as it was, with nothing else but the white of snow all around, the Foragers were even more surprised. Hanging beneath every ledge were flying-foxes, their claws gripping runnels and knobs of rock that had been formed aeons before and exaggerated by generations of the animals roosting under the protection of the protruding granite shelves. What had seemed to Dram as a cliff with life of its own was simply home to hundreds of the fox-faced bats. As they quarrelled and shifted position, the solid rock had appeared to be moving.

The Foragers had never before seen a flying-fox. That didn't trouble them. They saw food.

Time and time again, Dram and Snotty aimed and fired. Leather-winged creatures fell silent to the base of the cliff, their blood soaking the snow.

"Dram, we can't carry any more. That's enough."

She agreed and with her knife began to slit stomachs, cleaning the animals and also reducing the weight she and Snotty would have to carry.

Tired of watching her, he took from his pocket the compass left by the ancients who had excavated the cavern and made the arch with the stones that should fall down.

"Snotty, what are you doing? Help me with this."

He showed her the compass and how, no matter which way he held it, the arrow of the needle always swung to the south.

Dram asked to play with his toy and she too marvelled at the way the needle preferred to point south. "Why does it do that?"

"I don't know. It just does. Wherever I am, it's always the same. The arrow swings about, but ends up pointing in a southerly direction."

"Can I play with it?" she asked.

"Yeah." The compass meant nothing to Snotty. He'd tired of it anyway.

Dram made the arrow spin, watched it come to rest and put the toy in her pocket, thinking of the sketches that had been shown on the screen. Somehow the way the earth had wobbled had changed something and in some way the needle was obedient to the power of the planet. Dram did not know why, but there could be no other explanation. Never mind why, of greater interest to her was the fact that the needle knew where south lay.

Kneeling together they slit and cleaned and skinned.

Snotty ran an intestine between his fingers, squeezing out its contents. He repeated with another, poking at the food that had been digesting. "These things eat fruit, look."

It was the same with every bat they opened. Seeds and pulp came out of the digestive tract. "They must feed in the forests of Kaldor. There's no where else."

With nothing to be seen but snow, Dram agreed that Snotty had to be right. "So maybe Kaldor is not so terrible."

"I guess we'll find out, but I'm not worried about going into Kaldor."

The trek, the skinning and cleaning of so many bats had made Dram hungry. She cut a fillet from a carcase. "Let's have a snack before we get going."

"Yeah, okay, but they seem to have shrunk." With fur removed the naked bodies were quite small, with little meat on their frames.

Dram tossed him a slice. He chewed for a moment before spitting the flesh from his mouth. Cautioned, she licked the piece she had cut for herself and tentatively bit into it. "Ugh."

Still spitting to rid his mouth of the taste, Snotty looked at the number of bodies chilling in the snow. "Maybe they're better when they're cooked?"

The row of glazing foxy eyes seemed to be looking back at him, daring him not to be too sure.

Backpacks heavy, slowing them, Dram and Snotty arrived late in the afternoon. Laid out on a fur rug was the meagre booty brought by those who had returned earlier. A cry of joy rose from the expectant crowd as the flying-foxes were tumbled on to the fur. There was no doubt in the minds of their admirers that Dram and Snotty had the edge when it came to hunting.

Mangrove and Tasha were the last to return. The product of their day's work was a pair of leverets, young hares that they had dug from a burrow, a pitiful result for the hours of labour. Shallow applause was their reward. The hungry gathering had expected better from their Queen.

Disappointing as it was, the result from the Foragers had to be accepted. In the final hour of daylight, the Camarilla stood around the fire, enjoying the smell of roasting meat, salivating in anticipation. A flying-fox was taken from the spit and the first slice offered to Tasha. Dram and Snotty watched her grimace, chew for a moment longer and then spit the masticated mess into the fire.

"I can't eat this. No one is to eat the meat from these bats. They could poison us all." Tasha directed the bodies to be buried and other food prepared.

As the light drained from the day, a multitude of flying-foxes flew high, darkening the sky. In an act of accusation the bats cast their droppings on the huddled Camarilla so that brown stains slashed the snow, sullied furs and dirtied those unfortunate not to dodge the falling excrement. By this act of disrespect, the bats avenged their dead brothers and sisters.

"Good one, Snotty," Mangrove shouted, wiping his sleeve. "How did you and Dram manage this? Bats are inedible and now look."

"They were not to know." Tasha admonished him.

Amid grumbling, the small band of human beings, the last of their race, lay down to sleep. Kaldor awaited them.

Chapter 16

Long before dawn, Cloud's cries awakened those sleeping near her. Snotty was first to her side. He put his arm around her, cradling the moaning girl, rocking her from side to side.

"What is it, Cloud?"

With eyes wide open, yet not seeing him, seeing things he could not see, her lips moved, formed words silently and then she spoke. "Phantoms known and those unknown. Circling days in circular ways, no beginning and no end."

"Cloud, what are you saying?"

"One of us and two of us become one of us. Devils playing in the rock."

"There, there," he said. "Wake up. It's okay. I'm with you."

Sola came. With a boy gently patting each shoulder, Cloud emerged from her trance. With a shivering sigh she peered in her myopic way at the onlookers.

Tasha came to Cloud and took her hand. "Explain to us what you saw, Cloud."

"I never really know. I see pictures that come and go."

"Try for us. Try for me."

Tears misted Cloud's eyes. "The Camarilla will lose its Queen."

The prediction hit Tasha like a club. Shocked, she reeled and had to reach for Sola. He steadied her and smiled. "It was only a dream, Tasha."

But everyone present knew that hidden within Cloud's dreams lay the truth.

Returning to their sleeping places all could hear Ingamo's muttering. "I waited for Mali. She didn't come back. I keep telling you. No one has ever returned from Kaldor. We are lost."

Jemma tried to quieten him, but her efforts were half-hearted. Cloud's pronouncements had struck deep. For the remainder of the night worry would not allow her eyes to close.

In her sleeping place, Tasha too pondered the future, wondering what fate held for her and what would become of the people she led.

Lying under covers, Dram repeated Cloud's words, questioning what they might mean. Finding no answer, she snuggled deeper and slept soundly.

The smoke that continued to rise into the air long after the travellers had gone was a symbol of the life that had been, but the rising column had its own life. Giving the illusion of weightless mist or fog, the smoke — a myriad of minute particles that had once been wood or peat — drifted high and blew far with the breeze. Ultimately these particles floated back to earth to lie as ash, or unseen, fill the air with the unmistakeable smell of past burning.

Smoke, as Mangrove had feared, arouses interest and lays a trail.

On the summit of what had been Home Mountain, Torterats rummaged through the remains of the funeral pyre and in the desperation of hunger, with teeth grinding them to powder, swallowed Avon's blackened bones.

Homecave had advantages for the Torterats. They saw it as the new base from which they could roam the countryside. Living at the hub of territory that had previously been restricted to forays from afar, and with competition from the humans removed, the Torterats knew that for a time they could survive. When that time expired there would be but one option: if food was to be found, it would be to the south. When that became necessary, every Torterat was aware that somewhere along the way they would overtake their enemy. At that place and at that time scores would be settled. None of the Camarilla would live to walk away.

The forest of Kaldor was very close, but no obvious pathway into it, no break in the trees, could be seen. The caravan stopped and heads turned to Tasha for direction. She called the Foragers into conference. With nothing to make one way preferable to another, the decision was jointly taken: the group would cleave to the straight line they had been following. To ensure as little deviation as possible, two Foragers would go ahead for a short distance. Never to be out of sight, they would be the reference point for the imaginary horizontal plumb line. When the band joined them, the manoeuvre would be repeated.

The sleds were no longer useful. To drag them around trees and over the great roots that radiated from the trunks would be impossible. Loads were transferred, backpacks were jammed tight and the wooden sleds broken up to be carried for fire making. Parts that were judged too heavy to carry were abandoned.

Skis were exchanged for snowshoes, and strapped across already heavy loads. Like pack animals, the Camarilla waited for the signal to move.

Sola and Situ were chosen to be the first scouts. Without thinking about possible dangers, they entered Kaldor and held to the agreed straight line. To do so was not easy. The forest was old, thick with tree trunks of great girth that bore the weight of a dense canopy, so dense that after progressing a short distance, the light had dimmed.

The twins turned and called the others to come on. The stop-start journey had begun.

Within an hour there was no hint of the open expanse of plain the group had left. Throughout the morning, Sola and Situ led the way deeper into the trees, always attempting to forge a straight path, making allowance for the obstacles in their way. From the bole of every tree, thick roots clutched the snow and dug down into the ground. The task for the twins was to navigate a passage that would not be too arduous for those that followed, yet held to the line south. They did the best they could.

Observing the effect the effort was having on her people, Tasha called a halt. They had stumbled over unseen objects and laden with heavy packs climbed over interminable barriers. The travellers needed rest and they needed to eat. She chose a miserable area, a place where the trees were less thick, but where the canopy allowed no peep at the sky.

The rations distributed were slim — there was no knowing how long it would be before game or seeds or anything edible would be found — and over a fire quickly lit, so little food was quickly cooked.

Mangrove sat by Tasha. "We may need to be even meaner with the food."

"I know," she said. "But the going is so hard. I didn't imagine it would be like this."

That was the problem. Effort required energy. Energy required food. Insufficient food converted to poorer effort. It was a problem they had always lived with, but never in circumstances as bad as the present. The harsh truth, which Manny and Tasha now faced, was that they were committed to go on. Irrespective of the small quantity of food in reserve, irrespective of the difficulties, they could not retreat.

"If only Dram and Snotty had caught something decent instead of those stinking bats."

Tasha calmed him. They would have to make do with what they had.

Leaning against tree trunks, tying to stretch the rations by eating slowly, making the most of the break, talking amongst the clan ceased and some dozed.

"Hey, what was that?" Biscetti's yelling shattered the silence.

"What?" Snotty called to her.

"There."

Sleepers abruptly awake, all alert, watched Snotty walk in the direction she was pointing.

Biscetti cried out again and so did Ulan. They could see willowy figures among the trees. Then the shapes took form, smiling, beckoning the watchers to join them.

In slow motion, holding their arms from their bodies, the figures in the trees seemed to sway. They came toward the group now standing mesmerised by what they were seeing. The approaching dancers had the appearance of people, yet as they swayed in front of trees, their bodies did not hide the trees. Through the filmy shapes whatever lay behind was faintly visible. The wraiths came closer and in their outstretched hands held pieces of bread that were not transparent, but real, solid, appetising.

The Camarilla stared at the wavering wisps and at the offerings. To eat would be such a pleasure. For food to be so freely given and by such entrancing figures created a longing, a desire to touch the dreamy outstretched hands and to take with gratitude the proferred gifts.

In silence the ghostly dancers weaved among those they had entranced.

"Mali." Ingamo stepped toward one, taken back in time, scarcely believing what he saw.

The wraith smiled and held out her hand to him.

"Mali, it *is* you."

Ingamo went to embrace her, his head full of questions. She floated away from him, still smiling, saying nothing. The old man stared at her and in doing so stared through her. The transparency was strange, inexplicable. Even more strange to Ingamo, Mali had not aged. The gossamer girl looked exactly as she had done when he had last seen her, long-legged, strongly built, her face serene and beautiful. As she moved, Mali's hair swirled, billowing below her shoulders just as it had done all those years ago.

He took another step and the wraith, light as air, drifted backward. Mali, smiling, offered the bread in her hand. Ingamo reached to take it.

"Ingamo, come here." Jemma's stern command blew away the bridge spanning half a century. The old man obeyed and withdrew to the present. On Mali's face the inviting smile remained, on his, a sad regret.

Mali floated to Ulan, welcomed him to come to her and held out the bread so tantalisingly close that Ulan could smell its richness. He took the piece from her and bit into it, savouring a flavour he had never before tasted, wiping saliva trickling from his lips, licking crumbs from his fingers.

Fascinated, the Camarilla watched his enjoyment, thinking that to fill their empty bellies they only needed to accept the offerings from the apparitions drifting around them. It was so easy, so delightfully pleasant, to be entertained while they ate.

For the moment, those around him vicariously shared Ulan's pleasure. Soon they too would take and eat, but as they watched, Ulan began to fade. His face, his entire body gradually dissolved, until like Mali he became transparent. He smiled and wafted to dance with the other ghostly figures and was given bread which he then offered to Kadich and to Dandle, pirouetting around them, silently urging them to share with him.

"No." Tasha's cry was so loud, so anguished that it shook the leaves of the canopy above so that flakes of snow dislodged and fell.

Startled heads swung to look her way, to see her running to Dandle and Kadich, dragging them with such force that they were pulled to the ground.

"No," she shouted again. "You mustn't eat. Don't you see? That's how Mali was lost to Kaldor and now Ulan has joined her. He will dance forever with these ..."

Tasha broke off. Her face paled. She looked at Ingamo and at Mali and her gaze travelled from one dancer to another to another, "phantoms known and those unknown."

All knew that she was quoting Cloud, that once again Cloud in her unfathomable way had foreshadowed misfortune.

Tasha shuddered. A feeling of foreboding flushed through her. Cloud had also said that the Camarilla would lose their Queen. *Will I die or will I, unable to resist, fall victim to the phantoms' gifts?*

The wraiths ignored the violent interruption, continuing to float among the group, smiling kindly, offering enticement. It was as though Tasha's outburst had not happened, or that the filmy figures knew that over time her authority would lose effect.

They will always be here, Tasha thought. They will follow us, drift among us, offering, yet out of reach. *We have no means to drive them away and in the end ...* Tasha saw the situation clearly. The hunger trap would close on the Camarilla. Will to resist was the only defence, but when the last morsel was taken from the last backpack, one by one her people would fade before her eyes. *But before then I may be gone.*

Kaldor was a cursed land. Ingamo's words kept recurring in Tasha's mind: *We are lost.*

"No, no. Never." Tasha gritted her teeth.

She humped her pack to her back. "We're going. Snotty, Manny, take the lead. Take us south."

Making the most of the break, Snotty lay on his back, staring at the branches above.

"Snotty, I said let's go."

He sat up. "Tasha, maybe we don't have to starve. Food is all around us."

She looked at him as if he had gone mad. "The phantoms?"

"No." And Snotty explained how when cleaning the bats he had found partly-digested fruit inside them. "Listen," he spoke with excitement, bubbling with the idea that within minutes he would feed them all. "The bats must come into Kaldor to feed. Where would they find fruit?" He turned his eyes to the foliage above. "Up there."

"Is it possible?" But her heart leapt. Perhaps growing in the greenery high over their heads was fruit that would fill stomachs.

Snotty was already at a tree, searching for footholds. "It has to be."

His fingers found crannies in the trunk. Clinging to them, feeling with his feet for places to take his weight, he climbed until he had hold of a sturdy branch. From there Tasha caught only glimpses of him as he moved higher and was lost among the leaves.

Snotty could no longer see the ground. Untroubled by the height he brushed aside leaves to clear his line of sight, twisting his head so that he might examine every bough and twig. He searched with the hope that he would find the answer to hunger and with the thought that finding the fruit would redeem him after the blunder with the bat meat.

He was very high in the canopy, disturbing the topmost leaves and branches so that snow was constantly falling into his face. He brushed aside another branch and there he saw the fruit clustered at intervals along its length. Each piece was as big as a coconut, but with the appearance of an acorn. A gourd, a hard shelled cup, held the fruit and Snotty saw that some had been part eaten, munched by bats in their nightly feeding. *Yeah, this is what they come for.*

A hanging gourd parted from its stem as he tugged at it. His legs spread, his back hard against the trunk of the tree, Snotty held the gourd in both hands and bit into the fruit. "Agh!" He opened his mouth wide, spitting out the mush. "Agh," he cried again and spat repeatedly. The fruit was foul, worse than bat flesh. He flung the gourd into the mass of green and heard it crash its way to the ground.

Snotty came down from the tree, the hurt of disappointment an aching ball in his chest. "I was wrong, Tasha, sorry. It must be the fruit that makes the bats taste so terrible. We can't eat them and we can't eat what they eat."

"That's okay, Snotty. You tried." Tasha comforted him, but to lose the one chance she might have had to save everyone from starving hit her hard. She hid her feelings and quietly reminded him that it was time to go.

Wherever they stood, Foragers, elders, the very young, shouldered loads and waited patiently for Snotty and Manny to blaze the trail. Waved on, the trek recommenced.

The system was mechanical: a constant rewinding of the navigators going forward and the main party catching up. All the while, among the trees on either side, the smiling phantoms floated easily, knowing that their time would come.

Snotty stopped at a small clearing, where the canopy did not quite close, leaving gaps above. He dropped his pack and sat beside it. "Are we sticking to the line?"

"Well," Manny said. "As best we can, but when the phantoms get too close, we edge away from them."

"Yeah, but we don't stray too far. We'll be right. Anyway it's time we camped for the night."

The straggling procession joined them. Packs hit the ground.

Biscetti wandered among those resting, searching. "Where's Dumperty?"

Dram stood and went from group to group. Some remembered talking to him prior to the appearance of the filmy creatures. Others said he had stood by them and when they looked again had gone.

"He's not here. Tasha, Dumperty's missing."

Like the breaking of a wave, fear spread through the clan. The little boy was well loved. Had he eaten bread? Was he already floating out there behind, between, the trunks of trees?

Snotty shook his head. "Dumperty wouldn't have taken from them. Tasha, we have to look for him."

Again a problem put Tasha in its vice. Of course a search should be made for the little fellow, but where? Back along the path travelled had he fallen unnoticed, had he wandered off, tempted by a wraith or just to explore so that he might tell others of what he'd seen? And who should she send, perhaps to lose the searchers too?

It was like being at the crevasse again with Biscetti deep between the walls of ice. Better to lose one than four, Dram had said. Was the right decision to sacrifice Dumperty and so avoid the risk of losing another? The arguments squirmed inside Tasha's head, but the face of Dumperty pushed them aside, grinning at her, holding up his arms to be cuddled. Whatever the risks, she could not abandon him.

"Yes, Snotty. Will you do it?"

"I'll go with him." Dram said.

Tasha thanked them and the two Foragers were soon hidden by the trees.

Chapter 17

Dumperty had seen the wavering apparitions as the shock of Biscetti's scream shattered the quiet of the clearing. Turning his back on the spectres, he had run. They, in their actions should not have been frightening, but the transparency of their human forms was incomprehensible. The phantoms were there – Dumperty could see them — yet they did not exist because he could see through them. Fear overcame the boy and he ran.

He gave no thought to where he might find sanctuary. His action was the simple reflex to get away from the floating figures, to put distance between them and him, to put himself out of their reach.

He ran, hurdling low lying obstacles, his snow shoes awkward as he clambered over the arching roots of trees, desperate to get away.

He ran. Not thinking that he alone was rushing away, that others were not around him or following with the same intense urge to escape.

Fear lent Dumperty speed and gave him the power to keep moving. The little fellow ran and ran, a single figure racing through the trees, his only plan to get away.

Finally Dumperty stopped, bent with hands on knees, gasping for the air pumping in and out of his lungs, his chest thumping with the rapid pounding of his heart. He stayed like that for some minutes before he straightened and looked about. Only then did he realise that no one else was with him, that there had been no wild stampede, only he running madly and that totally alone he had no idea from whence he had run, nor how he might return. That realisation brought a new fear. He was lost, lost in the forests of Kaldor.

The gnarled trees crowded close. He examined them, seeking some recognisable feature that might suggest direction, the way back to his friends. None was apparent. Dumperty shivered. Frightening as the wraiths had been, to be lost and lonely was far worse.

He inhaled deeply. If one day he was to be a Forager, he had to show that he had the stuff to be one. He had to think rationally, overcome the panic of flight and of loneliness. Snotty or Manny would not behave badly, neither would he!

Dumperty surveyed the forest again. One tree caught his eye. It looked different. He approached the great girth of a trunk that had split and in continuing to grow had the shape of a gothic cathedral, its doors wide open. He came closer. The tree had not split. It had grown around some pre-existing stone work that was now sheltered by the living tree. Dumperty stood within the gothic vault and saw that the stone work had been made by man, that it was the upper part of a shaft. By standing on tiptoe he could look into it.

A concrete cylinder, the shaft dropped vertically into the earth. Curious, he removed his snow shoes and pulled himself up until he straddled the rim. Rungs of steel had been fixed into the wall of the shaft, a ladder, that Dumperty guessed was the means of entrance to, or exit from, whatever lay underground. With his foot he pressed on the top rung to test its strength. Set into solid concrete, free of corrosion, the rung was as solid as rock itself. Some five or six metres down, he could see the bottom of the ladder where it rose from a level floor. That was all. If he wanted to know more, he would have to climb down.

In their search for Dumperty, Dram and Snotty had at first retraced the path the group had travelled that day. They had seen nothing of him, nor gained any clue as to the way he may have gone.

"We're doing this the wrong way, Dram. We have to think. I wish Manny was here, or Tasha."

"We don't need *them*," she said. "*We* can find him. He has to be somewhere."

"Yeah, but where?"

They rested and tried to work out what Dumperty would have done. What if he had seen the wraiths? How would a little boy frightened by the ghostly figures react?

"What would you do, Dram? In his position, at his age, what would you do?"

"I'd go in the opposite direction. And he must have taken off as soon as he saw them."

Snotty nodded. "Yeah."

As best they could from memory, the two reconstructed the scene in the clearing when Biscetti had screamed. The wraiths had appeared from one side, not from ahead or behind.

"Then he would have hared off to the other side. Dram, we've come the wrong way." Snotty waved an arm at the trees. "If we're ever to find him, that's where he'll be, somewhere in that direction."

Dram agreed. That's where they should be searching. "But we don't know what may lie out there. There could be more wraiths or maybe worse."

"You have your bow. I have a knife." The implication that no matter what they came across, they could handle it.

Dram frowned, but said nothing.

Taking an oblique angle, they left their position. Snotty led the way. He had no fear of the unknown. What troubled him was the difficulty of finding the little boy in the vastness of Kaldor's forest. He silently prayed to the stars that luck would favour them.

Dumperty stared into the hole. Down there he would be safe from phantoms and from the weather. Perhaps food had been stashed there. He considered the situation. If a search party was sent for him and he was hidden below ground, he might not be found.

The rungs were alluring. What did they lead to? He could take a quick look and re-climb the ladder to check for any sight or sound of a search party. They would be shouting his name. He would hear.

The stories of the hollowed mountain told by Snotty and Manny had made their impression. The shaft, like the dwelling in the mountain, had been built by the ancients; could it reveal the answer to the mystery of Kaldor? At the bottom of the ladder maybe he would make some miraculous discovery that would take the clan to safety.

Anything was possible, but below ground he would find nothing without light.

Dumperty left the cathedral tree and searched the forest floor. With the solid stub of a branch, resin balled at one end, and fire to set the resin aflame, he would have a torch. It took time, but with a long, thin twig as his spindle, a handful of moss and dry leaves he created the flame and the torch was lit.

Taking care, testing each rung as he went, Dumperty descended the shaft.

At the bottom he held the torch high. He was in an ante-room from which doorways led. He chose one and walked through.

Flame sputtered from the torch. Flickering light danced around the chamber, giving Dumperty an incomplete idea of what was close and merely hinting in a coming-going way at what lay in other parts of the large room.

He thought that he could see the outline of a person sitting at a table and moved closer, holding the torch ahead with outstretched arm. Light and shadow played on the figure. With open mouth Dumperty lowered the torch. He gasped and his trembling reflected on the body of the seated figure. In the quivering light Dumperty gazed on a man dressed in uniform, his hands and face shrunken, mummified, dark as old mahogany. As if to attract the man's attention, the boy touched the uniformed arm and where his fingers rested, the fabric disintegrated and fell in a grey powder to the floor. Dumperty held the torch in front of the man's face and unseeing eyes beamed back the dancing flame.

The boy left the seated mummy and, more adjusted to the poor light, saw that there were many seated figures, all in similar uniforms. They sat at consoles arrayed with dials and large, round buttons. At the level of their dead eyes were the flat panels that Dram had described, the screen on which she and the Foragers had seen the pictures. Each of the figures — Dumperty saw that some were men and some women — had the same dark, shrunken faces and hands, yet they sat as though alive, intent on the screens and dials and the duties required of them.

Although impossible for him to know it, Dumperty had entered the control room of a military complex set up during the wars of the twenty-first century. The people at the screens were soldiers, trained to operate equipment that would track the guided missiles of the enemy. So dangerous were the weapons used in warfare, that, with their families, these military people lived and worked underground. It had not saved them. A missile from a technically superior enemy had evaded detection, and its neutron warhead had exploded with deadly effect. A cunning weapon, designed to be harmless to solid buildings, the neutron bomb left no obvious wound. It relied on shock and sub-atomic particles to rupture the internal organs of those in the subterranean shelter. Instantaneously the life of man, woman and child was extinguished, each dying at the spot where he stood, or sat or lay. Ironically, sub-zero temperatures and an atmosphere free of moisture had preserved the bodies of the dead.

Not knowing how or why these humans had been banished to Endless Night, Dumperty explored the bunker assigned so long ago to be their home and workplace.

He passed from the chamber and entered another. Here were beds, some tidy as if freshly made, but from the pillows of others mahogany faces stared at the ceiling. The skin of every face had shrunk so tight that Dumperty could see the bone of skull and cheeks and noses pressing sharply from the inside as if the bone would cut its way out.

Chamber was connected to chamber. Dumperty passed to the next and saw that it was a place for the preparation and consumption of food, a cafeteria in which more people sat at tables, upright or sprawled with head resting on arms upon the table. Whatever had been served on the plates had long evaporated or become minute dried pips. He searched in ovens and what had once been refrigerators. Nothing edible remained.

He came to the last of the chambers and found children sitting at desks. In front of them a whiteboard with words and numbers written on it. The writing meant nothing to Dumperty. The children, like all the people he had seen, were desiccated figures from the past. He looked at these silent pupils thinking that some of them would have been Foragers had they lived with the Camarilla. It did not matter that thousands of years had passed since these children had last moved or spoken, that their bodies were dark and shrunken like meat smoked for preservation, Dumperty saw them as he saw himself, young, small, kids with whom he could have happily played.

The flame of the torch threw light on a plastic poster decorating a wall of the classroom. Full of colour, the pretty picture of trees and rocky spires and mountains appealed to him — a gift for Dram or Tasha if he ever joined them again. He took it down, folded it and placed it inside his jacket.

Dumperty looked again at the children frozen in time at their desks. One was a boy no bigger than himself, blond hair neatly combed and parted, eyes forever fixed on an object lying by his hand. The thing appeared to be made of many parts and from it a small chain lay coiled with a clip at its end. He lifted the chain so that the fascinating object dangled, weighing heavy. Dumperty dropped it into his pocket. He would examine it later and play with it just as the blond boy must have done.

Retracing his steps, he stood again in the first chamber he had entered. This time, like a bowerbird, he searched for things that he could add to the trophies he had taken from the classroom. Nothing lay on the tables and consoles but a pair of spectacles, put down at the time, ready to be placed upon an ancient nose when needed. Dumperty examined the spectacles and slipped them into his pocket to join the heavy object with its chain.

He held the torch at each uniformed figure in turn. One wore a leather belt with a holster. Dumperty laid the torch on the table, raised the flap of the holster and took from it a pistol. He held it awkwardly. The gun was heavy, too big for his small hands. He juggled the gun, tried to stop it from falling, but did not have the strength. He clutched at the black metal of the trigger guard. Two of his fingers caught the trigger, but the gun continued to fall.

Dumperty did not pull the trigger, the weight of the gun as he tried to hold it, pulled downward. The trigger cocked with a click which he heard, and then uncontrolled his arm flung away from his body. His ears rang with a sound that stuffed his head to bursting. Dumperty fell to the concrete floor and heard no more.

Chapter 18

Dram tensed and swung her head to look at Snotty. The sound of the gunshot had come like a whiplash and as they stared at each other, echoed and re-echoed among the trees. They waited, thinking that the sound of thunder would be repeated, but the echoes became fainter until they were gone entirely.

"Snotty, there was no lightning."

"Hmm. Perhaps that wasn't thunder."

Dram paled. "If not, what else?"

"We'll look," he said. "Whatever made the noise was not far away."

With Dram at his side and unwilling to be separated from him, Snotty probed among the trees around them.

With quiet resumed, the noise had left no tell-tale evidence of its presence. The first sign that there could be some connection between the blast and Dumperty came when Snotty saw the spindle and the blackened ash, the boy's preamble to entering the shaft.

"Dram, he was here. For some reason he made fire." Snotty bent and riffled with his fingers in the ash. He touched pieces of resin that had melted and dropped into the snow, held them to his nose and sniffed. "Dumperty made a torch."

Dram looked at the trees around them. The overhanging canopy shielded the light to give a gloom to the forest, but no torch was necessary. She narrowed her eyes, slowly turning in a circle, seeking detail.

"Snotty." She pointed to the cathedral tree.

Together they stood within the thick walls of its trunk and looked at the stonework. They could smell the smoke of resin, but mingled with it was another more pungent, cordite, the powder that had propelled the bullet from the pistol.

Tall as she was, Dram was able to look over the rim of the shaft. Smoke from the still burning torch was wafting upward from the chamber below and the smell of cordite was stronger. "There's a ladder. Dumperty must have climbed down."

"Then so will we."

For a moment Dram considered letting Snotty climb down alone. No, she thought, not a good idea. "Okay."

She let him descend a few metres and followed.

Snotty stepped off the last rung of the ladder to the floor of the ante-room. Sputtering light from the control room led him through the doorway. He surveyed the chamber in a rapid appraisal of what existed and what might confront him. Light and shadow flickered on the still figures in uniforms. He saw that they had long dwelt in Endless Night, incapable of threat. His eyes travelled over the consoles, the dials glimmering, reflecting the flames of the resin.

Where is he? The room smelled strongly of cordite and burning resin. Snotty could see the lighted torch. He could see the preserved corpses, the artefacts and machines from ancient times. The child he sought had to be somewhere close, but where?

"Dumperty!" The shouted name boomed in the enclosed space.

No answer came.

"Dram, I can't see him."

Watching from the ante-room, Dram stepped into the control chamber and lifted the torch, holding it high in an attempt to gain more light. "There," she said.

Dumperty's foot protruded from below a table.

Snotty knelt and touched the leg. "He isn't moving. Give me more light."

Dram too sank to her knees and the flame lit Dumperty, lying still, eyes closed, his limbs twisted in unnatural positions. Dram's eyes filled with tears and her voice quavered. "He's gone. Endless Night has claimed him."

Snotty could see a dark patch where the boy's head lay. Grief surged in Snotty's chest and the taste of iron rose in his throat. Slowly he dragged Dumperty's little body from where it lay, just far enough to be able to lift him and place him gently on the table.

Blood had clotted in the hair at the back of Dumperty's head. Snotty gently parted the hair and with his fingers felt for the wound from which the blood had run. He found no hole in the skull, no fracture, just a tiny split in the skin. *Maybe, just maybe* ... Hoping that if there was no other injury, the little fellow had survived.

Kneeling low he held his ear to Dumperty's chest, heard the beating heart and felt the rise and fall of his chest.

Snotty raised his face to smile at Dram. "He's alive."

"Dumperty, Dumperty can you hear me?" Snotty shook the small shoulder, shouting the name, asking the question repeatedly.

Dumperty stirred and his eyes opened. "Snotty." Smiling, he put his arms around Snotty's neck. "What happened?"

"You tell us."

Dumperty looked for the pistol, saw it lying on the concrete by the leg of the table and warned Snotty and Dram not to touch it. "It barks and it bites."

Both Dram and Snotty examined the black metal of the gun. It looked harmless, but Dumperty had been knocked unconscious and had a bleeding head to prove otherwise. "Okay we'll avoid it, but what is this place?"

"I'll show you." And he led them from room to room.

Snotty was spellbound by the fact that he was surrounded by history, actually walking in places inhabited by the mummies of the people who had lived and worked in them.

The control room fascinated him the most. Resisting Dram's urging that they leave, Snotty touched dials and levers and wondered what their purpose had been. He looked at notices attached to the walls. They made no sense. That did not matter to Snotty. The bunker was a museum. He held the torch to shed light on more things of interest.

A series of diagrams held his attention, simple drawings whose instructions he could readily understand. The figure of a man lay flat on his back, another knelt beside him and, frame-by-frame, cardiopulmonary resuscitation, heart massage, was demonstrated. One diagram allowed Snotty to see inside the chest, to see the heart and how pressure externally applied with rapid rhythm forced a heart no longer beating to recommence its pumping. Snotty shook his head in wonder. The message was perfectly clear: dead men could be brought back to life.

He would have stayed longer, satisfying his curiosity, but the resin was burning low, the light fading.

"I don't want to be down here in the dark," Dram said. "Let's go, okay?"

With no reason to stay, or to return, the three climbed the ladder from the bunker. The dead would be left in peace to continue their everlasting vigil.

Standing in the shelter of the tree, his back resting on the stonework, proud that he could show the Foragers his unusual find, Dumperty took the object with the chain from his pocket. "Look what I found." He handed it to Snotty.

Snotty hefted the thing, feeling its weight. It seemed to be made totally of metal, red and silver and he could see that it was actually a thing of many parts, each folded to fit snugly within the red covers, yet each with a groove that would allow it to be extracted from its resting place by a thumbnail. He turned it in his hand and saw that on one side the red was decorated with a silver shield that held a cross. As Dram and Dumperty watched with open mouths, Snotty began to pull the parts from within the covers.

One by one the Swiss Army Knife revealed its secrets.

Sharp blade after sharp blade rotated to stand rigid from its casing. Snotty continued, raising a file, saws and measures. He tested the saw on the spindle Dumperty had used and with four or five quick strokes cut through the wood. "Oh that's so good."

A screwdriver and a corkscrew came from their hiding places. What their purpose was he could not even guess. He peered through the magnifying glass, got the hang of it and intently held it close to his finger nail and saw how his skin was roughened at the quick.

"Look!"

In turn, Dram and Dumperty saw the enlargement and then held the magic glass to their own fingers.

Snotty took back the knife and pushed the blades and tools down, watching astonished as each needed no final pressure, but sprang into its casing.

Happy with the stir he was creating, Dumperty showed the spectacles. "What do you think this is?"

Dram opened the arms of the frame. Holding one in each hand, looking at the clear lenses and the rests for the bridge of the nose, it seemed natural to her to place the spectacles on her face and to tuck the curved ends of the arms behind her ears. She pulled a face, squinting at the blurred images of Snotty and Dumperty as they laughed at her transformed appearance.

"You look so funny, Dram."

Dumperty's giggling was infectious. Grinning, Dram handed the glasses to Snotty. "Show me how you look."

In turn, again and again, the glasses passed from one to the other for each to peer cross-eyed at the others and poke out a tongue, laughing all the while.

"That's not all I found." Dumperty held out the coloured poster with its mountains.

Dram admired it, pointing at the many colours in the picture.

"Would you like it?" he asked.

Dram smiled. "No, darling, you keep it." She glanced at the knife in Snotty's hand. "I would like to have that."

The request was unexpected. The knife with its many tools, the way they all lay hidden and yet could be brought out for use, fascinated Dumperty. The knife would be his prized possession, unique. No one in the clan had ever seen such a thing. He looked at the knife, unwilling to give it away, thinking that it was *he* who had found it and that the knife would be happy to be his because it had been owned in the distant past by a boy just like himself.

Dram saw the difficulty he was having. "I'd let you play with it whenever you wanted."

"But I found it and the knife was the boy's in the underground cave. It's really mine now."

Snotty opened the knife again and, pulling a hair from his head, ran it against a blade. The hair was cut in two. "Really, this is so valuable it should become common property, like the rope, and the big cooking pot. Dumperty, we have no knife that can compare with this." He drew his own knife from its scabbard. The stone-age tool looked so rudimentary beside the stainless steel of the knife with many functions. "I fashioned this knife, flaked it with a stone. It's a good knife, but flint snaps. It breaks. The knife you found will never break. The clan will have it forever."

Dumperty nodded. The knife would be a great benefit to all. Nevertheless, he didn't want to part with it. "Well of course anyone can use it, but someone has to mind it. I can do that."

"Oh, you're such a little boy," Dram said. "One day you'll be a Forager, but not for a while yet and a Forager should have the safe keeping of the knife. Think of it this way: if I hadn't seen the shaft within the tree, you would never have been found. Isn't that worth some reward?"

Dram persisted. She reminded him how she had always let him sit with her on Home Mountain and sometimes shared her meal with him. Everything she said was true he had to admit, but to give up the wondrous knife ...

Dumperty breathed a deep sigh. "I don't know."

He was thinking that if anyone but he was to be trusted with the knife, he would prefer one of his heroes, Manny or Snotty. He was very fond of Dram, but the boys were his favourites. He would grow to be like them, a Forager with the same wonderful reputation they had. "What if Snotty minded it? He found me too."

Snotty felt the rush of pride in his chest, his face aglow. Dram saw the smile tug at his lips. "Yes, do that. Snotty will take good care of the knife." She patted Dumperty's head. "And you have the picture and the thing that makes eyes go funny. That's fair."

For the tenth time, Tasha raised her eyes to the gaps in the leaves above, seeing the sky growing darker. The sun was going down and the coming darkness worried her. Dram and Snotty had been gone for hours. Finding their way back to the group would be difficult in daylight. At night it would be impossible.

Among the trees the phantoms floated with smiling, inviting faces, holding out their bread with its promise of ending hunger.

"Oh," she murmured. "And Dumperty, where on earth might he be?"

Tasha's shoulders slumped. The weight of her responsibilities was becoming unbearable. She looked around for Mangrove, needing his company and the counsel he might give. He sat alone on the massive skirt that bulged from the base of a tree. Tasha joined him.

"It'll soon be dark, Manny. Have we lost three now? Should I have bothered about Dumperty?"

"You did the only thing you could do. Dram and Snotty are experienced. Whatever comes up they'll handle."

Mangrove went on talking, soothing Tasha, assuring her that Dumperty would make his own way back or that Dram and Snotty would find him.

Tasha nodded, letting herself be convinced that he was right. "But how will we feed ourselves and there, look at them, the phantoms haven't left us. Oh, Manny."

An angry yell interrupted, burst across the clearing followed by another and then the clamour of shouting and people standing, running about, wiping at their heads and bodies. Above, circling over the gaps in the cover, bats were discharging their excrement on the resting Camarilla.

"Ah." Tasha leapt to her feet and wiped at the warm brown liquid running down her leg. "This is all we need, Manny." She turned her face to the circling bats and cried out to them. "I'm sorry some of you were killed. We're all sorry. Go away. Leave us alone."

But the bats were intent on wreaking their vengeance and with leather wings wide-spread, flew through the breaks in the cover to more easily foul the cowering humans, tired, hungry and now covered in filth.

Mangrove had had enough. He drew his bow and fired into the whirling mass, not aiming not to kill, but to frighten. The arrow did its job. The bats retreated through the canopy and into the darkening sky.

All around the camp site, unhappy people wiped themselves clean. They had little to look forward to. The meagre evening meal would not satisfy and they would eat amid the smell of the droppings and then be forced to lie and to sleep on the dirtied snow.

Tasha walked from one small gathering to another, speaking to individuals, trying to raise spirits and to mask her own unhappiness, assuring her people, in case they had forgotten, that they had no alternative but to carry on. There would be no going home, because home no longer existed. Torterats had seen to that.

Night fell and as the forest dimmed, as if to mock the plight of the weary, the wraiths came closer bearing their gifts. The little band watched the shimmering figures. Darkness overwhelmed the light and the outline of trees could no longer be seen and as this happened, the transparency of the phantoms tinged with blue. Gaseous blue flames, they floated, tempting the hungry.

Night was not to be a time when the wraiths would be invisible to the Camarilla. Every eye that opened, unable to sleep, would see the dancing flames and be reminded that an empty belly could easily be filled.

Chapter 19

Amusing themselves with the Swiss knife, laughing madly at the strangeness of spectacles, Dram, Snotty and Dumperty were slow to notice that the day was nearing its end. Only when dusk began to creep through the forest, did the realisation hit them that night was about to fall, that they were in an unfamiliar place and would soon be in total darkness.

"I hate it down there, but perhaps we should spend the night at the bottom of the ladder." Neither place was desirable to Dram. Indeed both filled her with misgiving. In the underground chambers, however, she felt less exposed. Kaldor's dangers lurked among the trees.

Snotty let Dram's suggestion pass unanswered and in the fading light made a cross in the snow. "Say that's where Biscetti first missed Dumperty." He drew a line from the cross, the imagined camp site. "We looked for him along this line north until it struck me that it was the wrong way to go." He marked another cross. "From here we angled toward the west, right?" He drew another line. "So where do you think we are now?" Inviting Dram and Dumperty to pick a spot on the line.

The boy had no idea. Dram put her finger on the line. "About here, maybe?"

"So if we take this course east we should hit the camp?" Dumperty watched a right-angled triangle appear in the snow and heard Dram agree that if they took the direction of the last line drawn, it was their best chance to be reunited with the others.

Dram too wanted confirmation. "So we wait until morning and then get going?"

Snotty shook his head. "I was thinking that if we had torches, we go now. You don't really want to spend a night in that tomb and I think I can find the way."

Dram looked into the trees, unable to see more than the nearest grey trunks. Behind those, nightfall was making outlines hard to determine. It seemed to her that soon they would be unable to see anything.

She thought more, not believing that Snotty could lead them back, not wanting to go down to the bunker. Dram sunk her hands into her pockets. Her fingers felt the compass. Momentarily striving to recognise what it was they touched she frowned, then her face cleared and ideas flowed rapidly in her mind. The flames of the burning resin might be sufficient to find a way around the hazards of the forest. The halo of light would never shine ahead to show the way, but...

Dram fingered the compass. "It's nearly dark. Can you —"

Her question anticipated, Snotty assured her that Dumperty's torch, left unwanted at the foot of the ladder, would still be useable. Resin could be added to it and in its light he and Dumperty could quickly make two more.

Thirty minutes later, dark strings of smoke were spiralling toward the canopy. Lit by separate flames, shadows jumped in triplicate, leaping at tree trunks, sliding around them and those who cast the shadows made their way along the difficult path that Snotty had chosen.

At Dram's suggestion, he led. With Dumperty to be protected front and rear, she would be last, the rearguard.

No moonshine, no starlight, penetrated the thickness of the canopy. The forest was tar-black and as Dram had foreseen, the light from the burning resin threw feeble pools of light at their feet and lit little else. The spreading roots, the bulk of trees that baulked their way, made progress far harder than Snotty had believed. The straight line he had drawn in the snow had a fine logic. In reality the line began to twist and turn as again and again he avoided the obstructions growing in his way.

With Dumperty and Snotty ahead and engrossed in difficulties, Dram took the compass from her pocket and lowering her light checked the needle that always pointed south. The goal that Snotty had set, and which in his calculations lay to the east, did not lie in the direction of the arrowhead, but at right angles to it. "Snotty, I'm sure you're drifting to the north."

"Yeah well, it's not that easy."

"I know, but from back here I can see when you move away from the direction we should be taking."

"Okay." Snotty turned to Dumperty. "Are you making out little guy?"

"Sure."

Dram stroked the hidden compass. Its magic would guide them and only she would know.

For five hours they struggled, three young people each in a fluttering cone of light hemmed by impenetrable darkness. Snotty would hold the line for uninterrupted periods, but whenever he strayed, Dram would correct him. When he asked her how she could be so sure, she said that she knew that it was hard at the front, but from where she was, deviations were more obvious.

"Yeah, I suppose."

"I'm tired," Dumperty said, "and I'm hungry."

"We're all hungry, but c'mon. You're doing very well. It can't be far."

They continued.

Snotty peered ahead. He blinked to clear his eyes. "Dram, look there. What's that?"

She caught up with him and joined by Dumperty, stared. Distant blue wisps floated like fluorescent plankton in the sea of darkness that was the forest. "I've no idea."

"I do." Dumperty had begun to shake. He grasped Dram's hand. "That's what Cloud saw. I ran."

"Yeah," Snotty said. "They must be the phantoms. How do they do that?" He shook his head, puzzled by beings that scarcely seemed to exist, were like air and yet now glowed. "Never mind. Don't take the bread and we'll be okay."

Dram squeezed Dumperty's hand. "We'll soon be with the others. Where the wraiths are, we'll find the Camarilla."

She was right. Passing among the swaying, soft-blue figures, resisting temptation, Snotty led Dumperty and Dram into the clearing and straight to Tasha. He touched her and drew the two others close so that as Tasha opened her eyes, she would know. The lost boy was found.

Smiling, relieved, Tasha embraced each in turn.

Snotty found his voice. "We have to eat, Tasha."

In the clearing, in the cold of midnight, friends woke and gathered by the fire. In their centre the three ate the small portions allotted to them and told of what had happened.

"How did you find us?" Tasha asked. "How could you see your way?"

Dumperty was eager to tell the story. "Snotty worked it out. He knew where you would be and we had torches, but it was Dram who kept telling him when he didn't stay straight." The little fellow was excited, rushing his words. "She was so good. Snotty was up front leading us, but Dram sort of guided him, told him to go this way or another way. We could hardly see anything but Snotty had drawn this line in the snow and Dram had it in her head. She put me between her and Snotty so that she was at the back and from there she could tell when Snotty went the wrong way."

Dumperty put his hand on Dram's arm. In the circle around the fire, whispers went from one to another. Heads nodded and eyes fixed on Dram. Without her skill, the three would never have returned.

"And look." Dumperty had his audience. He placed the spectacles on his nose. Laughter filled the clearing and the spectacles were passed from hand to hand, from nose to nose, everyone wanting to wear the strange lenses.

From her place at the fire, Cloud listened and tried hard to see what was causing so much mirth, but in the firelight her poor eyesight was even worse and she could make out nothing other than the indistinct figures of those around her who were bending over double with amusement at faces wearing spectacles.

Mangrove saw the girl straining to make some understanding of what was going on. "Please," he said and took possession of the glasses. "Here, Cloud, you share in the fun."

He gently placed the spectacles on her nose and looped the arms behind her ears and waited for her to laugh. Others watched, already grinning at the myopic girl who was gazing in wonder at Mangrove.

"Aren't they funny, Cloud?" someone called to her.

Cloud didn't reply. She looked a little longer at Mangrove as though seeing him as a stranger. She turned and let her eyes travel over the group seated around the fire, and began to smile. Cloud was seeing individuals sharply defined. Gone was the fuzzy overlay of multiple images that used to be. She looked up and laughed aloud. What had been a swathe of green had become a multitude of single leaves. "I can see," she shouted. "I can see."

With her fingers she touched the lenses. "With these eyes I can see."

To those around her it seemed incredible. For them, wearing the spectacles had distorted everything to a misshapen blur. Yet for Cloud, the effect had been a wondrous transformation from fogginess to clarity. It had to be true. Cloud was no longer straining to see. She was not asking who it was who spoke. A face, a voice were identified as belonging together.

Dumperty took Cloud's hand. "Keep the new eyes. They're yours now."

She kissed the cherubic face that in the past she had only imagined he would have. Now she was sure. "Thank you. Thank you."

"I found other things." Dumperty spoke to Cloud and to those at the fire. He unfolded the picture. "Isn't it pretty? I brought it for Tasha."

Cloud marvelled at the colours, at the clear contours of mountains and shapes that never in her life had she been able to see. As she handed the picture to Tasha, Cloud silently gave thanks to the stars.

The last item that Dumperty had souvenired from the subterranean complex, the army knife, was held in the air by Snotty. The clearing had become a cabaret, the midnight-return a stage show of entertainment. "Watch." And he opened every blade and tool so that the knife looked like a metal hedgehog, glinting in the firelight. As the knife passed from hand to hand, Snotty let everyone know that it was in his care, but the many uses of its implements would serve them all.

The show was over. In their ice coffins people returned to sleep.

Chapter 20

With morning, the amusements of the night were forgotten. Harsh reality returned, Sola and Situ again the forward scouts to navigate the way.

So it went day after day. Fighting hunger, strength sapped as the natural obstacles in their path were avoided or surmounted, resisting the urgings of wraiths that dogged their every step, the Camarilla struggled on.

Taking their turn as the vanguard, Mangrove and Snotty halted, beckoned the main band to come on and dropped exhausted to the snow. Flat on his back, Mangrove glanced at the hovering wraiths and closed his eyes. He sat up. Something was different. He sniffed the air and the faint smell of charcoal came to him. Turning his head, he sniffed again. He was not mistaken. The remnants of a fire, the ash, the blackened twigs, lay close by.

Mangrove tapped his partner. "Snotty." Cautiously whispering, indicating with his eyes.

Snotty looked and yawning rose to his feet. "What are you worried about?" He walked to the ashes, kicking them, spreading them. The burnt and broken thigh bone of a snow hare flipped from his toe. He picked it up and threw it to Mangrove. "This isn't the fire of a stranger. Manny, we've been here before."

"What!"

"Yeah, good one eh? We're back where we started."

To have endured privation for seven days and made no progress was heartbreaking news for the Camarilla. To many, slumped on the snow, bellies empty, it seemed a grave mistake to have ever left Homecave.

"Cloud warned us," Ingamo cried. "Circling days in circular ways, no beginning and no end. That's what she said. Oh, we'll never escape from Kaldor. We are doomed, doomed."

Deeply unhappy, fearing that Ingamo could be right, Tasha sat with her head in her hands.

"No, Ingamo, you're wrong. I can lead us out of Kaldor." It was Dram's voice, loud and confident.

Tasha looked up to see Dram standing, her arms raised. "With me as your Queen, the Camarilla is not doomed. I will lead you to safety."

"Avon chose Tasha. She is our Queen." A voice called.

"Avon was old and sick. She made a mistake."

Disbelief that Dram could say such a thing came audibly, an intake of breath through open mouths.

Dram went on, listing the errors that Tasha had made, blaming her for the shortage of food, blaming her for a strategy that had them turning blindly in circles. "Endless Night will claim us all unless you accept me as Queen. Only I can take you out of Kaldor."

Heads began to nod at the possibility. Dram added weight to her argument, reminding all that it was she who had found the shaft into which Dumperty had climbed. It was she who guided Snotty when bringing Dumperty home.

Mangrove had heard enough. "Stop it, Dram. Tasha is our Queen."

"Can Tasha lead us out of this mess? Can she lead us south?"

Guarded conversations began among the gathering. Small groups formed, broke up and reformed as individuals listened, gave opinions and went to hear what others might have to say. Tasha watched the milling about. Snatches of conversation came to her. Dispirited, she thought that perhaps Dram was right. The words of Cloud's prediction echoed in Tasha's mind: *one of us and two of us become one of us.* The enigmatic prediction made no sense, but Cloud had also said that the Camarilla would lose their Queen, a plain statement easily understood.

Tasha watched the politics of regime change.

Dram moved from group to group promoting her cause, smiling, standing tall, an imposing figure. She called Snotty to verify her claims and people listened. Some were persuaded. Some asked probing questions.

Mangrove called for order. The restless argument fell silent and all waited for him to speak.

"This talk of a new Queen is nonsense. It's dangerous. Tasha has been faced with terrible problems. To blame her is wrong. Kaldor has taken all who ever entered and we know why." He gestured toward the filmy shapes drifting near. "The phantoms have kept us from going south. Always they moved close so that we shied away from a true course. Without touching us the phantoms herded us so that we came full circle. Look at us. We are starving. The phantoms know that. They want us to eat and become one of them. None of this is Tasha's fault. Don't listen to Dram." Mangrove scowled. "She should know better than to attack our Queen."

Tasha rose. "When Avon chose me, she said that a Queen's duty is to guide and guard her people. I have done my best, perhaps not well enough, but I've tried. Avon made it clear that the Queen of the Camarilla must give wise counsel and have faith in her decisions. Wisdom is hard to judge at times like this. Who among you would have done differently? I have set an example, suffered as you have every step of the way. I thought I had gained your loyalty." Tasha looked at Dram. "Obviously with you I didn't succeed."

"Tasha." Ingamo came to the front of the group. "We followed you and it got us nowhere. We are hungry." He appealed to the faces around him. "Dram can take us out of Kaldor. She'll feed us."

"Be quiet, Ingamo." Jemma shouted. "How can Dram feed us? Perhaps she wants us to eat the phantoms' bread. Tasha is our Queen. The Camarilla have never overthrown a Queen."

Argument broke out and a babble of voices rose from the milling, shifting crowd.

Dram raised her arms again and as the hubbub dropped away, demanded that the group decide. "Dram or Tasha, what is your choice, to die with Tasha or live with Dram?"

Mangrove made one last try. "We are the Camarilla, the small trusted band. Without trust we are nothing. You mustn't throw away your trust in Tasha."

"Decide," a voice shouted and the cry was taken up. "Decide."

Slowly people gathered about Dram. Tasha stood alone. Mangrove came to stand by her side and watched Snotty join Dram. With his arms by his side, Snotty turned his palms upward and raised his brows, the silent gesture that said: *What could I do?*

In his heart Snotty knew that Dram had put gloss on the role she'd played, yet he had to admit that she had been first to see the stonework of the shaft and it was she who had kept them on the right track when bringing Dumperty back.

"Don't dump Tasha." Mangrove was angry, pleading for all to think before they did something for which they would be sorry. "Of all of us, she is the only one with the skills to lead us. Avon knew that. She could have chosen Dram, but she didn't. Avon chose Tasha for good reason." Mangrove's eyes travelled around the group. He looked at faces he knew so well, not believing that they could revolt against their Queen. He singled out Snotty. "Snotty, you and I are a team. Don't break us up, stay with Tasha."

Snotty frowned, troubled, in two minds, but did not move.

Jemma walked to be with Tasha. Ingamo lingered near to Dram.

"Ingamo, come here. This is where we belong." Reluctantly he obeyed his wife.

Dumperty turned from Snotty to Manny and back again, not knowing what to do. "Dram, can I spend a day with you and a day with Tasha?"

"No little one. You come with me."

The gap between the two groups became a no-man's land. On one side were those who remained loyal to Tasha, on the other those who favoured Dram. Within Tasha was emptiness. She felt as if she had been disembowelled, everything of value taken from her. The carpet of snow between her followers and Dram's was the physical gap that separated the two camps. It represented much more to Tasha. It was a void splitting the Camarilla, destroying the centuries of trust on which they had built their existence and on which they totally relied.

Tasha walked to the centre of the divide and addressed the people who for all her life she had known as dear friends. She expressed her sadness, not for the personal affront at their desertion, but for the break-up of the clan. "All we have is each other. Look at our few possessions, the things we share to survive. They amount to almost nothing and yet with them we have managed to live because we rely on each other to share, each for all and all for each. These possessions: a rope, axes, cooking pots, they are fine in their way, but the greatest thing we have is each other. There are so few of us, we can't afford to throw away the most precious thing we own. We've lost Ulan to the phantoms. None of us should want to lose another and yet if we split everyone will suffer loss."

Dram stepped forward to stand a metre from Tasha, two girls opposed, their factions seeing them like gladiators in the centre of the separating avenue of snow.

"I will be the better leader." Dram said. "Count the numbers."

Tasha had already done so. She and those around her made only eight. Dram had attracted fifty.

Dram smiled. "You come over to me, Tasha. Then nothing will be lost."

"I can't surrender the crown that Avon gave me. Her will was that I be Queen. Nothing can change that until I see my Endless Night approaching and I appoint my successor. You know that, Dram. That is our law." Tasha turned her attention to those standing behind Dram. "You all know that is Camarilla law. You should also know that Dram doesn't always tell the story the way it really was. She's a valuable Forager, great with the bow. Her arrows always fly straight. Sadly her stories are not as straight.

Dram bends the truth to give a crooked picture. Follow her and you may regret it."

"She talks of possessions," Dram shifted so that both groups could see her face and she could look into theirs. "Snotty has the wonderful knife. Show them again, Snotty. And I have this." She held the compass high. "With it I will lead us out of Kaldor."

Biscetti's anger boiled over. "You're a liar, Dram. You never tell the truth."

Tasha hushed Biscetti. "How will you do that, Dram?"

Dram held the compass in the palm of her hand and watched the needle swing and come to rest. "See for yourself. This is another of my straight arrows. This arrow always points south." She looked in triumph at Tasha. "With this is how!"

Tasha bowed her head, recalling the pictures in the mountain carved by ghosts, the cartoons of the world that wobbled and the forces that had swapped direction. Whatever it was that Dram held in her hand, it knew the secret of those forces. Dram and those with her would be guided by the needle and find their way from Kaldor.

Tasha turned to the seven who had shown faith in her. "I am your Queen. That cannot be changed, but if you wish to go with Dram, do so. I won't try to stop you."

Ingamo moved to cross the space to Dram. Jemma grabbed his arm. "We stay with Tasha."

Dram spent a moment looking at those with Tasha, shook her head and turned away. She consulted the compass and with her other hand punched the air toward the route her group would take. "Let's go."

"Wait," Tasha shouted. "You have most of the food. We should have our fair share."

"Come with me and there won't be a problem." Dram's throwaway line came as she turned and walked backwards for two or three steps, grinning at Tasha and the few with her. Getting no response, Dram turned her back on them and with her new-found followers moved off into the trees.

The eight remaining were alone. The familiar group they had known no longer existed. They were a remnant, cut off from the main body to fend for themselves. For better or worse, the twins, Cloud, Biscetti, Ingamo and Jemma and Mangrove had stood by Tasha. She questioned Mangrove whether the compass could really show Dram the way.

"Yes. From what I saw when Snotty found it. The needle swings about when you move it, but it always comes to rest pointing south."

"Then we must keep Dram and her group in sight." Tasha took control. "First, check what food we have."

Packs were opened and dried meat, nuts and seeds were laid out for all to see. The stock of provisions was pitifully small. Tasha looked into each face, already pinched, eyes she had known to sparkle now sunk deep in their sockets.

"We have little to keep us going. But we shall keep going. What you see will be shared equally by all. The ways we have known will continue. We eight will be open and truthful with each other, just as we have always been."

The food was placed in Mangrove's pack. Tasha got agreement that they would eat only once each day. To ensure total fairness, Mangrove, not she, would divide the portions for each meal and in turn, rotating from day to day, seven would choose a portion. The one remaining would be Mangrove's.

The main issue decided, Tasha and her seven took off after Dram. Like a dinghy tethered to a much larger boat, they followed along at a distance, just keeping the main group in sight.

At the end of the day, Tasha was convinced. With the help of the compass, Dram had followed a very straight course.

Chapter 21

Snotty watched as Dram divided the food, putting her own portion close to her side. It was the third day since the split and he noticed, as he had done at each mealtime, that Dram's portion was slightly bigger than the rest.

"I'm bigger than all of you," she had said. "My body needs more."

He took his share and walked away to sit alone. Gnawing at the bone, stripping the last tiny shreds of meat from it, Snotty thought of Mangrove. The meat he ate was little enough, but he knew that Manny would have less. Using the butt of his axe, Snotty smashed the bone and sucked the marrow from it. His meal finished, he used a sliver of bone to pick pieces of meat from his teeth, swallowing them, wasting nothing. He had a pretty good idea of what Tasha's group had and it troubled him. His stomach rumbled and he ran a hand over it feeling the hollow between his hip bones. He felt his ribs and walked his fingers over them counting the ridges they made in the skin of his chest and the valleys in between. I'm a skeleton, he thought, and Manny will be worse and Tasha and Biscetti. *All of them will be starving.* Guilt flushed through him so that he closed his eyes, ashamed that he had deserted Tasha and his best friend. He touched the knife in his pocket, fingering the chain that secured it to his belt. *Manny and Tasha have nothing. I'm going back.*

Snotty rose, went to where his backpack lay and slung it to his shoulder. He approached Dram and told her that he was joining Tasha. "And I'm taking my share of the food."

"No you're not."

"Watch me!" Snotty knelt and with his pack beside him, placed into it what he estimated as his fair share. "Come with me, Dram. Let's all return to Tasha."

Others watched and listened from where they sat, silent, not wishing to be involved. Only Dumperty showed alarm.

"You're joking. I'm the Queen now. Let them come to me."

"Dram, you're not right for the job. Be told, Avon made no mistake. Goodbye."

Rising, Snotty felt a tug at his sleeve and saw Dumperty, tears in his eyes, holding him, pleading with him not to go.

"I can't stay, little one. I'm sorry."

"Then take me with you."

Snotty placed both hands on Dumperty's shoulders and bending, looked into the eyes swimming in tears. "You have to stay. There's not much to eat here, but with Tasha there will be less. It's for your own good, Dumperty."

"But I want to be with you and Manny."

"I know, but it's better for you to stay, believe me. Unless ..."

Snotty lifted his pack and appealed to the onlookers to join him. "Think of what you are doing. It's wrong. We should all be with Tasha."

They remained impassive, mere onlookers, more interested in what uneaten particles might be found as tongues slid over teeth and gums. Without comment, they watched him kiss the weeping Dumperty and go.

So did the wraiths. They came to Snotty, cajoling him to eat the offered bread, smiling in welcome, promising to satisfy his hunger and to make him a member of their family. He lunged at the transparent bodies, only to see them waft out of reach and he wondered what might happen if he was ever able to touch a phantom. Would he feel anything, or would his hand go through the shape as though it were not there, like a rainbow, simply a drawing in the air.

He recognised the face that Ingamo had said was Mali. She came to him, tantalisingly close, the ghost of a Forager that had hunted with Ingamo. Snotty could see the beauty that had never aged. He spoke to her, called her by name and asked why she tempted him, for what reason did she want him to become a phantom?

Mali smiled and hovered closer, swaying, as if moved by a puff of air. She beckoned him and with her arms, in her waving, weaving way acted out the charade of clutching him close as her friend. Ulan came, a Forager he knew well and liked, and from his actions he knew that Ulan in the same way as Mali, would welcome him as a brother dearly loved. The phantoms did not speak, their flowing actions telling Snotty all he needed to know.

He shook his head and backed away from Mali, but Ulan followed him, offering the bread. Other wraiths drifted around him, coming at him so that he was forced to twist and turn, looking for a way through the wall of airy figures. He rounded on those behind him and they faded to be a little further off, but others closed in at his back.

Isolated, taunted here, taunted there, Snotty became confused. With constant turning he no longer knew which way he should go. He was isolated, deep in featureless forest, the plaything of phantoms. His heart beat faster, his breathing quickened and for the first time in his life Snotty knew fear. He sucked air to fill his lungs until his chest expanded.

"Manny," he cried, expelling the air in a blast that sent the shouted name to echo into the trees. "Manny, help me."

The sound travelled, passing around the grey trunks, penetrating the forest, slowed a little by the frigid air, but moving outward in every direction. Its loudness diminished with distance and with the obstacles that deflected or absorbed it, but Snotty's cry came clearly to Manny. He glanced quickly at Tasha before turning his head toward the sound. Trees partially blocked his view, but among them he caught glimpses of Snotty, appearing, obscured, appearing again as he whirled in the centre of a cloud of phantoms

"Snotty, I can see you. I'm coming."

Through the trees they called to each other, one assuring, the other now assured. Snotty broke out of the barrier and ran toward Mangrove.

"Oh Manny, am I glad to see you." He wrapped his arms around Mangrove and hugged him. "Where's Tasha?"

"Not far away. Come on."

In a few minutes Snotty could see Biscetti and Sola and Situ walking toward them. A little further off, waiting, with belongings scattered about, Tasha stood with Jemma and Ingamo and Cloud. The warmth of happiness enveloped Snotty. *This is where I belong.* He could hear his own voice within his head telling him, and he asked himself why he had been so foolish as to walk out on Tasha and Manny.

Snotty was welcomed. Smiles and laughter so spontaneous, so generous, that he knew his behaviour was forgiven and forgotten.

"I'm sorry, Tasha."

"You're back with us, Snotty. That's all that matters."

"Here." He opened his pack and showed the food he had brought. "I thought you would need this. It isn't much, but ..."

The smoked meat, the handful of nuts lay in front of eyes that calculated how many meals they would provide. Snotty's gift was mentally measured in portions, no longer for eight, but now to feed nine. Tasha thanked him for his foresight. The food would add to the span of days before they were left with nothing.

"How is everyone faring with Dram?"

"Unfairly! Dram is not like you, Tasha."

"But they all survive?"

"So far! No one would leave her to come with me. Dumperty would've. I made him stay because of the food."

"Yeah." Manny said. "We understand."

Three days had seemed an age of separation and the conversation quickly widened so that they were all talking. Snotty was asked a myriad questions about individuals who had gone with Dram, and whether the compass ever faltered.

From his report it was obvious that both camps suffered similar conditions. Food was the prime concern, but with Dram's compass to guide them, the people with her clung to hope. "The needle points the way, better than the sun, better than the stars."

"It's strange that the needle can do that, always point to the south even after it's been shaken about," Mangrove said. "I wonder what magic it has."

Tasha suggested that the magic had something to do with what they had seen on the screen. "But we'll never know."

"Yeah," Biscetti said. "The ancients were smarter than we are."

Tasha smiled at what she saw as her sister's naivety. The pictures they had watched had given Tasha understanding. With all their cleverness, the ancients' gift to the generations that followed was starvation and Kaldor.

Chapter 22

Dram watched the phantoms weaving among the trees. *They never leave us.* And as darkness closeted the forest, the airy shapes took on their nightly form, glowing blue, never still, drifting with their mocking smiles. Dram stared at the wraiths, wondering if her destiny lay with them. She weighed time against the food now remaining and on the scales in her mind, time weighed heavy. Food had little weight at all. The imaginary scales were tipped hard against success.

She crossed her arms and with her hands, pulled them tight to her sides as if this might protect her from the problems she faced. Snotty had been gone for four days. Dram clamped her jaws, her teeth grinding on the thought that all the best Foragers were now with Tasha. She lifted her head, looking at the canopy. *What does it matter? There is nothing to hunt, nothing to find.* If there were, she comforted herself, *I have my bow.*

The dying campfire flickered light and shadow over her people. Weary from never-ending trudging and clambering over the forest's awkward, impeding growths, they looked at Dram and all that filled their minds was the thought of food. With the air they breathed, hunger rose from bodies like an odour and showed from hollowed eyes.

Blue shapes danced closer and Dandle rose from her sleeping place. "I have to eat."

Janus got to his feet with difficulty, his face contorted with
pain. Bending, he helped his wife from her ice coffin. "We too
will eat. We no longer care."

Holding hands, the old couple stood by Dandle and Janus
took her hand. Together, fingers entwined in their last human
moments, the young and the old moved from the light of the
fire, took the bread offered and ate. Slowly the substance of their
bodies dissolved to a blue transparency. Content at last, Janus
and Tang danced. Smiling, Dandle swayed, looking back at the
camp fire, offering her bread.

Those who had watched said nothing, too tired, too weak to
speak. Dram had let Dandle go, had not tried to stop her nor the
old man and his woman. They wondered why a Queen would act
in this way and if the same fate might await them all.

But the loss of three did have its impact on Dram. In much
the same way as Tasha and Mangrove calculated the effect of
the food Snotty had brought to them, Dram knew that less was
more. Fewer mouths to feed meant more for those remaining. In
a morbid way, that brought satisfaction.

"Go to sleep," she called. "Tomorrow is not far away."

The sepia tones of morning subtly lightened the forest. Dram
woke and thought that in Kaldor, dawn had no certainty. She
longed for daylight that came with brilliance, lit the landscape
far and wide so that she could see where she stood in relation to
it all. Around her, shadow draped the forest in never-changing
gloom. Dram caressed the compass, feeling its power. *Take us out
of this dreadful place. Take us out soon.*

She rose and stretched and called to the stirring sleepers that
it was time to go.

By noon Dram could sense a difference. The snow was no
longer as thick on the ground and in some places bare earth
showed in dark patches. Trees had become less densely packed
and cloud could be seen increasingly through a canopy that had
become ragged. She felt warmer, opened her jacket and looked
back at those following her. Some had removed outer layers of

clothing and stuffed them untidily into backpacks in order to move more freely and in comfort.

Ahead the trees were thinning more and through them the shapes of distant mountains could be seen. A breeze stirred the leaves with warmth that none of the Camarilla had ever experienced.

"Dram." She heard her name shouted and then cheering came from all around as people took her hand or touched her in their joy. "Dram, you have led us out of Kaldor. We've made it."

She smiled, squeezing hands that held hers, returning kisses. Someone cried out that the phantoms had gone and for a moment there was silence as everyone searched the way behind them. It was true. Among the sparse and separated trunks there were no writhing shapes. The cheering began again.

The sound of celebration filtered through the trees.

"What's excited them?" The noise surprised Mangrove.

Biscetti laughed. "Maybe Dram's broken a leg."

"Yeah, well ...," but he grinned.

Keen to keep moving, Snotty looked around the group. "Let's go."

"Not yet, Snotty," Tasha said. "We can't crowd Dram. We'll wait a while."

The arrowhead of the compass in Dram's hand pointed at the strangely coloured mountains.

"There," she said. "This is the way we go."

Her followers stood with trees at their backs and looked at what lay ahead. They saw a scene that was hard to comprehend. No snow lay upon the ground. For as far as they could see, the earth was bare. Between where they stood and the red line that rose under cloud at the horizon, the ground was the colour of yellow ochre. Disbelieving, some turned to face the forest and where snow lay white between the trees. Dram had led them from Kaldor. She had also brought them from the white world into which they had been born, to a land free of ice, free of cold, a land painted with colour.

No one had ever imagined that earth could exist without the deep mantle of snow, yet here it stretched before them, different from anything that they had ever known. Excited as children, exclaiming to one another, they gazed on the new land and claimed it as their own; a place where the air was no longer cold and even the earth looked warm and welcoming.

Gathered around, the group dropped packs, sat by them or on them and while they waited for Dram to say what should happen next, talked among themselves about how to lighten their loads, what should be taken and what left.

"Dram, do we need our skis?" Kadich asked.

She looked from him to gaze across the yellow land, flat, unbroken by growth of any kind. "Probably not, but we'll take them anyway. Fuel for the fire may be hard to find. If need be the skis can be burnt."

"Should we gather more wood?"

Dram nodded and sticks and dried and broken branches were taken from the forest floor to be bundled together. Jackets, taken off with the change in temperature, were wrapped around the firewood and the sleeves tied. Secured to packs, the extra load sat high, added weight, but assured the makings of a fire.

Dram went from person to person, checking that ties were secure, having a quiet word, instilling confidence. At the head of the column she called out, asking if all were ready. The answering cry of *yes* came loudly.

A new leg of the journey began.

The ground had no green among the yellow, no weeds, no blades of grass, but scattered everywhere were stones. Boots that had been made for snow and the smooth earthen floor of Homecave were unsuitable. The stones were lumpy underfoot or sharp so that feet bruised. Within a short time walking became difficult.

Dram heard the groans and looked toward the distant line of mountains. In the otherwise featureless landscape, she had no way of telling how far off they were, or how long it would take to reach them. Perhaps there the going would be different, but walking was so much slower than skiing.

With the passing hours, the heat of the day increased. Cries came to Dram that they should rest, rest and drink.

The realisation came that without snow there could be no drinking. So used to quenching thirst by bending down for a handful of snow to be eaten or melted, no one had spared a thought for water. Dram looked back. If water was to be had, it was lying frozen, crystalline in the forest. She detailed Hock, Zita, Belle and Vellum to go back and collect sufficient for all.

"Dra-am?" Belle's astonishment gave the name two syllables. "How do you reckon we'll carry melting snow?"

"You'll find a way." Dram was angry that she had not thought of the need for water, angry that until it arrived, the rest of them would be waiting, uncomfortable in the sun.

Chapter 23

Sunlight came in shafts through the disappearing canopy. Sola and Situ quickened pace, getting ahead and soon calling back to Tasha and the others that earth was showing through the thinning snow.

"We're out of Kaldor," Snotty cried. "That was the reason for the shouting and hurrahing." He gave a joyous cry. "This is where the torture ends."

"Perhaps," Tasha said.

"Come on, Tash," Biscetti was grinning. "Look, this is the end of the forest. You can see mountains. They're far off, but they're mountains all right."

"Yes." She was looking across the yellow earth at the distant figures of the group led by Dram, feeling the air warm on her cheeks. "But maybe there's more to Kaldor than forest."

With a few paces Mangrove moved clear of the trees and surveyed the territory that lay ahead. "I won't be long."

The others watched as he walked into the yellow country that stretched to the red horizon. He went on for three or four hundred metres, stopping every now and then to kick at the earth or to bend and rub at it with his hand.

"What's Manny up to?" Biscetti asked.

"He's touching the ground." The spectacles that Cloud constantly wore gave her an equality she'd never had. She gave a running commentary, not yet fully aware that others with naked eyes could see quite clearly what she described. They let her continue, enjoying with her the pleasure it gave.

"He's feeling it and now he's picking up a stone."

Mangrove returned and held out his palm to Tasha. She touched the dirt he had collected and rolled some between finger and thumb. The yellow earth was as dry as dust.

"It just goes on like that," he said. "And these stones are everywhere."

Tasha let the dirt fall from her fingers. "So dry, how can we survive out there?"

She looked to where she had last seen Dram and the people with her. They were still moving away, tiny figures getting smaller. "If they can't find water ..."

"Yeah," said Snotty. The implication being that death marched alongside Dram and those who had gone over to her.

He searched the country with a hunter's eyes. The yellow terrain was not uniformly flat, but with little undulation there was no chance that a creek or a watercourse of any kind would be found and with nowhere to drink the possibility of game was low. The cloud above the far off mountain range probably meant water existed in its valleys. Water would attract animals or at least fish, but until the mountains were reached water would have to be carried.

Mangrove had reached the same conclusions. "So what do we do?"

"We use the gourds."

"But —"

"Not to eat, to hold water."

"Will that work?"

Snotty gave him a wry grin. "I dunno. I was wrong about the bats and wrong about the fruit, but I just think —"

"Let's find out."

They spoke to Tasha, letting her know what they had in mind.

"Good idea. Get plenty. Those with Dram will need water too."

"Eh?" Snotty questioned her.

"They are our friends. They are still my people."

As they made their way back into the trees, Mangrove thought about life and its many contradictions. Dram had been cruel to Tasha, but Tasha was still doing all she could to help Dram and the deserters with her. At a personal level, he and Snotty had suffered great privation in the forest. For days on end they had striven to escape from it, yet now they were hurrying over ground they had hoped never to see again. Stranger still, their purpose was to pick fruit that was impossible to eat, but would keep them alive. He shared his thoughts with Snotty.

"Yeah," Snotty said. "But look at us and how things seem to happen. You and I get into awful trouble and never really know what the outcome will be, but it always works out." He grinned at Mangrove. "Is it fate, or the stars shining on us and giving us their protection?" Snotty laughed aloud. "Or maybe together we're just plain lucky."

"I guess so." Mangrove had really wanted to get across the idea that circumstance could alter attitude, that bad could become good, that what had been avoided could be keenly sought. He didn't try to explain any further. He knew Snotty's view very well. To Snotty life was simple; accept it as it comes and it will all work out. For Mangrove the current situation was far from simple and no one knew what lay ahead. Still, if you took Snotty's approach, you just got on with it.

They climbed trees, yanked gourds from their stems and let them fall to the ground. As he worked, pulling the extras needed for Dram, Mangrove compared Dram with Tasha and knew that Dram would not have done the same for her.

Much of the fruit was smashed as it ricocheted from branch to branch and finally thudded to the ground. That was of no consequence, the gourds remained intact.

Attacked with knives — Manny using his flint and Snotty the blades of the Swiss knife — the fruit was swiftly scooped out. Each gourd became clean, no longer part of a plant, more like a rounded polished bowl with a lip that curved inward where it once had gripped the fruit.

Manny admired their handicraft. "You were right. These gourds are great. The way they fold over at the top should prevent the water from spilling. Well anyway, it will help a bit."

"That's what I reckon and —" With his fingernails Snotty lifted the corkscrew from the Swiss knife. "I figure that if we bore a couple of holes in the lip with this, we can thread a line through them; make a sort of handle."

"What sort of line? What've you got in mind?"

"Well, you saw how thin and flexible the new growth was at the top of the trees. I could cut a few stems and then from each, slice three or four strips. The stems are so green the strips should turn out just like twine."

Mangrove agreed that they should give it a try.

The Swiss knife proved its worth again. Snotty deftly ran a blade the length of each switch, sliced a thin, narrow strip and repeated the action until he had a sheaf of green strings.

At the edge of the forest, everyone was busy jamming snow into the newly-made water containers, pushing it down hard to maximise the melt water that would quickly come with the higher temperature.

"This was a great idea, Snotty," Biscetti said and, as a movement caught her eye, looked out over the yellow land. Coming closer were the four that Dram had sent for water. "We've got company."

Cloud dropped the snow she held into a gourd and raised her head. "Belle, Hock and," she concentrated on the approaching figures. "Yes, with Zita and Vellum. Do you think they've left Dram?"

Mangrove tilted his head, doubt on his face. "Maybe. More likely they've come for water."

The filling of the gourds ceased. Interest centred on the Foragers trudging across the stony, yellow earth.

Tasha stood to greet them. Belle waved from a distance.

"Look at them," Biscetti said. "They've turned yellow."

Belle and her party had changed colour. Dust, kicked up as

they walked, had settled on clothes and skin so that the four appeared to be powdered in yellow talc. Sweat had run from brows to carve dark, damp lines on faces and necks.

Laughing, Biscetti put a finger on Zita's nose and wiped a spot clean. "Hi, grubby girl."

Zita pushed her hand away.

"Biscetti!" Tasha was terse. "Get them all a drink."

The four were given gourds of melting snow and sitting, held cold water in their mouths before swallowing, eyes closed, relishing its cooling effect. They held snow to their brows and wiped their faces with it, seeing the snow turn to yellow with the dust. Belle glanced at Tasha then looked away, ashamed. The Queen she had deserted was showing compassion, providing her with cooling water, not accusing her of treason. Hock, Zita and Vellum, their thirsts now quenched, sat with eyes downcast. They too knew that they did not deserve the kindness shown to them.

"We'll come back to you, Tasha," Belle said.

Tasha shook her head. "No, you must take the water you came for and return to Dram. Without it, those with her will die of thirst."

The four protested. Tasha would hear none of it. Filled gourds were hung by their green strings from straight lengths of timber, poles that Snotty and Mangrove had fashioned from branches. With Vellum and Hock in front, Belle and Zita behind, a pole would rest on each shoulder. Like the coolies of old, they would bear the load of water now dangling in the gourds.

Hock asked if Tasha would come with them.

"No. We'll wait for the sun to set. It will be cooler then. You should suggest to Dram that she do the same; rest by day and travel by night."

"Then we should wait with you for nightfall. We could all go together."

"Get going," Mangrove said. "You heard Tasha. Those you left behind have waited all day in the sun. They need to drink."

Chapter 24

Sitting on the stony ground, her jacket over her head to keep off the sun, Dram looked into the distance, wishing for water. Those around her sat with heads on knees, jackets draped over them. Some had worked hard to set up wigwams, digging into the yellow dirt so that skis could stand upright and clothing used to create some shade. No matter how they tried to avoid the sun, its heat was inescapable.

Dram peered through lashes coated in dust. Her tongue was a dry lozenge, thick in her mouth. She tried to lick her lips, but she had no spit to moisten them nor to swallow.

The shape appeared small at first, a mirage-like blur made up of parts that hung together and moved as one. Dram narrowed her lids, trying to identify the shimmering image gradually growing in size as it came toward her. She stood and shielded her eyes with her hand. The parts were taking form, becoming separate figures. Relief swept away Dram's dejection. She could see Hock and Vellum. She could see Belle and Zita. They were joined by the load they carried on their shoulders. It had to be water.

Dram called hoarsely to those around her and they rose from makeshift shelters to watch the arrival of the water carriers.

The mood of the camp changed from despair to joy. Dram ensured that the distribution of the water occurred smoothly. She played the role of Queen, walking from group to group, advising all to drink sparingly and to keep in mind that the water in the gourds was all they would have until more was found. That could be days away.

Belle listened, and taking courage, passed on Tasha's suggestion. "She said that we should travel by night, save our strength and our water by resting when the sun is up."

"Really? Here you'll do as I say."

No one else argued. They agreed with Dram's counsel, and talked among themselves saying how wise she was. She had saved them. She could be relied on to get them safely south.

Dram stood tall and proud, accepting the congratulations. "You have placed your trust in me." She held a gourd high and let water stream into her mouth as proof of her genius. "As you can see, I haven't let you down. As for Tasha, where is she and her little group?"

Dram got the response she sought; the laughter of her subjects. She glanced at the sun low in the western sky. "We'll eat now and camp here for the night."

With sunset the air cooled and in the twilight Dram's followers welcomed the comfort. The meal had been small, but thirst no longer troubled them and the heat was gone. Many spent time looking at Dram. With her to lead, the future was looking good.

In good humour, simple sleeping places were prepared. Stones were cleared from the ground and a skin lain over the dust. Packs served as pillows. The atmosphere was one of holiday. The cooking fire glowed. Around it all prepared for sleep, calling to one another from where they lay, joking, happier than they had been since leaving Homecave.

The first of the stars made their pinpricks in the darkening sky and the temperature eased further. Hands reached for jackets, but without cloud to retain some of the day's heat, the air cooled rapidly. Grumbling, people fumbled in packs for furs and wrapped themselves in the old way. They were learning the lesson that cold was not always accompanied by snow. As they snuggled into furs, the crescent moon cast a feeble light over the yellow earth and over the cartwheel of sleepers with the dying fire at its hub.

A scream shattered the stillness of the night. A shuddering, repeated screaming that punctured dreams and brought people instantly awake.

"What is it? What's wrong?" Dram sat up and looked about to see from where the cry had come and why. But others were jumping to their feet and brushing at their clothing and from them sounded the same wavering cries of horror.

"There," a voice shouted. "Dram, there on you."

She looked down and on her chest, its tail curled ready to strike, pincers held wide, a scorpion stared back at her.

The first animal to leave the pre-historic oceans, an arachnid related to the spider family, the scorpion for more than two hundred million years had roamed the land. Armed with powerful grasping claws and venomous toxin, the scorpion survived by paralysing its prey and then eating it alive.

Dram had no knowledge of scorpions, but ten centimetres in size, longer than the palm of her hand, the menace of the arachnid terrified her. Dram shuddered and in quick succession knew why screams were all around her and that she had to get the strange and awful creature off her chest. Her own cry of alarm rose into the freezing air as she plucked at her jacket.

Afraid to touch the scorpion, she tried to shake it free, but it clung with its eight legs and curled its tail even further. Dram's eyes were fixed on the thing, ignorant of what it was, whether it was an animal or an insect or another creation of evil from Kaldor, but with no doubt at all that its purpose was to harm her.

Mesmerised, her mouth wide with fear, she saw every detail. In the weak moonlight the trunk of the animal shone brittle, as though it were armoured. The arched tail was made up of separate nodules jointed together and Dram recognised that this allowed the tail great flexibility. Like a whip it would lash and the needle-like sting would pierce her and inject its poison. As she looked the scorpion reared, opened the twin claws of its pincers and with tail bent fully forward, readied to attack. Dram drew a long juddering breath. She had to act or she would die. She flicked quick and hard with the back of her hand, knocking the thing from her chest. Shaking with fright she watched it scuttle away and at that moment, when she thought that danger had passed, the noise came to her.

Through the commotion of screaming all around, the rustle of crawling insects came from the ground, a constant scraping of many legs on the yellow earth. Dram looked down. The ground was crawling with scorpions. She felt the hair on her scalp rise in fear. Her eyes widened. All around her people were lifting their feet, spinning giddily to avoid the creatures, searching the yellow dirt to find a place free of the spread pincers and the arching stings.

Dram heard Hock calling to her, begging her to tell them what to do. She was their leader, they were overrun. How could they save themselves?

Another, lighter voice cut through the racket. "Dram."

That's all she heard, her name cried out by a child in a terrified cry for help.

"Dumperty, where are you?" But the campsite was a confusion of whirling bodies and screams, making it difficult for Dram to locate the little boy.

She ran a few paces, turning her head from side to side, hoping to find him. Under her feet she heard a popping. She took a few more steps and heard the sound again, a short, sharp crack. Through her leather boot she felt something hard, felt it give and heard the sound of a brittle body crushed.

"Hock," Dram shouted into the melee. "Jump on the creatures, smash them with your feet. Hit them."

The slaughter of the scorpions began and Dram searched for them, squashing them, hearing the bodies snap even as her eyes roamed the uproar for Dumperty.

She saw him, still lying at his sleeping place, wrapped in his furs, one hand holding the fur to his chin for warmth. On the little hand a scorpion had its pincers gripping Dumperty's skin, its tail arched so that the sting was held above the scorpion's head ready to strike.

"Dram, it's hurting me." Tears welled in his eyes.

"Don't move."

Dram stood above Dumperty, shaking with her own fright and for fear of what was about to happen to him. She loved the child. She could not lose him. What was she to do?

Belle saw Dram standing over Dumperty, saw the unmoving actors in the tableau and came to them.

The tail of the scorpion, like a piston, thrust back and forth as if testing its aim.

Belle was puzzled, wondering why Dram made no effort to get rid of the scorpion, to kill it or swipe it from Dumperty's hand. Belle could see the pinched skin clamped in the claws and the threatening movements of the tail. Dumperty was in mortal danger yet Dram stood as though carved from rock, doing nothing.

Belle backed away, hearing the bodies of arachnids crush under her feet.

Chapter 25

The stars were familiar, although some seemed to be higher in the sky. Mangrove and Tasha questioned why that should be so and concluded that they had now travelled a long way south. It was they who had changed position, not the stars.

The sliver of moon gave some shadow to the stones so that the yellow earth had a roughened appearance. The band of nine could not avoid the stones, but the night air was preferable to the heat of day and the exertion of walking kept them warm. Water was carried in the way Snotty had devised, and by rotation each took a turn to shoulder the poles. Old as they were, Jemma and Ingamo insisted that they take part in carrying the burden. Tasha agreed. With everyone sharing the load unselfishly, the bond between them became stronger.

Using the Southern Cross to guide them, the tiny caravan moved steadily through the night hours.

"That must be Dram's fire," Snotty said. The lone blip of light was far ahead, directly in their path. He glanced at the sky.

Mangrove saw the movement of Snotty's head and knew that he was checking the bearing. "Yes, Snotty, Dram's needle shows the way as accurately as the stars."

Automatically everyone raised eyes to look at the gleaming points of the Cross. It was their lodestar, but in every mind was the thought that should the sky become overcast, they were lost. Only Dram had the needle that never failed.

Tasha broke the silence. "Dram's fire comes and goes. See how it's there and then not there."

In the weak light of the crescent moon and too far off to distinguish detail, Tasha's view of the campfire was being interrupted by bodies rushing about in panic.

Curiosity aroused, unable to guess what was causing the here-again-gone-again glow, the party quickened pace. With the distance halved, the faint sounds of shouting and screaming came through the still air.

"Sola, Situ, Manny, Snotty, come with me." Tasha was already running toward the commotion.

When closer still, they were able to see the wild contortions of people stomping at the ground, but only when near enough to recognise faces did Tasha and the boys begin to hear the scratching of hard-shelled bodies on dusty earth. The sound came to them in a constant, low crackling. Their running feet began to pop the scorpions and the popping cut sharply through the background static and over that again were the louder cries of the people who had cast their lot with Dram.

In the chaos, Snotty saw Dram standing over Dumperty. The picture of her frozen with uncertainty, the boy lying at her feet, his face pleading for help, the scorpion poised to strike, was suddenly all that Snotty saw. He ran, pushing others aside to get to Dumperty and as he ran, his fingers tugged the chain of the Swiss knife. Still running, he felt for a blade, flicked it out and in one swiping lunge sliced through the body of the scorpion. The force of the blow sent the segmented tail flying to the yellow earth, where twitching, it oozed toxin into the dust. With the point of the blade, Snotty eased open the clutching pincers and using his thumb and forefinger, crushed the head and thorax, grinding them in anger. He wiped his hand on his jacket to rid himself of the mess and picked up the sobbing boy.

Dumperty, his whole body shaking, wrapped his arms around Snotty.

"It's okay, little guy. You're safe now." Snotty held him tight. The wild execution of the arachnids continued. Belle had taken a burning brand from the fire to drive the scorpion from Dumperty. Seeing him in the arms of Snotty, she began hunting down the scuttling creatures and searing them. The scorpions curled and sizzled in puffs of grey smoke. Those that had escaped the stomping and the burning fled to hide under stones or to disappear into holes burrowed in the ground.

Dram's group had survived.

In the aftermath, as furs were shaken and packs emptied to ensure that no scorpions had taken refuge in them, Snotty confronted Dram, accusing her of doing nothing when Dumperty was in danger; of standing by, gaping, as the scorpion prepared to strike.

Dram's voice broke as she tried to speak. "I wanted to. I wanted to get it off his hand, but ..."

"You did nothing, Dram. If I hadn't arrived he'd now be in the Endless Night."

Dram became defensive. "Don't blame me. You could have ended his life with the knife." She held out her arms to Dumperty. "Come to me, darling. You know I'd never let you be hurt."

The child shook his head and clung more tightly to Snotty.

Tasha had listened to the two arguing and intervened. "The fact is, Dram, you did nothing for Dumperty. You choked, didn't you?"

"I did not!"

People who had been hunting the last of the scorpions stopped what they were doing and moved nearer to better hear the interchange.

"You did." Tasha spoke calmly. "I've seen you like that before. You told Avon a different story, but I was there, remember?"

"Rubbish."

"It's true, Dram. And you don't think ahead. You don't prepare. For goodness sake, did you bring water with you today? No you didn't."

"I sent back for water. We're okay aren't we?" Dram sought support from the circle of listeners.

Most nodded and many answered that water was not a problem, blaming the scorpions for any discomfort.

"Dram, had it not been for Snotty and Manny, you would have nothing to drink." Tasha looked into the faces of those around her. "Snotty had the idea that if he removed the fruit, the gourds could be filled with melted snow, so he and Manny gathered enough for us and a lot more for you. Belle and Hock, Vellum and Zita, they couldn't have brought you a drop of water without Manny and Snotty."

Belle listened and hung her head. That was not the entire story. She was grateful that Tasha mentioned nothing more.

Dram was defiant. "I told Belle what to do. She did it."

"Dram, be honest. You ..."

Tasha got no further. Dram took a step toward her and smacked her hard on the face.

"Oh." Tasha staggered back, but the cry she made was drowned by the gasp that rose from the Camarilla. Never had one of them struck another.

Shocked, Jemma went to Tasha and put her arm around her. Jemma could not believe what she had seen, but the evidence remained; the pink imprint of Dram's hand on Tasha's cheek.

"Get out of here, Tasha." Dram was breathing heavily. She turned in full circle, catching every eye so that no one could misunderstand. "If any of you think of joining her, remember that I have the magic needle. Only I can find the way south."

Belle took a few paces to be with Cloud and Biscetti.

Dram watched. "Anyone else?"

Hock nodded and moved to stand alongside Belle. The foursome had broken up.

Dram's ultimatum had worsened the division of the clan. She had brought an ugly edge to the disagreement and was about to find that major upheavals impact differently on minor players in the drama.

The four were witnessing the disintegration of close friendship that had seemed eternal. Their co-operation in the completion of daily chores, their reliance upon one another, the ideas they shared, were being ripped apart. Their group, a sub-set of the Camarilla, was experiencing at a closely personal level the break up of the larger population. Dram's rebellion had until now not really affected them. They had remained together, carrying out their duties. Now, two looked at two from opposing sides.

It was too much for Zita and Vellum. Tasha had refused them earlier in the day, but they knew she had done so from selflessness. Tasha had put the welfare of those with Dram ahead of her own ambition. Zita and Vellum made their choice. They crossed over to stand with Belle and Hock.

"Take them, Tasha and go."

"Wait a minute," Snotty said. "We want a share of the food."

Hock tapped his pack. "It's okay, Snotty. We're carrying ours with us."

In the moonlight, in the cold night air, with no sound but the scrape of packs against clothing and the slosh of water as poles were lifted to shoulders, Tasha and her party that had now grown to fourteen, left Dram and those who had reaffirmed a wish to stay with her. The moon, a feeble light reflected from its saucer's edge, looked down on the separating bands of humans, one settling down for what remained of the night, the other marching over yellow earth toward the Southern Cross.

Snotty led the loyalists. Dumperty walked beside him, now and then skipping in order to keep up. He was glad to be again with his hero.

Periodically positions changed, so that the tiring task of shouldering the laden poles was evenly distributed. Belle, Zita, Vellum and Hock were pleased to be so readily accepted and offered to do more than their share. Tasha shook her head. All but Dumperty would take a turn.

As the hours slipped by, the moon set. The way was darker, but the stars glinted, lighting the way. Underfoot the yellow earth petered out. What had been hard ground became softer, no longer providing stability. It puzzled Mangrove. He had become used to the absence of snow, but this experience was different again. The day's firm footing had gone. The ground gave, so that on occasions he seemed to slip, unable to get a firm footing. He bent and showed Tasha a handful of sand. Grains slipped through his fingers. Mangrove could not understand. The ground they were walking upon had become an elusive conglomeration of individual particles.

Chasing the stars, with ample time to think, Mangrove ran through his mind the experiences encountered since leaving Homecave. He concluded that beyond the world of ice into which he had been born and which he had grown to know so well, there were lands whose existence he could not have imagined, even in his dreams. Hard as his life had been as a Forager in the snow, he had known what to expect and how to best survive. He scooped up more sand and with misgiving let it dribble from his clenched palm. The unknown could be more worrisome than reality.

They walked until the sun had risen well above the horizon, taking advantage of the cool air of early morning. Only when the sun began to burn and the ground to heat, did Tasha call a halt. They would bivouac until evening.

Mangrove gazed at the orange-red range, trying to estimate how far off it was. It seemed to him that despite walking for most of the night and into the morning, the distance had scarcely diminished. The initial thought that the mountains would be reached in three days might be optimistic. From where he stood, the sand was level for a kilometre or so, after which it rose in a dune. What lay beyond that was hidden by the height of the wind-rippled sand.

"Snotty, I'm going to take a look."

A lonely figure, Manny walked across the sand. At Tasha's direction, makeshift shade-cloths were erected and the remaining food was laid out. How long it would last would depend on the picture Manny painted on his return.

Cloud looked at the bits and pieces that were meant to sustain them; so little for so many. Her glasses brought her companions into clear focus. Working with jackets off let her see how thin they were. Had her friends always been so skinny? In the past, had her poor vision prevented her from really knowing them? Cloud felt the bones of her own arms and realised that she was just as thin. She wondered if her eyes were like Tasha's and Biscetti's, sunk deep in dark hollows.

Everyone had a few sips of water before it was placed in the shade. A little to drink, a little to eat, that was the regime Tasha had lain down and to which no one objected. If they were to survive, conservation of supplies was imperative.

At the top of the dune, Mangrove looked toward the distant red line that was the next goal in the journey south. The hill of sand he had climbed was but the first. Between him and the mountains there were many more. Row followed row, reminding him of patterns seen on rare occasions in the clouds.

Mangrove turned away. His footprints, depressions in the sand, led him back.

"Well?" Snotty asked.

"A few hills of this stuff," Mangrove kicked at the sand. "Quite a few." He took the drink that Snotty offered. "I didn't see a sign of water."

"Hmm. There'll be water in the mountains. How many days do you reckon it'll take to get to them?"

"Hard to tell. Four, maybe a bit longer."

Snotty grinned. "We'll be right."

"Yeah, I know. With our luck ..."

"Manny, we need luck," Tasha said. "We'll count on four days." She distributed portions of food accordingly.

The meagre meal was quickly consumed. Lying in the shade they slept.

An advance guard of Torterats milled about, the snow pockmarked by their backward and forward running. Noses close to the snow they tried to identify the source of the smell that had attracted them. Scratching, digging to get a stronger scent, despoiling the pristine beauty of the frozen land, the Torterats uncovered the carcasses of the bats that Tasha had buried on the night before entering Kaldor.

Had Mangrove known, he would not have found sleep so easily. The Torterats were on the move, following the tell-tale signs that the Camarilla had left along the way.

Flying fox meat that the humans had found so disgusting had quite a different reaction from Torterats. They ate greedily and went searching for the colony from which the frozen bodies had come.

Chapter 26

The invasion of the scorpions, the interruption to the night's rest, caused Dram and her people to sleep beyond daybreak. They lost the advantage of the cool morning hours, hours when walking was comfortable and distance more easily covered.

"Never mind," said Dram. "We'll make it up as we go."

Dram was wrong. Carrying belongings and fuel for the fire, toting gourds swinging from poles, made speed impossible. Progress slowed further when the hard ground turned to sand. Nevertheless, Dram urged the stragglers on, continually referring to the compass, keeping to the course.

Late in the afternoon, Tasha's campsite came into view, not directly ahead, but hundreds of metres left of the line Dram was taking. Again Dram consulted the magic needle. She smiled. The stars were not proving true for Tasha. She, Manny and Snotty and their little group had wandered off the correct path.

Others had also noticed. From behind, a voice called to Dram asking whether Tasha should be told.

"No. She had her chance."

"But Tasha might change her mind."

Dram replied that if Tasha had her eyes open, she would see her mistake plainly enough. She would see Dram passing and come to join her.

Those with Dram looked across the desert toward the cluster of shelters where their former friends were camped. Dram was no doubt right. Only one could lead. The one they had chosen possessed the needle that knew the way.

The caravan continued, struggling slowly up dunes that rose for forty or fifty metres to a broad table top, sliding and slipping down the far side to walk across valleys of sand and climb again. From the valley floors, all that the travellers could see was the slope of sand behind and the slope of the next hill to be crossed. From the crests, the rust-coloured mountains loomed in the distance, drawing them on. Far to the rear, Tasha's camp was lost from view.

Sand found its way into boots and with the occasional stumble, into mouths. Dram ignored the complaints and insisted that there be no pause until nightfall.

On the ridges and in the troughs of the valleys, Dram eyed the ground carefully for sign of scorpions or any other annoyance, animate or inanimate, that might disrupt the quiet hours necessary for sleep. Satisfied that no threat existed, with the dunes casting long shadows, Dram declared that they would pitch camp in the valley below. Should the wind rise during the night, the hills of sand would offer some protection.

Pleased that the day's labour was at an end, the group descended. As each foot ploughed into the slope, the sand disturbed cascaded like a sandy tide that flowed from above to cover grains lower down. Fascinating as it may have been at some other time, to the people anxious to be at the bottom, the sliding hillside was of no interest. Their thoughts centred on water for a dry mouth, food for an empty stomach and sleep.

With the sun almost set and the air cooling, Snotty opened his eyes and stretched. He nudged Mangrove. "Time to get going."

The sound of his voice and Mangrove's yawning woke Tasha and the others. Each ate the portion of food allocated and sipped the ration of water. The small quantities would be all they could consume until the following morning.

Cloud breathed on the lenses of her glasses and wiped them clean. Testing that they were clear, she looked around, feeling as she always did, the joy of sight that Dumperty's gift had brought to her. She paused. The smooth face of the dune was scarred and it had not been that way when they had lain down to sleep. To be sure, Cloud fogged her lenses again and polished them with the inside of her jacket. There was no doubt. It was far off and difficult to see, but a ragged line ran from the bottom of the dune to its top.

Cloud tugged at the sleeve of Biscetti who was repacking her gear. "Look."

Biscetti squinted, peering to where Cloud was pointing, just able to make out a faint mark on the otherwise plain sand hill that like an endless sausage stretched as far as she could see. "I can't — oh yeah." Biscetti laughed loudly. "Cloud, you see better than I do now."

Sola and Situ stopped what they were doing and asked the girls what they were looking at, but everyone had heard the laughter and as Cloud pointed to what had caught her attention, Mangrove saw and immediately knew the truth.

"That's where Dram crossed over the hill of sand." He looked at Tasha. "She's moving away from us. I wonder..."

Tasha didn't let him finish. "Do you think the needle is a better guide than the Cross?"

"I don't know, but we talked about the stars. They're not where they used to be. They're not quite the same since we left Kaldor."

Tasha nodded, troubled that the permanence on which they had always relied had deserted them and that the boundaries of Kaldor might not yet have been crossed. "But we've come a long way from Homecave, that's why. That's what we decided."

"We did, but maybe the magic needle is more accurate."

The possibility that he had left the certainty of Dram's direction to become lost in the strange environment worried Vellum. "Hey, why don't we use Dram to show the way, follow her tracks?"

Mangrove looked at Vellum as though he were demented. "We're travelling at night! Sometimes we're ahead of her."

"Yeah but ..."

"No buts, Vellum," Jemma stepped between him and Mangrove. "We'll do just as Tasha says."

Tasha calmed the situation, praising Vellum for the idea, also making clear that they were travelling as Dram's group slept and vice versa. "And if we follow in Dram's footsteps, we might as well join her. She'd demand I surrender to her and recognise her as Queen. I can't do that."

"No one wants that," Snotty said. "And what's it matter if we steer a course that's different from Dram's? We've got away from the Torterats, we've got away from phantoms, let's keep aiming for the Cross. We'll be right."

Tasha looked from face to face, gauging reactions. The consensus seemed to be that there was no alternative. "Okay, we'll continue to put our trust in the stars."

With all their worldly goods loaded once more on backs and shoulders, the tiny band set out for the first of the dunes. Above, the sky turned from blue to velvet black and the brighter planets showed like silver buttons. One by one the stars of the Cross emerged and, so that no one could mistake the constellation for what it was, Alpha and Beta Centauri pointed to it.

All in Tasha's party knew that the night would be one of constant toil. Mangrove had briefed them well on the rows of dunes that lay in their path. Nevertheless, the going was harder than expected. The sand provided no real grip. It slipped from under feet that sought to climb the slope and gave no support when coming down. As Dram had found, the sand was a shifting surface that could not be trusted.

Determined to keep up, Dumperty's legs were pumping, taking two steps for each one that his heroes made. Getting to the top of the hills was very difficult for him. Whenever he pitched forward into the sliding sand, either Snotty or Mangrove would quickly take an arm, josh him that he was falling down on the job, making him laugh so that he did not lose heart.

Ingamo and Jemma slogged on, not complaining, setting an example for the younger ones.

After hours of exertion — grunting as knees bent to lift feet from clinging sand in the upward climb, leaning back to avoid falling on the downward slope — the party stood on the level top of yet another dune. Belle flopped to the sand and appealed to Tasha for a break. Tasha glanced at the sky above. The red planet, Mars, had set and the pattern of the stars indicated that the night was drawing to a close. As yet there was no indication of dawn, but on Tasha's reckoning daybreak would not be long in coming.

She smiled at Belle, telling her how well she had done and that if she could manage a little more effort for an hour or two, they would then stop and set up camp for the day. The words of encouragement, the thought of rest when the sun came up, were enough. Belle got to her feet.

The unsteady lurching downward, the stumbling climbing, recommenced, the sand always collapsing under the pressure of weight, slithering downhill to gather in the valleys.

Mangrove walked beside Snotty as they crossed a valley. What had been the easier part of the journey, the traversing of the hollows between dunes, had become progressively harder. Their feet were sinking into sand where previously it had been relatively firm. "Snotty, this reminds me a bit of Torterats."

"When they were taking us back to the hollow mountain?"

"Yeah."

Snotty laughed, remarking that there was no chance of Manny icing this time.

They pressed on.

In the east the sky began to lighten. From the top of a dune, Mangrove surveyed the mountains, satisfied that through the night good progress had been made. No longer just a distant line, the mountains were a silhouette grown larger.

"One more hill, Belle and then Tasha might call it a night."

Belle gave Mangrove a wry smile. Resting could not come quickly enough.

"Yes," Tasha said. "We'll stop on the other side of the next hill."

"What about we camp on top of the hill, Tasha?"

When she questioned why, he suggested that the table top of the dunes was much firmer than the sand in the valleys. "It's softer down there and with every new hill the sand on the valley floor is finer. Crossing the last couple we were up to our ankles."

Tasha quizzed Snotty and Biscetti as to their opinions. They agreed with Mangrove.

"And we've got a view from up there," Snotty said.

"Wonderful, Snotty. We can see a whole lot more sand." Biscetti laughed and sent some flying with her toe.

Abreast, in an uneven line, the sand sliding with them as they went, the band went down the slope. Making their way across the valley to the hill on which they intended to spend the day, Mangrove's observations held true. The sand *was* softer and gave more. The four carrying the water found the going tough. At times they sank to their shins in the sand. Tasha questioned Mangrove as to why it should be happening.

"I've been thinking about that and I can't be sure," he looked back at the hill they had just descended. "But these hills aren't stable. Look there."

The light breeze was blowing sand in a fine spray from the crest. The sand fell to the slope and Tasha stopped walking to watch mini-landslides occur along the face of the hillside, slippages that measured at most thirty or forty centimetres, often much less.

"See what's happening," Mangrove said. "The wind blows toward the mountains. The sand is constantly moving in that direction and the closer we get to the mountains, the deeper the sand in the valleys."

Tasha looked down at her feet. They were so deep in sand she could not see them. "It's softer too." She wriggled her feet and sank lower.

"Yes, just like a new dump of powder snow."

They moved on, hurrying to catch up with the others who were already struggling up the next slope. Making a game of it, Sola and Situ competed to be first to the top. As they scrambled ahead, the new day's sun shone on the ridge and soon after, fingers of sunlight poked down the long valleys. The climbers' shadows, like dark, mimicking monkeys, climbed beside them.

Chapter 27

On the table top of the crest, the intended resting place for the day, the shade structures were put up in a routine that from habit had become fast and efficient.

Dumperty lit the cooking fire and in twos and threes, people squatted by it to sear their portion of dried meat, sniffing the aroma of cooking that made the little meal more appetising.

The sun rose higher and with its warmth the breeze lifted, carrying with it fine grains of sand. Tasha looked across the fire and nodded to Mangrove. The grains were gently peppering her neck as they blew from the northern side of the dune to drop to the southern slope.

Smoke twisted into the air, the breeze catching it, curling the smoke as it rose higher, a streamer reaching out toward the mountains in a gesture of friendship.

Cloud watched the drifting smoke, marvelling that she could see the furthest flimsy wisps as they thinned, dissolved to nothing and disappeared. Her reverie was broken when Tasha called to her that it was time to rest.

"Okay." But Cloud was unable to resist one last look at the mountains and the hills of sand before she lay down. Her eyes lingered on the rust-red range then moved to gaze at the long rows of dunes and valleys that ran east. The table top on which they camped ran straight and wide for as far as she could see, as though it had no ending. Cloud leaned forward, concentrating.

Something was moving, coming along the flat top of the dune, coming fast. She waited a moment to be sure.

"Tasha, someone is coming."

Cloud's cry had the tone of anxiety, of uncertainty as to why someone should be running toward them. She caused the whole camp to sit up and look, to stand in order to better see who or what was approaching. It was a call sparking everyone to sudden alertness, ready to act in case of trouble. All strained to put shape and a name to the advancing figure.

Snotty raised his hands to shade his eyes. "It must be one of those who went with Dram." He stepped a few paces forward, his hands still above his eyes.

Cloud ran to join him. She too held her hands to ward off the sun. "Kadich. It's Kadich."

"He's come to his senses at last," Jemma said. "Come running to join his true Queen."

Kadich kept running until, exhausted, he would have fallen. Mangrove caught him by the arm to steady him. Kadich bent over, put his hands on his knees and dragged air into his lungs. Sweat dripped from his face into the sand.

"What's wrong, Kadich? Why are you here?" Mangrove brought him some water.

Kadich sat and drank. "Dram's in trouble." He was gasping for breath. "She's being swallowed by the sand."

Mangrove knelt beside him and pointed to the next valley. "Down there?"

Kadich nodded. "We were crossing to climb the next dune. Dram was leading and the sand was really soft and then she started to sink into it. She tried to get out, but the more she struggled," Kadich paused for breath, "the deeper she went. We tried, but we couldn't get her out. The sand will swallow her."

"No," Tasha said. "We won't let that happen. Have you burnt your skis for fire?"

Kadich shook his head. "We tried to get to her with them. They were no good."

Tasha gave quick orders. Jemma and Ingamo would stay at the camp with Dumperty and look after Kadich. The rest of them would find Dram and get her out.

"If we're in time." Mangrove was slinging his pack to his back.

Tasha had a quick look around, thinking of what they might need. "Biscetti, get the rope."

Snotty grabbed his bow and a few arrows. "How far to Dram is it Kadich?"

"Along the dune for fifteen hundred footfalls, from there you'll see her in the valley."

"Let's go," Tasha said and as they began to run she wondered for how much longer she and those with her could continue to punish their bodies. Weeks of physical and emotional strain, heightened by poor diet, were taking toll of strength. Running was hard. None of them could keep it up for long, but they must force themselves or the sand could take Dram into Endless Night.

Again opposing forces challenged Tasha. She was putting them all at risk by stretching physical tolerance to the limit. Why am I doing this? she asked herself. The answer was plain. Dram's life was at stake. *But she challenged me, she* deposed *me.* Tasha wiped the thought from her mind. Dram was one of the Camarilla. She could not be left to die.

Tasha called to Sola and Situ. If they had the strength, could they make the effort to run ahead, to count their paces as Kadich had done and then try to spot Dram in the valley? When they saw her they should stop, signal, then wait and rest until she and the others caught up.

Sola and Situ took off, happy to be given the responsibility, counting as they went. They pushed themselves, hearts pumping, muscles hurting, covering the distance until they saw the drama below. Situ waved to Tasha and pointed into the valley.

Dram was below. Her followers had moved back and were grouped at the bottom of the slope staring at her. The girl that they had chosen as their Queen was buried to her armpits in sand.

Tasha and the slower runners joined Sola and Situ and spent a moment taking in the scene in the valley.

The sand held Dram fast. She was making desperate, fitful movements, trying to claw her way out, but with each futile grasp at the surface of the sand, it rose a little higher.

"Dram's digging her own grave," Snotty said. "She should stay still."

Biscetti looked down on the girl who would have deserted her in the crevasse and knew exactly what Dram was thinking: that before much time had passed she would be beneath the sand, and in the black emptiness of Endless Night. Pity flooded Biscetti's heart. "Tasha, we have to get her out."

"We will." Tasha led in a wild plunge down the unstable, sliding slope.

On the valley floor she quickly checked the efforts that had been made to get to Dram. Skis had been tried. The hope had been that the flat area of the skis would support a rescuer on the shifting sand. They had floated on the surface until weight was put on them. As a rescue device, skis were useless.

"We'll get the rope to her and pull her out." Tasha said.

"Yeah, give it to me." Snotty took the rope from Biscetti and walked in ankle deep sand toward Dram. As he progressed he coiled the rope, hefting it in his hand as he gauged the distance to where she was. Dram cried out to him, calling his name, begging him to get her out.

Snotty felt the soft sand giving under him, in a few strides he had sunk to his knees. *If I go any further, I won't get out. We'll both be stuck.* He stopped and with difficulty took two backward steps to stand on slightly firmer ground.

Dram watched him retreat and cried out in anguish.

"Stay still. I'm not leaving you."

Between Snotty and Dram were twenty metres of sand that would swallow anything that went upon it. He began to swing the rope, letting it out through his fingers so that it made an increasingly larger circle. Dram could hear the whir as it swung through the air, realized what Snotty meant to do and lifted an arm to catch the end when he hurled it. She felt the sand rise a little higher and screamed to Snotty to hurry.

Swaying with the rhythm, building the energy in the whirling length of rope, Snotty looked at Dram and let the rope go. It flew toward her. She stretched to reach it. The distance was too great, the rope too heavy. It fell short.

Snotty dragged it back and tried again. Again it fell short. The sand inched to Dram's shoulders.

Mangrove took a fishing line from his pack and began to tie it to an arrow. "Tasha, I'll fire the arrow to Dram and tie the other end of the line to the rope. With the line she can pull the rope to herself and then we can drag her out."

Dram's scream echoed between the dunes. Sand was above her shoulders. One arm remained free, but her chin was almost resting on sand.

"There's no time, Manny. The rope has to be taken to her. This is something I must do myself."

"Tasha, you can't."

"Manny, it's my duty."

"You'll never make it back." He watched her go with sadness choking him.

Tasha took one end of the rope from Snotty. "Give me enough to tie around Dram. All of you will have the strength to pull her out. When that's done tell Manny to shoot the line to me."

"But Tasha, no."

She smiled at him. "Do as I say, Snotty."

Holding loops of rope in her hand, Tasha began to make her way to Dram. She appeared as though she were walking in water, her arms not by her side, but lifted with elbows bent, swinging as the sand became softer and deeper. The thought in her mind was that she must have time; time to save Dram, time to seize the rope when the arrow with the line was fired to her, time to be dragged free before the sand sucked her down, took her from the daylight and the air she breathed. In the space of seconds, events of Tasha's life flashed through her mind; good times, bad times, all the hurly-burly of her short life. Time, she thought, short or long, that's really all we have.

The sand resisted Tasha. She forced her way, closing the gap to Dram, gradually sinking deeper. She could hear Dram gasping,

and knew that it was because the sand constricted her chest.
Tasha could feel the force of it, like a press squeezing her own
body. She reached for Dram and pushed the end of the rope under
the surface and under Dram's arms, searching blindly with her
other hand until she found it, lifted it free and tied the knot.

"Pull, Snotty, pull."

Where Snotty stood, others had come. Many hands grasped
the rope, feet dug for a foothold and, as if in a tug-of-war, the
Camarilla — united again for the moment — pulled with all
their strength. Stumbling backwards, they hauled Dram from the
quicksand and at the rope's end she came slithering free.

"Hurry!" Manny loosened the knot from Dram's chest and
in quick half hitches secured the fishing line to the thicker rope.
Taking aim he shot the arrow over Tasha's head. The line fell,
brushed her hair and rested at her side. Already up to her waist,
unable to move her legs, Tasha, hand over hand pulled the line,
watching the rope coming closer. She took it and as she had done
with Dram, knotted the rope around her chest and cried out to
Snotty to pull. The sand held tight, not wanting to let her go. The
rope became taut, vibrating to sing like a wire in the wind and
Tasha felt it bite into her flesh. She was being pulled apart; the
rope applying an unbearable pressure to her upper body, the sand
gripping her legs, her waist. Those heaving on the rope would not
give in and their success came in a strange sucking sound. Tasha
was plucked from the sand like a cork from a bottle. Gripping her
lifeline, she was reeled in by eager hands. Out of danger, Tasha
stood, removed the rope and walked to where Dram lay against
the slope of the dune.

Dram had been perilously close to dying. The evidence was
there to see. Sand remained sticking to her clothing and to her
hands and neck. It had gathered on her scalp, showing through
her hair and grains flecked her face. As Tasha approached, she
could see Dram working her tongue around her teeth to find and
spit out sand that had got into her mouth.

Tasha smiled at Dram and spoke her name, saying it in a soft
and gentle way that with the one word implied many feelings:
sympathy for the ordeal that Dram had suffered, the hope that

she was recovering and would have no after effects, friendship offered without rancour and previous arguments forgotten.

Dram looked at Tasha and said nothing. She slowly got to her feet and with both hands brushed sand from her clothing and tried to clean it from her face and neck. With her nails she scraped sand from her scalp and drew her fingers through her hair.

People from both factions stood around, spectators intent on what might develop. They waited with anticipation for an end to the quarrel, an end to the division of the Camarilla family.

Dram spat sand from her mouth. "This changes nothing, Tasha."

Tasha shook her head in disbelief.

Mangrove stepped forward from the onlookers. "Dram, Tasha willingly traded places with you. She risked her life to save yours."

"I am the Queen," Dram said. "It's my right to be protected. Every one of you has that responsibility."

"Dram, you are not Queen. Avon chose Tasha."

The benevolence that had enveloped Biscetti was gone. She was angry, shouting at Dram. "Without Tasha you'd be under the sand, looking into the darkness of Endless Night."

Dram ignored her and held the compass in the air for all to see. "I still have the magic needle. I am the true Queen, the only one who can safely lead the Camarilla."

In the amphitheatre formed by the hills of sand there was total quiet. Every face remained passive, eyes fixed on Dram, but with no acknowledgment that she had spoken. The belief in her as a leader had evaporated. The loyalty she had won now lost. People who had supported Dram had witnessed the willingness of Snotty and Mangrove to go to Dram's aid. They had seen Tasha's selflessness, her actions as a person who in the most dangerous circumstance put Dram's welfare ahead of her own. That all of this meant nothing to Dram, that she had not given Tasha one word of thanks, stunned everyone.

Snotty broke the silence, putting into words the thoughts that all shared. "Dram, you don't know how to act as Queen. For those few days I was with you, I saw how greedy you are. You're greedy and you're proud. You think you're too good for us and you're not. You're tall and beautiful, but inside you the real Dram is not very nice. I saw through you some time back, now everyone has seen you for what you are."

Heads were nodding and there was a mumbling that Snotty was right. A Forager came to Tasha and kissed her on both cheeks, recognising her as his Queen. His action prompted others so that a queue formed. Person by person, the ritual was repeated. Tasha was re-confirmed as Queen of the Camarilla.

Ignored, Dram watched the defection of those who had supported her. She felt the hurt of isolation. Friends with whom she had always lived, and who for a time had obeyed her, said not a word to her nor even looked at her. For them she had ceased to exist.

Dram considered her alternatives. She could kiss Tasha in the ceremony of recognition and be absolved from the sin of disloyalty, or she could refuse, become an outcast, live on the perimeter of society to pick up whatever scraps might be thrown to her and like a mongrel dog follow in the wake of the travellers.

No. I am better than Tasha. Dram picked up her pack and without a word left the gathering. Hurt, angry that she had been discarded, thoughts tumbled in her mind and among them Biscetti's accusations and Snotty's criticism kept recurring, stinging like acid because she knew that they had spoken the truth.

Dram kept to the base of the dune, walking away, not looking back, too proud to admit that she may have been wrong, that she should have thanked Tasha and the whole clan for saving her. *I'll go alone. I have the needle. Tasha will have to come to me.*

She examined the valley floor as she went, looking for firm ground and when she thought that there was the possibility that she might get across, she prodded with her foot, testing its reliability. After many disappointments she found a place where the sand held together. Slowly, one tentative step at a time, she reached the next dune. At the top, the mountains seemed suddenly closer. The sight of them strengthened her resolve. She held the compass on the palm of her hand. The needle brought further comfort. It held steady, pointing south.

Chapter 28

The crowd milled about, uncertain what to do. Embarrassment lingered, few willing to speak to Tasha and those who had remained loyal to her. They talked in low tones to each other and waited.

Mangrove and Tasha watched Dram leaving. "She's going toward our camp." Mangrove said.

"Yes, she's trying to find a place where she won't sink into the sand. She's so stubborn that girl. All alone, it will be so difficult. I should go after her and persuade her to come back."

"No way, Tasha, *she* must make that decision. Don't waste your time." Mangrove looked at the crowd, sitting, standing, waiting for direction. "Do we send for Jemma and Dumperty and the rest or do all of us join them?"

Tasha was still watching Dram's efforts to find a way across the valley. "Look, Manny, Dram's found firm ground. She's getting across."

They saw Dram pick her way to the slope of the dune and begin the hard climb upward.

"We'll cross there too," Tasha said.

She called to Sola and Situ and asked if they were strong enough to return to the camp.

"Sure." The two boys in willing duet, smiling broadly.

"Thanks. Take Belle and her crew with you, there's quite a bit of gear to pick up. Meet us where Dram crossed. It's safe there."

"Okay."

An hour later, united with Snotty and Mangrove, Dumperty was pleased. The split in the Camarilla had troubled him. A child, with a child's view of the world, he disliked change. The departure from Homecave had been traumatic for him. His life, the settled existence that he had known well and loved had undergone dramatic upheaval. The anxiety he felt had worsened when he had become lost, found and then left with Dram. He had not enjoyed any of these experiences. They had shaken his faith in the stability he had always known and which he believed would last forever. But he was again with those he loved and he felt relief that among them his life would regain the regularity on which he could rely. Only Dram was absent.

Dumperty listened intently as he heard the story of the quicksand and how she had voluntarily gone into exile. He made no comment, but wished that Dram would return. His world would then be complete, returned to normal, the way it had always been; the way he liked it.

Relaxed at last, Dumperty yawned and lay on the sand.

Mangrove smiled as the boy fell asleep. "He's flaked, Tasha."

"I know how he feels. We'll climb the next dune and rest. Spend the day and overnight there, before we go on. The mountains can't be too far off, so from here on we'll travel by day."

"Yeah, good idea."

They both understood the difficulty of finding a way over the mountains in the dark, but as Mangrove was nodding his assent other words were repeating in his head. The words that Cloud had spoken as she awoke from her trance before they had entered the forest of Kaldor. *One of us and two of us become one of us.*

Mangrove repeated them for Tasha. "It's uncanny. Her prediction has come true. The Camarilla was united, broke up to become two and is now one again. Dram split us, but that's over. We are as we used to be."

"Except for Dram." Sadness was in Tasha's voice. "And Cloud said more." Tasha could remember clearly the scene in the dark hours when Cloud had said that the Camarilla would lose their Queen. That was behind her, now resolved, but she recalled other words. "*Devils playing in the rock.* What did she mean by that, Manny?"

"I don't know and often Cloud can't explain what she sees, but one thing's for sure. Sooner or later we'll find out."

"Yes." The words ran around in Tasha's head. *Devils playing in the rock.*

The trek recommenced with the Camarilla herded together, treating the valley as though it were a dangerous river where a step either side of the path taken by Dram would see the unwary disappear into the sand. Mangrove carried the sleeping Dumperty, finally laying him down on the flat ground that topped the dune. Quietly so as not to disturb the child, Zita and Hock erected a shade to cover him.

Mangrove conferred with Snotty. The range, rust red, was now close enough for them to see the gorges that twisted among the heights. In clefts the green of leaves appeared as dark blotches against the rust, but the sight was one of rugged rock rising high from winding ravines.

"Snotty, I don't like the look of that. How on earth will we find our way?"

Mangrove expected the usual breezy, confident answer, but Snotty was examining what lay ahead, section by section, looking for some chink, some clue, as to how they would overcome the massive obstacle.

"There's gotta be a way." Snotty was still looking, hoping that somewhere a passage existed. "Hasn't there?"

Mangrove shrugged and said that they were both too tired to consider the problem. "We'll sleep and talk about it then with Tasha."

Along the crest, in the shade of improvised shelters conversations gradually ceased. Some slept, some simply rested.

Mid-afternoon the camp stirred with people rising, thirsty and hungry. Dumperty came to sit by Tasha. Wanting company, he stared her awake.

"Hi, little guy, how are you?"

"Fine. What are we going to do now?"

"What would you like to do?"

"I don't know." Dumperty thought for a moment. "We could look at the picture I gave you."

Tasha smiled and patted his cheek. "Okay."

She found the folded poster and laid it out on the sand. Dumperty pointed at the ravines, finding them unusual, moved his finger to the various peaks of the mountains, exclaiming how high they were and how some had odd shapes.

"This one looks like a sleeping hare." He looked to Tasha for her reaction.

"It does." She moved her finger over what could be imagined as the nose and laid back ears of a hare sitting peacefully at rest. "And it's red, just like the mountains out there."

Manny came to see what amused them.

"See," Dumperty said. "This mountain looks like a hare that's fallen asleep."

Mangrove followed the outline of the mountain, agreeing that there was a likeness. He stared intently at the other features of the poster. At the configurations of the lumpy hills that surrounded the sleeping hare. At first glance, the impression was that the picture had been painted to pleasure the eye, but Mangrove was intrigued at the detail: jutting peaks, the vertical faces of escarpments, the fissures that creased otherwise plain walls of rock. And the shape of the hare was unmistakeable. More than that, the mountains in the picture were red.

Mangrove looked up to examine the range. He stood and taking the poster with him, walked to where he and Snotty had been before they slept. Referring to the printed sheet he followed the pattern of the range, constantly comparing it with the actual scene before him. Drawn from a slightly elevated perspective, Mangrove could see the hills surrounding the hare, those before and to either side. The winding ravines and creeks or rivers, had been included. The pretty poster that had attracted Dumperty was a picture of the terrain they must cross.

"Tasha, get Snotty and come here."

"Why?"

"Just get him."

Dumperty ran to Mangrove. "What's up?"

"You'll see."

Mangrove held the poster, aligning its edge with the base of the rust coloured range. Tasha and Snotty, with Dumperty in his arms, listened to Mangrove and as he highlighted the features imprinted on the sheet, saw the reality that had been captured there.

"This is a picture of the range and what lies within it. Every detail has been captured." Mangrove was excited.

"You're right." Snotty ran his finger across the mountains, sliding his way along saddles and around peaks. "We can use it to find our way."

"I found it," Dumperty said.

"And that was very clever of you." Tasha smiled at him. "Snotty, look here." She indicated an arrow, almost insignificant in the bottom right hand corner of the poster, an arrow that could have been a replica of the magic needle. The arrow was pointing at the range and all beyond. At its point was the letter 'S'.

Tasha was ignorant of writing. That letters could be arranged to form words and that each word had a meaning were unknown to the Camarilla. That words could be written and later read was a concept that Tasha could not imagine. She knew that likenesses were made of living creatures because the walls of Homecave were decorated with drawings of animals. As a child she had watched Avon and Jemma put lasting images on the rock, but writing appeared only as lines and squiggles.

Tasha studied the sign, the 'S', and recognised that it was the same as the one in the compass. Whoever had drawn the picture was looking south when he did so. He had left the mark so all would know. The 'S' had to be a symbol meaning south.

"What's it matter?" Snotty said. "The arrow points south and that's the way we want to go."

"Yes," Mangrove said, "but Tasha's right. We don't need Dram and the needle now." He looked again at the sleeping hare and the shape of individual mountains. "We can plot our course from the picture, updating it as we go."

Dumperty glowed with pleasure. He had found the picture that would guide them. That neither he nor the Foragers had ever seen a map before was irrelevant. Tasha and Mangrove had made observations, linked symbols with the power of the compass and drawn the conclusion that they held in their hands not only a view of the land, but a means of planning the path they would take. The map, in a way, gave them a view of the future, foreknowledge of what awaited them.

Tasha re-folded the map and tucked it away in her pocket. The picture with its many colours had acquired a new identity. It had become essential to the safe passage of the clan. "I think we should celebrate," she said.

The evening fire was lit early, a centre of warmth, a focal point to which people were drawn. They came from the sleeping places already prepared and stood or sat around the fire, listening to Tasha explain that in her hand she held an image of the land they would walk upon. The map was examined, passed from hand to hand to give everyone the opportunity to look at it close up and fully comprehend the startling idea that with it they would know exactly where they were. Rather than being blind to their surroundings, they would know what lay beyond the next towering ridge. They would see it on the map. The compass, whose magic had seemed to be irreplaceable, had been pushed aside.

Mangrove, with reservation, accepted the congratulations that were heaped upon him for making the discovery. "The picture doesn't tell us everything. It will guide us faithfully over the land we see within its frame, what lies beyond the edges remains unknown."

Snotty grinned and assured him that luck had never deserted them. "Anyway, all's well now. Let's enjoy ourselves."

Mangrove made no comment. Despite stringent rationing, the food supply was almost exhausted. He could understand why Tasha wanted to take minds off the situation they were in, and the map did provide some insurance for the near future, but time was running out. Predicting when or where the journey might end was impossible. *We don't even know what we're looking for. How will we know when we find it?*

Staring fixedly, focusing on nothing, Mangrove contemplated the future. A cry from Biscetti abruptly interrupted his thinking. She was kneeling by Cloud and as Mangrove hurried toward them, Biscetti cradled Cloud's head on her lap.

Others too had heard Biscetti and a crowd gathered around the two girls. Cloud lay quite still, her eyes closed.

"What happened?" Mangrove asked.

Biscetti was stroking Cloud's hair. "We were talking, then for no reason she became quiet. Her knees folded and she collapsed. I just caught her."

Cloud's eyes opened and she began to speak, her voice sounding as if it came from far away. "All above, one below, but not alone. Death falling from the sky."

Biscetti continued to stroke Cloud's hair, comforting her, but Cloud saw no one but the figures in her dreams. "A land alive to lift and shake. Liquid fire that rivers make."

Leaning over, with her face close to Cloud's, Biscetti tried to rouse her, talking sweetly, assuring Cloud that she was with those who loved her and that she would come to no harm. If Cloud heard she gave no recognition. She began to tremble and then screamed as if terrified by the things she saw in her mind.

Mangrove knelt and gently shook Cloud. "Wake up. It's okay. It's okay."

Gradually Cloud returned from the frightening places of her dreams. Blinking, she looked around and the images inside her head were replaced by the reality of the dune and the friends looking down at her.

"What does your dream mean, Cloud?" Mangrove was worried. There was already too much he didn't understand. The things Cloud had seen in her vision made no sense, yet he was filled with foreboding.

"I don't know."

It's always that way, Mangrove thought. Cloud can't explain, but fear now walks with us. Terrible events are waiting to happen.

Tasha had witnessed the drama. Cloud's predictions had blown away the good mood, the optimism that the map had induced. That mood had to be regained. The flute would do it.

Tasha began to play and winking at Snotty, moving with the rhythm, she nudged him to get the party going.

Snotty's mood was infectious. He moved from group to group, his presence raising spirits, his good humour, like a tide, lifting expectations.

Tasha read the change and played bright tunes. The words of happy songs echoed over the dunes and rose into the darkness of the desert night. When sleepiness finally ended the singing, Mangrove sat with Tasha by the fire and put to her the question that troubled him: to where was she leading them?

Tasha gazed into the flames, held her palms to warm them and smiled. "I don't know what we're looking for, but when we find it we'll know, Manny. We'll know."

"And what of Cloud's dream?"

"Who can interpret the revelations of a dream, Manny? All I can say is that we must be strong. By believing in ourselves we will succeed and so survive."

She spoke so confidently that he was reassured.

On the flat top of the dune the Camarilla slept. The flames of the fire dwindled until only the glow of embers marked the presence of these suffering human beings. Above, the stars wheeled with the turning of the earth.

Chapter 29

Waking, for a moment not sure of where she was, Dram sought to find some recognisable feature. In the darkness, the fire at which Tasha and Mangrove warmed themselves showed its distant, dancing light. The sight of the fire chilled Dram, bringing home to her that she was alone in the night. She wrapped her arms across her chest, now aware that she lay at the foot of the range and that with daylight she would need to find her way over the red mountains. Under the furs, her hand fumbled in her pocket and gripped the compass. Her fingers rubbed along its surfaces, feeling the shape, reinforcing the belief that the compass with its magic needle was her salvation. For the moment she was alone, but before long Tasha and the others would come looking for her, crying that they were lost, begging her to lead them south.

Comforted in the knowledge that only she could find the way, Dram breathed more easily. Her loneliness faded. *I am alone, but that is the fate of a leader.* She remembered the times Avon had asked others to leave her so that in solitude she could make hard decisions. Yes, Dram thought, I'm like Avon and clutching to that idea she closed her eyes and slept until the sun had risen.

The first rays hit the rocky outcrops of the range, lit them in red and bounced off to shine a pink light on Dram's face. She blinked and shielded her eyes until they became used to the rosy glare.

Sipping water, chewing a strip of dried meat, she pushed to one side the last of her provisions. Staring at the single gourd, now almost empty, at the two hardened wafers of smoked hare, Dram dropped her head and sighed. The self-confidence she had inspired during the night drained away. The pathetic scraps of food, the mouthful of water, would be gone by nightfall. She knew that Endless Night would enfold her soon.

She sat for a long time, bowed by the prospect, but gradually her attitude changed. Picking up the meat she ate heartily. If this day was to be the first of the few remaining to her she would go at it with vigour. At least for a day, hunger and thirst would not gnaw at her gut and dry her throat. She drained the last of her water.

Dram looked at the mountainside that grew from the sand and angled its smooth sides toward the sky. Rising to her feet, slipping her pack on her back, she walked a few hundred metres along the base of the mountain searching for faults in the rock that might provide footholds or a place where it was less steep. Nothing gave her any hope.

She retraced her steps and walked in the other direction. "Yes," she cried aloud. A ravine opened like a great gash in the mountain, offering a pathway. Dram entered, and as she walked she looked with wonder at the walls of the gorge that rose high on either side. The gorge continued to widen, transforming into a small valley before it narrowed again further on.

From the middle of this open area sunlight was glinting, reflections of light dancing on the rock wall of the gorge. Dram quickened her pace and then began to run. The empty gourd jiggled at her belt, her pack jolted rhythmically on her back. Uncaring, she ran on. The sun was bouncing off a sheet of water larger than she had ever seen. It has to be, she thought, and as she ran toward it she pictured in her mind the water that ran below the ice, but that view had been restricted to the size of the fishing hole. Other liquid had come from melted snow and had steamed in the cooking pot. Those sightings gave only a hint of what she saw before her.

A waterfall dropped from the top of the cliff, falling in white drapery to spread into the lagoon from which the sun reflected to attract her attention. Scrubby trees, low, woody, grew close to the rock face, a fringe at the edges of the gorge, but the overall impression was a shining sheet of water.

Dram lay full length on the bank and drank directly from the lagoon. She dipped her face under to let water wash cold around her cheeks and eyes. Dust and sand that had clung stubbornly to her hair and scalp came free. Eyes open, she looked at the pebbles on the bottom and through the water saw the shapes of fish.

Getting to her feet, Dram wrung water from her hair and dried her face on her sleeves. She took her bow from her pack and drew on the string, testing its resilience, feeling the latent power. The idea of starvation blew away. Dram fitted an arrow and waited.

Curious fish swam to where she had disturbed the sand. Dram sucked tiny pieces of meat that had stuck between her teeth and spat them to sink slowly in the water. The fish darted, competing to gulp a morsel before it was swallowed by another fish. Dram fired, murmured her satisfaction with her aim and lifted arrow and impaled fish to the bank. Repeatedly she fitted an arrow to her bow and fired. The catch mounted.

It took her fifteen minutes to gather kindling from among the stunted trees. In another fifteen her fire stick was smoking and, crouching low, Dram blew the flames into being. Spitted on a green stick, the fish dripped fat into the fire.

Her belly full, she leaned against her pack. All was well. She would catch more fish, spend the day smoking them and pack them for the weeks to come. The sound of the waterfall was reassuring. She would fill her gourd as a precaution, but the mountains would provide run-off. Water should not be a problem.

Dram was content. The threats were gone. With green leaves on the fire, fish, so easily caught, were curing in the smoke. There was no rush to move on. The lagoon would be a pleasant place to overnight. She yawned and gazed about, thinking how quiet it was. Clouds were drifting overhead, increasing in number with the promise to fill the sky as the afternoon progressed. The moving cloud was the only indication that above a wind was blowing. Deep in the gorge, the air was totally still.

But not everything was still.

Dram tensed and watched. An animal had emerged from the narrow ravine at the far end of the valley. It stood with head raised sniffing the air, searching the sweep of ground with big eyes. Dram could see the nostrils flaring and contracting, and the cautious eyes moving in their sockets. Twin horns rose from the head, recurving, arching over shaggy hair.

The wild goat, an ibex, was unknown to Dram, but she willed it to come closer. Slowly, taking care not to startle the animal, Dram strung an arrow to her bow, held it in her lap thinking that fish was good, but that it had been a long time since she had licked the juice of fresh red meat. She bided her time, waiting for the beast to be sure that no danger threatened, waiting for it to come within range of her bow.

Smoke from the fire curled lazily upward. The ibex looked at it, surveyed the valley one final time and ambled to the lagoon to drink. Legs spread, head and neck stretched, the noise of its lapping sounded in the still air.

With her eyes fixed on the drinking animal, Dram, hugging the ground, edged her way closer, gauging the distance, wanting to be sure that she could not miss. The moving clouds gave her some assistance, their broken shadows running across the ground and over the water in fleeting changes of colour. All the while the sunlight was losing out to cloud, the darker patches growing until the sun was totally blotted out.

"Good," Dram whispered, happy that in the duller light her outline would blend with the earth.

Disturbed, suspicious, or simply ensuring all remained safe, the goat looked up, water dribbling from the tuft of hair at its chin. Dram froze, unblinking, and gave her entire concentration to the goat, silently begging it not to run. Assured, the ibex took a couple of steps into the water and bending, continued to drink. With slow, deliberate movements that were almost indiscernible, Dram resumed her stalking, her eyes never leaving her prey.

She saw the water suddenly erupt, huge jaws clamp on the spread forelegs, heard the bellowing of the goat and watched as the monster that had come from below the surface rolled and rolled in the shallows, thrashing the water with its own bulk and the body of the screaming goat. Amid the noise Dram could clearly see the terror in the goat's eyes and then the bellowing ceased and the goat's tongue flopped from its mouth, never to taste another thing.

The monster stopped its rolling and where Dram had seen intermittently the white underside, she saw now only the raised scales, the dark armoured skin that with the swishing of its long, thick tail backed into deeper water. The last thing she saw was the body of the goat held tight in the jaws before it disappeared below the surface.

Dram sucked in air through her open mouth. The fact that a crocodile was previously unknown to her only added to her alarm. Huge as it was, the suddenness of its attack was terrifying. She swallowed. In her mind was the memory of dipping her face into the lagoon, of looking at swimming fish. She saw herself standing up to her knees in water, firing arrows and fish bleeding as the arrows skewered them. Her body began to shake uncontrollably as she imagined the giant jaws closing, tossing, over and over, crushing her, drowning her, dragging her from the light.

In panic, wishing only to get away from the lagoon and the monster that, unseen, could attack without warning, Dram ran to the curing fish. Coughing in the smoke, she stuffed the greasy, gutted bodies into her pack and as she did so thoughts tumbled in disorder: the beast had legs, she had seen them, it moved suddenly and fast, there could be more than one, he or they could be eyeing her, readying to surge from the water and take her down.

The image filled her brain. Her whole body was shaking. Smoke was making her eyes water and in fear Dram looked towards the water. Her eyes were stinging so that tears added to the difficulty of seeing through the haze. Oil from the fish was falling into the fire, spitting and sizzling, thickening the smoke and giving it the strong smell of cooking. With a waving hand Dram tried to clear the smoke so that she might see. It continued to rise and through the coils that eddied with her waving she

thought she saw the scaly monster coming from the water. She
rubbed a sleeve at her eyes and strained. There was no doubt it
was there, leaving the water, coming for the fish, coming for her.

"Ohhh." The cry came in a shuddering, trembling sound.
Dram's instinct was to flee. She could see herself as a lone figure
with no one to come to her aid. Her bow, her arrows would be
useless against the armour of the scales. She should run, but
without food she would die. The big croc was scrabbling toward
her. Dram could see mud flicking from claws and from the thick
tail that trailed weaving from side to side. It left the water and she
could hear the scraping sound of its body on the sand.

Rushing, jamming stuff into her bag, Dram scooped up the
gourd on its string and took off. There was no going back to the
desert. That way was now barred. She made for the far end of the
valley, running in a wide circle, keeping well clear of the water,
her single aim to escape.

Dram ran fast, long legs extended, arms pumping. She ran
through the defile, the corridor where the gorge narrowed, not
looking back, putting all her effort into speed and distance;
running, running, terribly afraid.

The cliffs of the defile fanned out, kept on spreading and Dram
entered a place that was completely different from the valley she
had left. There was space, an amphitheatre of five or six hundred
metres in diameter, the arc of its perimeter a succession of pillars
of red rock that towered to the sky. The big gorge was no more.
It split into ravines that ran between and around the rocky
pillars. Like the fingers at the end of an arm, or the river that
divides and sub-divides at its delta, the gorge had lost its
single identity.

Dram ran toward the geological oddity, wondering at the
strange shapes that reminded her of stalagmites. She could not
know that when dinosaurs ruled the earth, white water had
already gouged its way through the mountains. But columns of
harder rock had withstood the wearing. The torrent of the river
had flowed around the columns, further eroding earth and stone
as it went, deepening the ravines.

The dinosaur reign ended with extinction and the lagoon was a mere memento of a once mighty river. Everlasting, the towers of rock remained.

Running was taking Dram's strength. She looked over her shoulder. No monster was following. She slowed to a walk and, breathing heavily, took stock of her new environment. The problem she now faced was which of the many alternative routes she should take. From habit, Dram glanced at the sky. Dense grey cloud was all she could see, with no inkling of where the sun might be. *Never mind, why did I bother? I don't need to know the position of the sun.*

Taking the compass from her pocket, Dram held it flat on her palm. The magic needle would show her the way. She waited expectantly for the needle to swing to the south and hold steady. It did not, but gyrated wildly, turning three hundred and sixty degrees clockwise and abruptly reversing to complete another sweep of the circle.

Dram watched in alarm and shook the compass. The needle continued its mad, uncertain spinning.

"Stop! Stop!" She stared in disbelief. The panic she had experienced at the lagoon returned. Flight then had been the response to fright. Now to run, to walk, to proceed on her way was possible, but to where, by which path? Dismay engulfed Dram. She shook the compass again and again, trying to bring some sense, some stability to the needle. It continued to whirl about; a thin, black dervish, no longer sane.

Dram held her palm flat and still, hoping that peace would return. Nothing changed. The needle continued to dazzle her with its wild, irregular motion. She looked up at the rust red towers of rock and at the red mountains from which they had been carved. She felt antlike in their presence, a tiny human enclosed by walls that could not be climbed, confronted by a maze of pillars through which she had to find her way.

Stricken with fear, she stared at her surroundings. The cliffs, the towers, were playing with her, closing her in and treating her like a caged animal to be tormented as whim took them. Thinking this way, Cloud's prediction burst into Dram's head; the memory of the night spent in sight of the forest of Kaldor. *Devils playing in the rock.*

Dram sank to the ground and cried.

There was so much that Dram did not and could not know. The compass lying on the ground beside her twitched in unpredictable swings because of the overwhelming attraction of the iron in the surrounding rock. The mountain range — weathered to its rusty colour by the iron ore of which it was largely composed — overruled the magnetic field of planet earth. Within the domain of the red rock, the compass was as lost as Dram.

She sat for a long time clasping her knees, her head bowed. Finally, knowing that she could not stay sitting, Dram rose, pocketed the compass in the hope that it would regain its magic and slung her pack to her back. She ran her eyes over the array of towers and the number of ravines; all were equally inviting, all offering passage from the amphitheatre. One, maybe more, maybe all, would lead her south.

Dram walked straight ahead, aiming for the gap opposite the defile. From her reckoning it was aligned with the course she wished to take. She passed between two of the rock towers, leaving the arena of the amphitheatre behind and entered an entirely different and confusing place.

The ravine ran straight for fifty or sixty metres, there it met another column of rock and divided so that Dram had to elect which way to go. She chose left and the ravine almost immediately split again, teasing Dram with which fork to take.

The towers had been formed from the top down through aeons of erosion, but to Dram they grew uneven from the floor of the ravines, columns that blocked the possibility of seeing any distance. Like giant chess pieces rising high, they checked her progress. At each new obstacle a fresh decision had to be made. Dram went this way and then that, walking on, becoming increasingly unsure, lost in the meandering passages that an ancient river had cut through the rock.

What am I to do? She held her head in both hands, trying to think, reaching the conclusion that her real decision was not whether to turn right or left, but to determine her objective. Should she press on, hoping that eventually she would find her way out of the maze? Should she try to find her way back to the amphitheatre and from there brave the monster and retreat to the desert? Should she give up, sit down and wait for Endless Night to claim her?

The pillars surrounding her, rough and red, gave no encouragement and no clue. Dram looked at them and could not tell from where she had come. For all she knew the twists and turns might be leading her back to where she had started. She wished that Snotty was with her. His boundless optimism would lift her spirits. Come what may, together they would make their way south. But Snotty was not with her.

Dram made her decision. She would be like him. Take destiny by the scruff of the neck and keep on going. A path out of the maze had to exist. She would not give up. She would find her way out. Endless Night would not be her lot, not for a long time.

Thirsty, she reached for the gourd, frowning as she lifted it that it did not seem heavy enough. A quick examination confirmed that the gourd did not contain the amount of water she expected. Dram shook her head at the loss, realising that water had been slopping from it when she had run. She took a niggardly sip. The need to preserve her resources was paramount.

Dram sniffed the air. The smell of fish was strong, coming from the pack that lay by her side. Flies, attracted by the smell had settled on the pack, some crawling, looking for entry. Dram waved them away. They rose buzzing in the air and returned. She opened the pack and the smell came strong and pungent. The fish she had plucked in such a hurry from the smoke had stuck together in an oily lump. Dram pulled at the mess and put a piece of flesh in her mouth. The taste was fine, but she knew that would be short lived. Only partly cured, the fish would decompose unless the job of smoking was completed.

Tears welled in Dram's eyes, the determination with which she had buoyed herself gone. Nothing was going right.

Chapter 30

On the table-top of the dune the Camarilla gathered to eat a communal breakfast. Despite the short rations, spirits were high. The map would be their guide and surely hunting would be good in the mountains.

Had there existed an observer with the ability to view far and wide from above, he would have seen the band busy gathering belongings prior to departure and in the valley of the lagoon he would have seen Dram, the archer, loosing her arrows at the fish.

The Camarilla gave no thought to Dram. Their thoughts were self-centred, with the hope that luck would favour them on the next leg of the journey.

Standing apart from the crowd occupied with packing furs and utensils into backpacks, Tasha, Mangrove and Snotty consulted the map and surveyed the range.

Snotty pointed to the left, to the opening of the gorge that Dram had elected as her pathway south. "That might be the easy way to go."

Tasha shook her head. "Look here." She held her finger on the map. "The gorge becomes a tangle of ravines that seem to run in knots. I don't like it."

Mangrove agreed and looked toward the sleeping hare. "We should aim for that mountain. It's recognisable."

Snotty leaned across to study the map in Tasha's hands. He made the point that with the rise and fall of the range, they would be traversing ridges and valleys and not always able to see the sleeping hare.

"But we can mark our way on the picture," Tasha said and explained her thinking. They would plan the next move from each ridge and plot progress on the map. By doing so they would have some idea of current location, perhaps not completely accurate, but satisfactory for the purpose.

She went to the ashes of the fire, picked out a piece of charred wood and tested it on the map. The charcoal smudged the paper.

"Hmm, wait on." Snotty used the Swiss knife to sharpen the burnt end. "Try it now."

Tasha touched the paper again. The 'pencil' worked perfectly. Mangrove and Snotty nodded approval, imagining a series of dots that would record their progress through the mountains.

Unlike Dram, who had tried to find her way from the base of the range, Tasha and the boys surveyed the possibilities from the top of the dune. The vantage point let them see further, but apart from the gorge, the range seemed to present an impossibly steep face of rock, too difficult to climb. Adding to the difficulty, the light was alternating from bright to dim as the sun was increasingly obscured by the same cottony balls of cumulus that were aiding Dram in her stalking of the ibex.

Biscetti, bored and impatient to get going, joined the group to ask when they would be on their way. Tasha shrugged, saying that so far the place to climb from the sand had not been found. "We can't see a safe way up."

"Cloud might," Biscetti said.

The mystical girl wearing the spectacles came at Biscetti's call. Walking along the dune, stopping to peer across the distance at the red rock wall, walking further, searching, Cloud finally pointed to where a tree splashed the red with green. "There."

A narrow cleft in the cliff, barely wide enough for a human body, would be the way to the top.

In single file, people made the ascent. In places, boulders had tumbled and become wedged, presenting an extra challenge to the old and the very young. Wherever the way was blocked,

Foragers gave assistance; lifting packs, providing a leg up. Eventually the climb was completed and while the last to make it were still catching their breath, Tasha pencilled a dot on the map and circled it. The dot had special significance. It was the starting point for the way over the mountains.

Ingamo watched Tasha make the mark and raised his eyes toward the sleeping hare. To reach it would require a lot more climbing. The spot on the map, the ridge on which they stood, was dwarfed by the altitude of the hare. Ingamo sighed. His bones felt old, his muscles tired.

Equally tired, Jemma bullied the old man to keep going.

Dumperty, struggling, but determined to keep up, saw defeat on Ingamo's face and took his hand. "You can lean on me when the going gets tough."

Ingamo smiled. "That's very kind. Let's help each other, eh?"

The old man and the little boy stayed close, doing just that.

The going was tough! On the second day every ridge was higher than the last. The ground at times crumbled underfoot so that slipping and sliding became commonplace, but the pilgrims were making progress, moving higher, seeing further. It was as though travelling south was taking them to the top of the world.

Climbing such rough, steep country took its toll. Not only Ingamo felt the strain, most were at breaking point, ready to lie down, perhaps never to get up. Tasha felt little better. A thin blue line on the map suggested that a river ran in one of the valleys ahead, but in getting to it, the Camarilla would pay the price of exhaustion and some might not be able to make it. She called a halt for rest.

Dirty from scrabbling up the steep slopes, skin and clothing had taken on the colour of the mountain range, so that lying flat, too tired to move, bodies merged with the ground as though sculpted from red clay. Looking no different, Tasha too lay down. She closed her eyes and would have slept, but a noise disturbed her, a falling stone that bounced and rolled by her head. Without moving she scanned the cliff above for the cause.

High up, animals were moving from one narrow ledge to another. Tasha marvelled at their sure-footedness. They seemed to stand where no foothold could exist, looking about, bending to nibble, moving on again, unconcerned. The ibex acted as though gravity had lost its power over them; that vertical cliffs held no danger because to fall was impossible.

Tasha raised her head and saw that Biscetti, with Belle and Zita, had also noticed the goats. As unobtrusively as possible, each was fitting an arrow to a bow. Tasha admired the care with which the girls moved. Fluidly, in slow motion, each knelt and using only signals from the eyes and almost imperceptible nods, selected individual targets. The opportunity would not be wasted. Three arrows would aim to bring down three goats.

Thirty metres above, unconscious of the developing threat, the ibex continued to gaze upon the mountain scenery or to seek a blade of grass that had succeeded to grow among the rock.

Without a word spoken, three arrows flew and three goats fell, tumbling down the cliff-face in a cascade of stones. Exultant, shouting their success, the girls ran to claim their prizes. Any chance of sleep was gone. Figures of red ochre rose from where they lay and cries of jubilation echoed around the mountains. The famine was over.

The smell of roasting goat drifted in the air. Mouths watered, knives sliced at flesh and hunger that had ached in bellies for months was at last satisfied.

Tasha let the band linger for a while, but with eating, the mood had changed. Strength had returned to muscles, and bodies revitalised were ready to move on.

Mid-afternoon, Snotty shouted from a ridge that he could see water. In fact the creek the Camarilla were approaching was the source for the waterfall Dram had seen. But the situation for the unhappy Dram could not have been more different from that enjoyed by the group now laughing, hurrying to be able to drink freely. It was not just an end to the miserable rationing of water that spurred people on, it was the knowledge that where rivers ran fish would swim.

And it was so easy. None of the back-breaking work to smash a hole in ice, just the baiting of a hook and a short cast into the stream. The fish piled up on the bank. Tasha walked among the fishers, congratulating this one on his catch, that one on the size of the fish she had landed. "Yes," she murmured to herself, "fortune is at last smiling on us."

With a stock of meat, fish and water and the probability that more might be found, the situation had changed dramatically.

Thirst and hunger satisfied, Snotty and Mangrove checked out the rising ground over which they would soon travel. Climbing a bluff from where they had full view of the sleeping hare, Snotty, like some lord in his private domain, took in the whole scene.

"So far so good and if ..." His words trailed off. Distracted, his eyes were fixed on something moving in the sky.

Mangrove followed the line of Snotty's gaze. High, very high, a bird with wings extended was soaring in lazy circles. The bird fascinated them and as they watched they saw others in the distance, all circling, rising in updraughts, slow and easy in a sleepy, effortless riding on air.

But the raptors were not sleeping. With eyes that could take in everything from horizon to horizon, or in a blink could, with telescopic precision, magnify anything of interest, they were scouring the mountains for what might fill their craws.

The raptor that had caught Mangrove's attention had also seen the two Foragers. In one graceful roll the bird folded back his wings and dived. With open mouths Snotty and Mangrove watched him plunge straight down, unfaltering. The raptor fell like a stone, dropping directly at them, faster than anything they had ever seen, growing larger with each passing second.

"Hey." The word from Snotty was recognition that they might be in trouble, a warning to take care. The raptor was a missile aimed at them, coming at speed.

Snotty felt for his bow. Not taking his eyes off the bird, he fitted an arrow. Alarmed, Mangrove tried to run, but he could not compete with the speed of the raptor that at the last moment lifted its head to flare, and with spread talons, slammed into Manny.

In a millisecond it was done. Mangrove lying unmoving, the big bird standing on him and then turning to face Snotty, wings fully extended, ready to attack again.

Snotty fired.

Too close to miss, his arrow struck the raptor in the breast with stunning force, entered flesh, broke ribs, pierced lungs, kept up its awful trajectory until the barbs of the arrow head stuck clear from the feathers of the raptor's back. The raised wings drooped and as his eyelids closed over the wonderfully sighted eyes, the bird dropped dead, his feathers a winding sheet draped over the inert Mangrove.

"Manny!" Snotty screamed, filled with fear that his greatest friend had been claimed by Endless Night. The size of the raptor and the force with which it hit its prey were designed to kill in one lethal blow. Snotty had recognised this too late to save Manny and, as he lifted the bird off him, it was obvious that evolution had perfected the raptor. Built for speed and to strike without warning, nature had completed the design with talons that could puncture and grip tight and a beak that could strip flesh from its kill.

Well you won't do that again. Snotty pushed the raptor aside, knelt by Manny and rolled him gently on to his back.

There was no rise and fall of Mangrove's chest. Snotty put his cheek by Mangrove's lips. He felt no breath. "No, no, please no."

Snotty placed two fingers at Mangrove's neck. There was no pulse. Mangrove lay still. Snotty could see the shadow of Endless Night beginning to fall across the Forager who had been his lifetime friend.

"Manny, no," he whispered. "Don't go."

Mangrove, lifeless, lay with eyes closed and in a flash of déjà vu, Snotty was in the military bunker, seeing the diagram on the wall. He was kneeling beside Manny and the drawn figures he recalled were in the same positions. The one kneeling had blown into the mouth of the one with eyes shut and in the next frame had pushed at the chest. In desperation, Snotty tried to recall the sequence of motions so that he might apply them to Manny, tried to bring to mind those simple pictures drawn to give an urgent message that could be easily understood without words.

He tilted Mangrove's head to clear his airway, bent low and blew into his mouth. Imagining the heart he had seen, he placed one hand upon Mangrove's chest and, with the other on top of it, his arms rigid, he pressed down with all his power, compressing the chest again and again. Mangrove made no response.

Snotty tried again, clamping Manny's nose as he blew into his mouth. He thought he saw Mangrove's chest rise. It was an illusion. Snotty switched to compression, using his strength to push down so that Mangrove's heart was squeezed and released repeatedly to pump blood around his body.

Over and over Snotty went through the cycle, feeling his arms tiring, fearing that he would be unable to continue, uncertain that what he did was correct. But Snotty's memory was good and through him, the ancients reached out across four thousand years to revive Mangrove. With a long, shuddering intake of breath, he opened his eyes.

Snotty leaned back to rest on his heels. "You're alive."

Mangrove groaned. His back ached from the impact of the raptor, his chest sore from the compression. The raptor about to hit him was the last thing he could remember. "I'd gone to Endless Night, hadn't I?"

"It looked that way," Snotty grinned in his usual way. "But you're okay now."

Mangrove persisted with questions. To be wrapped in Endless Night, to even *appear* to have departed the life he loved, was not something to be passed over lightly. "What happened to me? Why were you kneeling there, leaning over me?"

Snotty told him of the diagrams he had seen on the wall of the underground control room, how they seemed to be instructions for bringing the dead back to life.

"You're always there for me, Snotty, aren't you?"

"You're my friend."

That statement was enough. Snotty helped Mangrove to his feet. They looked at the raptor and Snotty withdrew the arrow from its body. "We'll eat him, eh?"

"Why not? He'd have eaten us."

Plucking the bird was quick and efficient. Snotty held its naked body and gutted it. Mangrove, bruised and sore, looked on, the thought in his mind that after being washed in the creek, the raptor would make a fine meal. He took a tail feather and stuck it in Snotty's hair. "This is your trophy. You should always wear it so that no one ever forgets how quick thinking and how skilful you are."

Snotty liked the colours of the feather. He touched it, adjusting it to hold firm in his hair and laughed. "Yeah, I think I will."

Mangrove breathed deeply a few times, testing his ribs, trying to stretch away the soreness. He looked to where the other raptors had been making their slow circles in rising air. No longer taking advantage of lift, two were spiralling downward. They descended not in the vertical dive of attack, but in a leisurely way, their heads craning, turning to allow eyes to remain fixed on a point on the ground.

"What are they up to, Snotty?" Mangrove searched the area below the birds and saw the spires of rock formed and interlaced by the maze of ravines. From the height of the mountain, he could have been a bird himself, seeing the tops of the columns of rock and into the depths of the passages carved between them.

The two Foragers tracked the flight of the raptors until the birds, with occasional wing beats to maintain height, were flying in a tight circle around a single pillar.

"Maybe they nest there. I think I can see a dark patch on one of the columns."

Mangrove squinted. The cloud cover had diminished the light; that and distance was putting his vision to the test. "It's a funny shape, but yeah. Anyway, let's get this big chick back to camp."

Snotty settled the body of the plucked raptor on his shoulders. Mangrove, grateful that he only had the bow and arrows to carry, made his way with care. The way he felt, he reckoned that it would be some days before his bruised body was back to normal.

Seeing the boys returning, intrigued by the burden Snotty was carrying, Tasha went to meet them. Surprised, delighted by the size of the bird that would add new taste for palates to savour, she grinned at them. "How about that?"

Mangrove coughed and held his chest. Tasha's smile faded. "Manny, what's wrong? What happened to you two?"

Snotty related the story of the raptor attack and how he had resuscitated Mangrove.

"Are you really okay, Manny?"

He assured Tasha that he was.

She sighed and looked directly into his eyes, picturing him in the shroud of Endless Night. "Death falling from the skies. Oh, Manny."

Cloud's vision had become reality, only to be re-written. Through Snotty, the knowledge of the ancients had intervened to cheat Endless Night of her victim. Playing in Tasha's brain were the other words uttered by Cloud on the dune: *All above, one below, but not alone. A land alive to lift and shake, liquid fire that rivers make.* Did Cloud actually see a raptor diving to kill Manny, or did some shadow invade her mind, some hint that death would knock him down. As she pondered the impossible questions, Tasha cringed with guilt that she had dismissed Manny's concerns at the time by saying that the revelations of a dream could never be interpreted. She knew that she should have tried, but when Cloud spoke from the depths of her trance, the scenes she described could have been reflections from warped mirrors and those reflections wreathed in smoke so that nothing could be clearly understood.

Tasha repeated the words to Snotty and Manny. "What *did* Cloud see? What meaning is hidden in the pictures she draws? They are so vivid and yet so confusing."

They shrugged. It was too hard, but as Manny had found, concealed in Cloud's pronouncements were dangers that could prove lethal.

Chapter 31

The torments of Dram's predicament gave her no peace. She sat huddled in the ravine and took a tiny sip of water, the smell of part-cured fish reminding her that her food supply would last a day, perhaps two. The conclusion was inevitable: unless game came her way, in forty-eight hours her larder would be empty. She contemplated the last resort of chewing the leather laces of her boots and licking out the stained and oily lining of her pack. When reduced to that, she knew the end would soon follow. The gourd was light in her hand, mocking her with the fact that there was little left to drink. If by chance rainwater lay in some rock hollow, or a stream cascaded down the rock face of a mountain ... *If by chance* ... The dry dust, the red rock gave hope a hollow ring. Dram sipped again and made the promise that she would not touch another drop until nightfall.

Lost, alone, she bowed her head and reflected on the events that had brought her down. The fine times that she had enjoyed when Avon had been Queen, friends like Snotty and Manny, Sola and Situ, little Dumperty, even Tasha, all were stranded in the past. Dram saw their faces, saw herself with them racing over the snow and sitting around the fire in Homecave. Memories of the expedition to the hollow mountain came sharp, hurting so that she shivered at the thought that she would have abandoned Biscetti. Her face contorted with shame at the wrongs she had done Tasha. Dram folded her arms, gripped them and swayed back and forth.

Remorse would not leave her. She had taken advantage of Snotty, a good friend who would have done anything for her. Tears filled her eyes. Hitting Tasha, denouncing her. *She risked her life to save me from the sand. I didn't even thank her.*

Every incident played in Dram's mind, every detail stark. She shut her eyes tight, but the scenes remained, regret twisting its sharp edges within her. The full realisation stole over Dram that the plight she was in was of her own making; that she had made mistake upon mistake, offending all who had been close to her. If only, she thought, if only I could make amends. *But it's too late for that. I deserve whatever punishment is in store for me.* And she was certain what that would be. Endless Night would soon cast its shade.

A sound came faintly to her. She cocked her head, trying to locate from where it came. The possibilities were many. The sound could be coming from any one of the ravines and as she strained to hear, turning her head from side to side, the skin over her entire body prickled with fear. The noise she heard was the slithering of scales over sand and rock. The monster had left the lagoon to follow her. But where was he? From which passage would he appear?

Panic came again with racing heart and trembling limbs. Dram stood, frozen in fright. To run down any one of the ravines might take her straight into his jaws. The noise of the crocodile was getting louder. Dram looked for footholds in a pillar. She would have to climb.

Scales rasping on stone filled the air. Dram reached high, found a place to put a foot. She was shaking. "Stop it. Stop it," she muttered, knowing that her life depended on finding the knobs of rock and the crevices into which she could fit her fingers. She had to be able to think, to quickly appraise the uneven face of the pillar above, select a hold and go higher.

The crocodile, an animal evolved over seventy million years or more, had fixed in his tiny brain a picture of a girl. He had her smell and the smell of fish in his nostrils. Finding his way through the labyrinth of rock pillars was made easy.

Dram had climbed two metres from ground level, the rock rough on her hands and against her cheek as she clung close. She searched the rock face above. A possible handhold was beyond her reach. She tried again, her arm outstretched, fingers clawing at the rock. She looked down for somewhere to place a foot that would take her the few centimetres higher.

The senses of hunter and hunted were fully aroused. The sound of the animal was much louder. Dram could hear the harsh grunts of the crocodile, which could smell that his quarry was within reach. She, the human being, was spurred by the sound to escape. He, the animal, driven by her strengthening scent, was rushing to find her, then to eat her. Seconds separated them.

The monster burst from a passage. Dram turned her head, looked into his yellow eyes as he fixed them on hers and felt blindly for any slight protuberance of rock that might help her. She watched the jaws open wide, smelt the reek of crocodile breath and pulled herself higher. The crocodile ran and in one explosive, violent motion the front half of his body lifted and twisted. Dram saw it happening as if in slow motion: the giant jaws, the rows of teeth, the yellow eyes, the creamy underbelly. Her fingers found the projection. She hauled and at the same time reached with her other hand, glancing to where it might grab a hold. In unthinking co-ordination of arms and legs she lifted a foot to find a toehold in a crevice. She pushed herself higher. In Dram's mind, time had stopped. She glued herself to the rock, expecting jaws to clamp and crush her body, heard them snap shut and felt no pain. Sensation followed sensation. The tympanic membrane of her ears vibrated with sound so physically near that she could feel as well hear the noise. The arteries in her neck were pulsing, pressing at her skin as if to burst out. Her lips quivered, buffeted by the air she drew into her lungs and noisily exhaled. But she remained alive.

Dram clung to the spire and looked down. The heavy body had crashed to the floor of the ravine. She could not take her eyes from the huge animal, watching as it tried again to jump at her, but the croc could not repeat his effort and fell short.

Dram inched higher. What might have been a ledge had become the resting place for tumble down boulders that over centuries, eroded or struck by lightning, had been dislodged from further up the pillar. If she was to be safe, the place to be was with the boulders on the ledge. Dram ran a hand over stone, feeling blindly for somewhere to grip. The boulder rocked, teetered, leaned toward her as though it would complete its long-awaited fall to the floor of the ravine. Dram shut her eyes. It was the end. She would fall, dragging the rock with her. On its fulcrum, as though it were some stone metronome, the boulder rocked away from her. Lifted a little by the movement, Dram pulled herself all the way.

From there, out of reach, she could observe.

In frustration, in anger, or simply settling for what was available, the crocodile tore at Dram's pack and like a dog, flung it from side to side as if it were alive. Dram watched as arrows spilled from the pack, the bow, her jacket, the coagulated lump of fish. From above, she saw her last hope of eating vanish. In one gulp the fish were gone. Not satisfied, the croc chewed at the pack itself, grinding the leather until it too was swallowed. With one final rough movement the crocodile settled, crushing the gourd. Dust darkened with water that was quickly absorbed and the yellow eyes fixed on Dram.

The human and the animal stared at each other. The waiting game, the end game, had begun.

With abundant food and water, an air of calm enveloped the camp. The band was at ease, wanting for nothing. Mangrove's brush with death had laid bare part of Cloud's vision and dismissed the mystique. Forewarned was forearmed. Constant watch for raptors would not only avoid injury, it might add to the cooking pot.

The general feeling of well-being took away urgency. Tasha agreed. Continuation of the journey south could wait until the following day. The Camarilla would rest by the stream. Everyone would eat his fill and sleep content.

The cloud broke up during the night, becoming ghostly ships that sailed the sky, taking the light of moon and stars, sailing on to release the light to shine in intermittent bursts upon the sleepers. By dawn the sky was clear and with the sun the mountains lost the brown of night to burn again in rusty red. Mangrove stretched, grimacing as his fingers touched sore ribs and bruised muscles. Maybe I felt worse at some time in the past, he thought, but I can't remember when.

Snotty, still lying in his sleeping place, watched the play of Mangrove's expressions and laughed aloud. "Move around a bit. You'll be okay."

"Thanks." A sarcastic retort making plain that Snotty's lack of sympathy was not appreciated. "Oh, I hurt all over."

Snotty laughed again, but came to help Manny get his gear together. "You're upright and breathing. That's what counts."

Individually, collectively, around the campsite belongings were packed and food and water distributed. Tasha watched the smooth sharing of the communal load, happy that co-operation had fully returned. She was reminded of the old days, the days before the exodus had begun. *Well, those days will return. I know they will. We'll find a home and then ...* She tried to imagine what sort of place that might be and the unwelcome thought intruded that perhaps it lay at the end of the rainbow, a place always somewhere ahead, a promised land that kept moving away as the clan approached. *No!*

Tasha turned her attention to the matter at hand. The new day had begun and the sleeping hare beckoned. "Let's go."

The trek was underway again.

As the group approached the bluff where Mangrove had been attacked, Biscetti was curious. Walking beside Cloud, she suggested that they climb it.

"Snotty says the view is great from up there."

"Okay, but what about raptors?"

Biscetti scanned the sky. "Nothing. They won't be around until the sun heats the air and the updraughts start."

"I guess so."

The two girls climbed until the view spread in every direction. Biscetti spun like a ballerina to take it all in. She could see the dunes that from this height appeared like ripples in the sand. The dunes looked so small, not an obstacle at all, she thought, and yet they had been so difficult to cross and quicksand had almost taken Tasha and Dram.

Biscetti turned to look at the way ahead, at the sleeping hare. That view too had a benign appearance, as though any chosen path would be easy. *I hope so.* But experience had taught her that appearances could be deceptive.

"I can see Dram." Cloud's announcement came quietly, yet to Biscetti it hit like a thunderclap, out of place in the serenity of the mountains and the distance and the endless blue of the sky.

"Where?"

Cloud pointed. "On that ledge."

Biscetti strained to find Dram among the columns of rock and the patchwork of ravines. "I can't see her."

Cloud's glasses glinted in the sunlight. "There."

Biscetti stood behind Cloud and followed the extended arm and the pointing finger. Biscetti could see something. Perhaps it *was* Dram. Perhaps the dark spot on the ledge *was* the runaway, the would-be queen. Biscetti could not tell.

"What's she doing?"

"I can see something else, a big animal. Dram's on the ledge and the animal is in the ravine below her."

"I'm telling Tasha."

Biscetti yelled and waved. "Tasha, Tasha. Cloud can see Dram."

The news, shouted from the bluff, echoed like the cry of the muezzin, a call to the faithful from the minaret. The startled group halted, every head looking up at Biscetti.

"Wait here." Tasha motioned that all should sit. "Manny, Snotty, come with me."

The three joined Biscetti and with Cloud directing, made out the figure on the ledge.

"What's happening down there?" Tasha asked.

"Hard to tell, but Dram must have climbed the column of rock to get away from the animal." Cloud was concentrating on the scene far below. "It's huge and Dram's lying on a ledge above it. She has little space to move. Most of the ledge is taken up by a fallen boulder." Cloud turned to Tasha. "It's not a good place to be."

Mangrove's eyes were good, but he could not make out the detail seen by Cloud. "Does she have her arrows and her bow?"

"I can't see them. I don't think so."

Snotty sat squinting at the distant drama, putting himself in Dram's position, recalling a time he had been attacked by wolves. "Dram's had to climb to escape being eaten. In the hurry, she's had no time to arm herself."

"So it's one on one," Tasha said. "Dram can't defend herself and she probably has no food and water on that ledge."

Snotty agreed. It was only a matter of time for Dram. "Endless Night will take her if she stays on the ledge, and if she climbs down she'll meet the same fate."

"No," Tasha said. "I can't let that happen. Dram is a Forager. She's one of us."

"Tasha, I'm sorry for Dram, but there's nothing we can do."

"Yes there is. I'm going down."

"You can't." Biscetti and Mangrove spoke as one.

Snotty joined them and argued that Dram had made her decision voluntarily to go into exile, that it had been the culmination of a number of unhappy events. "Maybe we're better off without her, Tasha."

"Don't say that, Snotty. We grew up with Dram. We can't leave her."

"She wouldn't do it for you, Tasha." Biscetti was angry that her sister would put herself in danger to rescue Dram.

"And how do you intend to get to her?" Mangrove asked. He was shaking his head, believing that the idea, which stemmed from Tasha's humanity and the responsibility she felt for all the Camarilla, was noble, but it lacked practicality.

Tasha brought the map from her pocket. "We're here." She touched the spot on the map and explained her plan. The four on the pinnacle would accompany her down the mountain. The sides were steep, but Mangrove agreed that descent was possible until the mountainside dropped sheer into the ravine. "What then?"

"Then you lower me by rope."

"Tasha?"

"I can do it, Manny. And remember this: it is I who must do it." She looked at Biscetti. "Would you get the rope please?"

Manny persisted, wanting to know how Tasha intended to rejoin them. Her answer was simple. Dram and she would find their way back to the dunes and then follow in the footsteps that had brought them within clear sight of the sleeping hare. "I have the map, remember."

Tasha would not be dissuaded.

When Biscetti returned, as well as the rope she carried Tasha's pack. "You'll need this, but please ..." And in one last effort to have Tasha change her mind, Biscetti pleaded with her not to go. Argument was useless.

"I knew no matter what I said you'd go." Biscetti handed over the pack. "I put some meat in there. Who knows how long you'll be away."

"Thanks, little sister."

Carefully, with Snotty as pathfinder, the five picked their way down the slope. At one point, as they stopped to assess progress, Biscetti looked toward the rock where Dram had taken refuge. "That's Dram all right."

The figure was a long way off, but the tall girl, the long hair was unmistakeable.

Mangrove licked his lips and whistled with a piercing blast. Dram gave no indication that she had heard. He tried again in a long, unwavering note.

"She heard you," Cloud said. "She's trying to locate where we are."

Whistling and waving, calling her name, they saw Dram raise an arm in recognition.

"Well, she knows we've seen her."

Tasha studied the honeycomb of spires to pinpoint Dram's position. The rock columns were all so alike, she had to be certain. With the map spread, Tasha found the one where Dram was trapped and using the 'pencil' scored it with charcoal. The others watched her trace a winding path among the spires, the course that would take her to Dram.

Moving down the slope, one or the other would give a wave, but at lower levels Dram was lost to view.

Finally they stood at the brink of the sheer cliff. Once lowered to its base, it was Tasha's intention to follow the path she had drawn through the maze of ravines.

Mangrove was nervous. "It's not too late to go back, Tasha."

She smiled at him. They had come too far. There was no going back. Snotty gave her his bow and quiver. Tasha slipped them over one shoulder.

"Take this too." He handed her the army knife.

"Thanks, Snotty."

Mangrove lay at the edge and looked down to the valley floor. "The rope may not be long enough." He took it from Biscetti and let one end fall. As he thought, it dangled free.

"That's close enough." Tasha judged the rope to be a couple of metres short. She could drop to the ground from there. It shouldn't be a problem.

Mangrove suggested that when she was at the bottom, they would let the rope fall. "You and Dram may need it."

"Okay, thanks." Tasha looped the rope around her waist and began the descent.

The smooth wall of the cliff offered no difficulty. Tasha walked her way down, most of her weight taken by the group at the other end of the rope. As expected, it fell short.

Tasha eyed the drop. The challenge of two metres looked different from close up. She let loose the hitches and fell, watching the ground coming to meet her, bending her legs to cushion the shock. Hitting the ground, she rolled in an effort to take the sting out of the impact. Not so bad, she thought and stood to wave, letting the others know that she was okay. The rope snaked its way through the air to fall beside her.

As Tasha entered the warren of ravines, Snotty led the others back up the mountain. From the bluff at the summit, they might be able to follow events as they unfolded.

The charcoal line twisted among the columns. Tasha followed, laden with backpack, weapons and rope, looking like a soldier in the field or a mountaineer, ticking off her progressing position, wondering why Dram had taken such a meandering path.

Dwarfed by the rock pillars, Tasha walked in their shadow only to be lit by the sun, as though the chess pieces of the pillars stood on a checkerboard and she was stepping from white square to black as she closed on her objective.

Tasha took the bow from her shoulder and replaced it with the coiled rope. She fitted an arrow to the bowstring and shouted into the air. "Dram, can you hear me?"

"Tasha, where are you?"

"I'm coming for you."

"I'm so glad." Relief surged through Dram, only to evaporate. "How can you find me in this dreadful place?"

"I know the way. I have a picture of where you are, the picture that Dumperty found."

The girls were calling to one another, their voices echoing among the canyons.

"Tasha, there's a monster here. So huge, you can't imagine how huge."

"I have Snotty's bow."

"A bow is useless." On the ledge Dram looked down at the great length of the crocodile. The yellow eyes were no longer looking at Dram. The croc's head was swaying, the eyes searching for the opening from which Tasha would appear.

"Tasha, the monster knows you're coming. He's waiting for you. Run away while you can. And Tasha, I'm sorry for all I did to you."

"I'm not running. I'm coming for you."

"Then listen to what I say." And Dram described the monster to Tasha, told her how, despite his size, he could move fast.

Tasha remained still, listening, thinking how she might overcome such a beast. "Dram, I have the rope. We'll use it together."

The arrow was returned to its quiver, the bow to its place on her shoulder.

Still unable to see Dram, Tasha shouted her tactics. She would creep as quietly as possible and shielded by the towers of rock, get close to the one on which Dram was held hostage. Dram should look for her, be ready as Tasha hurled up the rope with the noose already tied. "Then I'll show myself, the lure to attract the monster. From above you drop the noose to me and hang on."

"Oh, Tasha, you have no idea of his size."

"Do you have a better plan?"

"No, but ..."

Tasha formed the noose with its slipknot. She slid the knot, enlarging the noose, making it big. They would have one chance to snare the monster, one chance only to draw the rope tight around his jaws, locking them closed. *Then I'll use the knife.*

With no real appreciation of what she would be up against, Tasha imagined that she would straddle the roped crocodile and cut its throat.

She looked at the map, imprinting on her brain the route she must take to get to Dram. The map went into her pocket. Tasha coiled the rope and crept around pillars of rock. She was almost there.

Tasha swallowed, hugging rock, letting one eye search for Dram. Dram saw her, raised an arm in caution and put her finger to her lips. Tasha hurled the rope. Dram caught it.

The great head of the crocodile raised and turned. The yellow eyes looked toward the slap of rope on flesh.

Tasha stepped from cover and Dram dropped the noose to her. Tasha stretched it wide, daring the monster to come at her, fearing that it would be the last thing she ever did. The experiences of her lifetime, hunting wild animals that were themselves crazy with hunger — and had she made a mistake would have eaten her — had not prepared her for such an encounter. She had never seen anything so big.

The crocodile ran at her on stubby legs, clawed toes scattering sand and pebbles, the great tail stretched. Tasha looked into the yellow eyes and held her ground, the noose circled, reaching from the rusty ground to the height of her shoulders. It was a hoop, thrust toward the charging beast, daring it to pass through and snatch the human bait.

To Dram, gripping the tail-end of the rope, looking down from above, it seemed a daring, impossible scheme. One tonne of primitive animal versus the slender Tasha could have only one outcome. Dram shuddered; so much depended on the noose. Tasha had to guarantee its placement and then she, Dram, had to have the strength to draw it tight, closing the jaws and keeping them closed. And what then? She had seen the monster with live prey. She had seen her own pack swallowed.

Dram foresaw what would happen. Her strength was pitiful in comparison with that of the monster. Once he was snared in the noose she would never be able to hold it tight. The picture was clear. She would be yanked from the ledge, falling to join Tasha, both of them to disappear into the jaws.

There has to be a better way.

Dram looked about for something, anything that would assist her to bring an end to the nightmare. As she searched other thoughts ran parallel, urging her to act before it was too late, before Tasha lost her life trying to save Dram's. *Come on, come on.* She eyed the boulder that had been her handhold. It had rocked, but it had held her weight. Dram flicked the tail-end of the rope around it, and around again, snapping the hitches tight and then leaning back, taking the strain. In the tug of war about to take place, Dram had added another to her team. She would be last in line, but the boulder would act as the real anchorman. Its mass combined with her effort might be enough to win the day.

A tremor ran through the noose in her hands, signalling to Tasha that Dram was holding firm. The ground under Tasha's feet trembled from the pounding as the monster ran at her. A wind blew at her cheeks and ruffled her hair, air disturbed by the headlong rush. The moment was almost upon her. The armoured scales, the rows of teeth, the absolute size and speed of the beast mesmerised Tasha. The jaws began to open. She stepped back, arms extended, and as the snout of the crocodile came at her through the noose the rope cracked taut. Tasha tried to leap away but missed her footing, staggering as lightning fast the noose shrank to grip the jaws of the crocodile.

From above Dram saw it all: the jaws forced together, Tasha stumbling backwards and then the monster driven insane by the clamping of the noose rising on hind legs, lashing this way and that to get rid of the binding.

The heavy tail whipped in frenzy and in a mighty clout knocked Tasha flying. Dram knew that she was witnessing the last minutes of Tasha's life.

The rope, meant to shackle the monster, relied upon the anchor of the boulder and the effort Dram could muster, but the boulder had begun to sway. The wild gyrations of the crocodile were being transmitted through the rope, exaggerating the rocking, tipping and tilting of the heavy boulder. The rope was cutting into Dram's hands. She held on, using all her strength and she too felt the power of the crocodile. The boulder, big as it was, was surging backwards and forwards and with every movement it jerked her from her feet. Time was fleeing, the last grains about to leave the hourglass. The rope had begun to fray.

Dram fought hard, her muscles burning, trying to slow the swaying of the boulder, losing the battle as the angle continually increased, watching fibres of rope unravel as they were cut.

This is not the way.

Like a burst of sunlight the idea flashed in Dram's mind. She shouldn't be fighting to dampen the oscillation of the boulder, she should add her weight, time her shoving to topple its mass over the edge.

Dram sat on the narrow ledge with her back hard against the rock face, her knees bent. The boulder leaned toward her, swung away and as it did she placed her feet on it and pushed. Her legs were pistons, contracting as the boulder came at her, extending as it swung away. The swaying of the huge stone gained momentum.

Dram pushed hard with her legs, relaxed, pushed hard again. The boulder teetered, the rhythm broken, and fell from the ledge.

The force against which the crocodile fought no longer existed. The taut rope was suddenly slack. Dram scrambled to the edge and watched. The crocodile, resistance removed, dropped to the ground. The rope, tied at one end to the animal and at the other to the stone, folded prettily down to drape the crocodile's head. The boulder immediately followed. In the time it took Dram to draw breath the monster had perished, his skull crushed.

A few metres from the scene of carnage, Tasha lay unmoving, one hand at her leg the other flung across her chest.

Dram climbed down from the ledge. In her whole life she had never experienced the emotions welling inside her. Tears of sadness ran slowly down her cheeks. Tightening her throat was the realisation that she had been far too slow to admit that Tasha was a real friend and that she, Dram, had been too late to make it up to her. Pain gripped Dram's breast and her breathing was uneasy, juddering into her lungs as she held back sobs.

"Oohhh." The cry of pain came from Tasha, travelled like an arrow to strike Dram and change her mood. Tasha had not gone to Endless Night, she was hurting, but she was alive.

Tasha attempted to stand, became almost upright and then sank back to sit on the red earth clutching her thigh. "Don't move, Tasha. I'm coming." Dram's sadness was gone, she was bubbling with joy. "We did it. We killed the monster, look."

"You did, Dram. Thank you."

Gently, Dram held Tasha's leg and examined the damage inflicted by the crocodile. Where the tail had slammed into Tasha, the shape of the armoured scales was left indented, depressions in her flesh darkening with bruising. The girls could see the external evidence of the blow. What they could not see were the broken blood vessels inside the leg, the blood welling to gather under the skin.

"We can't stay here, Tasha."

"Dram, I don't think I can walk."

"I'll carry you, but first, there is something I must do."

Dram leant forward and kissed Tasha on both cheeks. "You are my Queen."

"All is forgiven and now forgotten, Dram."

For a long moment each girl looked into the eyes of the other. The past had been buried.

"Okay, let me get what I can from the mess over there." Dram indicated the scattered remains of her belongings.

"And the rope, it's the only one we own."

Dram approached the monster. She untied the slipknot, the scales of the snout rough at her wrists. Close to her face, the yellow eyes, no longer bright with fire, looked at her and saw nothing. Dram patted the great stone, the silent executioner.

She salvaged her bow and arrows and her jacket. The gourd was smashed, lying in pieces in the stain from the water it had contained. "We have two bows and some arrows, but we have no food and we have no water."

Tasha moved her leg, grimacing at the pain. "There's food in my pack."

Dram opened it. "Wow, so much." She lifted a steak of goat meat and bit into it.

Silently Tasha gave thanks to Biscetti. There was more than enough food for one. Her sister had thought of Dram.

Tasha watched Dram tearing pieces from the steak, chewing with relish. "See, we've been in worse positions than this."

Dram raised her eyes to the rock pillars that rose like spears to hedge them in. Beyond them the mountain chain rose even higher. The prospect was daunting. She sighed. "If you're game, I'm game."

Tasha reminded her that she had the map. "We'll go back to the dunes and then take the route that will lead us to the others. There's no other way."

Dram knelt and assisted Tasha to climb onto her back. *No other way.* She was imagining the lagoon. There, they would have to pass by the dangers that dwelt below the water.

Chapter 32

"What can you see, Cloud?" Biscetti was anxious, her own eyes unable to make out the distant detail.

The four who had lowered Tasha into the valley of the spires had returned to the vantage point on the mountain. Cloud acted as commentator, relaying to Biscetti, Mangrove and Snotty the final events as they played out on the ledge.

"I can't see Tasha. Dram's on the ledge. She has the rope and it's looped around a big stone. The stone is rocking backwards and forwards."

Snotty was again putting himself in Dram's position. "Tasha found Dram and must have tossed her the rope, but where's the animal?"

"I don't know. It's not where it was. Wait, Dram's kicking at the rock on the ledge."

Listening to Cloud, not knowing what was really happening, Biscetti and the boys learned that the boulder had fallen and Dram had climbed from the ledge and could be seen no more.

"What's going on down there? Where's Tasha?" Biscetti's anxiety for her sister's safety sharpened her tone.

"Tasha's with Dram." Mangrove's matter of fact statement sounded to Biscetti like funerary words of solace, a gentle, understated way of saying that both girls had gone to Endless Night.

"What are you saying?" She screamed at him.

"Hey," Snotty stepped in. "We don't know what's going on down there, but Dram wouldn't have left that ledge if the danger still existed."

"Tasha's my sister. She's our Queen," Biscetti said. "I have to know what's happened to her."

"Biscetti, we have no way of getting down to the ravines." Snotty said. "You know that."

"I'll go back the way we came. I'll return to the dunes and find my way from there."

Mangrove shook his head. "This is madness. One by one walking off into the maze of ravines is suicide."

"I'm going, Manny. Get that straight."

They stood, their eyes locked, neither giving way.

"I'll go with her, Manny." Snotty broke the impasse. "Sola and Situ can come too."

Mangrove understood what was going on in his friend's mind. Biscetti had cast doubt on Tasha's fate. Her life might hang in the balance. It was Snotty's natural instinct to act. He couldn't bear to think that Tasha and Dram had been deserted when they might need help. "Okay," Manny gave in. "But arm yourselves well and take plenty of food and water."

"Take me too," Cloud said.

From Dram's back, Tasha gave a last glance at the monster. It lay where Dram had felled it, the boulder a tombstone at its head.

The map in Tasha's hand guided a path through the maze. Had she not drawn the charcoal line that snaked its way amongst the images of the spires, they would have remained locked forever in the confusion of ravines.

"Without you, Tasha, I'd never have found my way."

"Without you Dram, I'd be stuck back there with the monster, but please put me down. My leg is killing me and you need to rest."

Tasha wore her backpack into which all they had had been stashed, which meant that Dram bore the whole heavy burden.

Dram set Tasha down to lean against a column. "Let me look at that leg."

In the time since they had started out, Tasha's thigh had swollen terribly. Dram grimaced at the sight. "How's it feel?"

"Like it will burst."

Dram could see that. The skin seemed to be stretched to the limit, forced to expand by the blood and fluid gathered within and among the ruptured muscle cells. The point of impact, an indentation when Dram had last looked, had become a hard, purple lump rising above the general swelling. "You must be hurting."

"Hmm."

"It's really bad, isn't it?"

Tasha nodded.

"Give me the knife, Tasha."

Dram took the Swiss knife from her and with her thumbnail flicked open a number of blades. All were for cutting, not what Dram was looking for. She closed them and looked carefully at the other side of the knife. "Yes, this is what we need."

The short, narrow blade was honed to a sharp point. "You know what I have to do?"

Tasha nodded again. She could scarcely speak. Pain was overwhelming her. "Do it."

Dram plunged the rapier blade into Tasha's thigh. Black blood spurted from the wound, rose like a fountain and as the pressure was released, as quickly fell. Tasha's cry eased to a sigh of relief, the pain ebbing with the blood running from her leg.

"Oh that's so good." Tasha threw her head back and closed her eyes. The haematoma, the blood from crushed and torn vessels that had been dammed within her muscle tissue, had made its escape.

Taking a handful of sand, Dram wiped Tasha's leg clean of most of the blood. "Do you think you can go on?"

"Oh yeah. I feel a whole lot better."

"It's the pressure that causes the pain."

"I know," said Tasha.

Dram lifted Tasha onto her back and they resumed their march.

In the amphitheatre they rested again, the warren of ravines behind them. Dram pointed to the defile that would lead them to the lagoon. "Once through, we could face trouble. There might be more ..." She let the possibility hang in the air. Fear was already churning in her chest.

Tasha took her hand and squeezed. "We'll make it, Dram. We've beaten a monster once. We can do it again if we have to."

"Well ..." The thought, intended to be comforting, did not dispel Dram's doubts.

The amphitheatre had been a welcome release from the tight, restraining confusion of ravines and spires. Emerging from the shadowy defile into the open valley completed the change.

Tasha heard the sound of falling water. For the first time she saw a waterfall and as Dram had done, thought how wonderful it looked. "Since we left Homecave everything has changed." She gazed at the stream cascading from the top of the cliff, at the way it fell to hit ledges, rebounding in spray that rose like smoke to became a veil, gently floating to fall like rain into the lagoon. "Nothing like that was possible in our frozen world."

"It's different." White flecks had dried at the rim of Dram's lips, her tongue dry in her mouth. Standing under the waterfall would be wonderful. "And I really need a drink."

"Yeah, let's do that."

From her position on Dram's back, her head now higher than Dram's and feeling tall, Tasha looked around the valley. The expanse of the lagoon, feathered by the slightest of breezes, reflected the clouds. *It's so pretty.* Admiring the novelty of open water, Tasha sniffed. "I can smell smoke."

"Hmm," Dram said. "When I left here I was in a hurry. The fire I lit is probably still smouldering."

"Dram!" The cry sharp with alarm. The disarming peacefulness of the scene suddenly shattered. "Look there."

On the far side of the lagoon a crocodile lay at rest on the bank. As they watched, the big animal lifted its head, raised its armoured body and slid into the water.

"He's seen us." Dram's voice quaked with panic.

"Put me down, Dram."

"I can't do that."

"You must. Put me down and run to the fire. Please it's the only way."

"I don't underst—"

"Get a brand burning. Our arrows, our knives are useless, but fire may save us."

In the water a spearhead of ripples was coming toward them, parting to a widening chevron. Almost invisible, with only eyes and nostrils a fraction above the surface, the crocodile was closing on the girls.

"I'll walk as best I can. Dram, you have to go!"

Dram eased Tasha to the ground. "Okay." And she ran.

The remains of the fire gave off a faint heat. Dram knelt and with the end of a dry and leafless branch stirred the blackened debris, looking for coals whose faint show of red might be prompted to flame again. She blew, ignoring the flakes of ash that came away, hoping for the glow that would ignite the last of the carbon and give her the flame she needed. She prodded again and gas trapped in the burnt wood flared. "Yes, keep burning, keep burning."

The ragged end, where the stick had broken from its tree, sparked and thin splinters took fire. Dram twisted it so that the stump of the branch came alight and the flame licked up the length, heating the wood until a solid section was burning brightly. She looked up. Tasha was limping toward her, still one hundred metres distant. The vee of ripples that swept back from the nose of the monster had become a speeding dart aiming to strike Tasha.

Dram began to run to her, the flaming branch held high, sparks streaming behind. The monster reached the shallows and lumbered toward the bank, his great tail thrashing the water, his aim to cut Tasha off before she reached Dram.

The three figures were on a collision course.

On so many occasions in the past Tasha had seen the hunter homing in on disabled prey. That was the way with animals, go for the easy mark, energy had to be conserved. Now the law of the hunt was being applied to her. She cried with pain, trying to run.

The croc came from the water. The race intensified. Dram increased her stride, estimating distance, estimating time. She had to reach Tasha before the monster and as she ran, data raced in her brain, the calculation of the equation that involved the different speeds of the three involved and the distance each would cover. Dram had to pinpoint the exact spot at which the three would converge and she had to be there first.

The physics of time and motion, the geometry of moving bodies in space were being processed in her head, the quick-fire neurons of her brain connecting, receiving, sending signals, solving the problem as she ran.

Distance shrank. Dram drove her long legs at the ground, sprinting. Tasha was slowing. Dram could see the blood running from her leg. She watched Tasha fall and the computation was immediately altered.

Dram called on her body to move faster, screaming at the crocodile, drawing his attention away from Tasha.

It was enough. For a moment the big animal was distracted. Dram put herself between it and Tasha. She held the burning torch in front of her, held it like a weapon, her life and Tasha's dependent on a flame.

The crocodile opened his jaws and lunged at Dram. She thrust the fire at him, let him feel the heat. He roared: a deafening, rasping sound that rolled around the valley. But he backed away.

They stood opposed, pitted one against the other, Tasha a fallen bundle huddled on the ground behind Dram.

Tongues of flame flickered blue and yellow. Dram enticed the beast, teasing him with the torch, poking it forward, watching him rear back, jaws wide, the roar striking her ears. She waved the flame from side to side, making the animal sway to avoid it. Dram was asserting her superiority, driving him back.

The crocodile counter-attacked, rushing at Dram again, instinct driving him to take her in his jaws. She held the torch like a club and swung it to pass between the jaws so that the flame shone on rows of teeth and seared mouth-flesh.

The monster roared and hissed, retreated, then turned and, defeated, dragged his giant frame into the water of the lagoon.

Dram sank to the ground beside Tasha. They clung to one another, relieved, exhausted. Where the crocodile had disappeared from view, they saw bubbles occasionally rising to the surface.

"Oh, Dram, without you I'd be ..." Tasha imagined the rows of teeth crushing her, tearing her to pieces. "You were fearless." She gripped Dram's hands. "Thank you."

Dram stared at the rising bubbles. "There was a time when I couldn't have done it ... when I would've left you."

Memories of the crevasse, of the hollow mountain, of Torterats filled the minds of both girls.

"That was a long time ago, Dram."

"It was you who changed me, Tasha."

"Well ..." Tasha paused and smiled. "We're friends now."

"Yes." Dram looked at Tasha's wound. "We have to get away from here. Come, I'll carry you."

"We need to drink." Tasha could see the dried corners of Dram's mouth and her speech had thickened.

"But ..." Dram gestured toward the lagoon.

Tasha picked up the still burning torch. "This should keep unwelcome visitors away."

Holding the flame above the water, Tasha guarded Dram as she drank. "Fill your belly while you can." In turn, she dipped her own face into the water and drank deeply.

"Ready?" Dram asked and getting the nod from Tasha, hurled the burning torch far out into the lagoon.

With Tasha upon Dram's back, the two recommenced their journey. Through the gorge at the mouth of the valley they could see the dunes.

Despite the fact that the group had come over the same mountain ridges only a few days earlier, Sola and Situ were well ahead, the customary advance scouts checking the lay of the land.

Biscetti, Cloud and Snotty followed, commenting on landmarks that had made an impression on the outward journey when the going had been hard. Returning to the dunes was relatively easy. It was not a continuous downhill walk. Valleys intervened, slopes had to be climbed, but all agreed that coming down was a lot easier than going up.

Cloud was walking behind Snotty, looking at the trophy that Mangrove had stuck in his hair. "Will you always wear that feather, Snotty?"

He lifted a hand to lightly touch it. "Yeah, I think it's pretty sharp."

For another hour they kept moving, backtracking down the slopes that had been so difficult to climb. Snotty looked to the west. Through broken cloud the sun was casting long shadows. Daylight would soon be gone. He whistled to the twins, caught their attention and signalled them to stop.

"What are you doing?" Biscetti's question had a hard ring.

Snotty replied that it would soon be dark. "We'll make camp and go on at first light."

About to argue, Biscetti held her tongue. As much as she wanted to get to Tasha, to try to find their way in the mountains at night would be foolhardy. "Okay."

Sola gathered twigs fallen from the sparse scrub that struggled to survive in the rough terrain. With the fire going, they ate, prepared sleeping places and snuggled into furs.

Biscetti gazed up at clouds that seemed to brush across the stars, revealing them, hiding them. Every now and then in the southern sky she could see the cross. To Biscetti the four stars with their nearby pointers symbolised the purpose of the exodus, heavenly bodies promising a better life. And, she thought, Tasha is like the stars. She's the one leading us to our new home. But for a long time, worry kept Biscetti from sleeping. She could not help wondering where her sister might be and whether everything was all right with her.

Once through the gorge, Tasha slid to the ground. Dram dropped to her knees. She had borne the weight of Tasha and all they had in the pack and could walk no further.

The setting sun sealed the decision. Without preparing sleeping places they simply lay down. The day for each had been interminably long, full of action that had tested both physical and mental endurance.

In the twilight, before sleep overtook them, the girls talked, living again the dangers they had faced. Each was praised by the other for her courage. Occasional giggles interrupted as they made fun of situations that at the time they thought they may not survive.

Tasha became serious. "Cloud dreamed of you, Dram. We had no idea at the time, we never do, but I'm sure it was you she saw."

"What did she say?"

"Strange things about a land alive and liquid fire, and there was this riddle." Tasha repeated the words Cloud had uttered when in her trance: *All above, one below, but not alone.*

"I don't get it."

"We were on the mountain looking down at you. You had left us and gone off alone, but the monster had tracked you down. Don't you see? You were alone but not alone."

"Hmm," Dram said. "That's why you came for me."

"Yes."

Dram was quiet for a few moments, thinking. "I'm glad we're friends, Tasha."

"So am I."

The sky darkened and as stars began to show, their talking slowed and pauses intervened while one waited for the other to respond. The silences grew longer and finally nothing more was said. The girls had drifted into sleep.

Biscetti woke as dawn seeped over the mountains. Slowly darkness crept away and with its going, the hills and scrub assumed their form and colour and she could place herself in her surroundings. She stretched, yawned and rose from her sleeping place. There was no point in lying around. They had to get going.

Moving from one to another, Biscetti shook a shoulder or nudged a back with her toe. "Sun's up. We should be on our way."

Snotty peered up at her. "Where's the sun? It's not even proper daylight."

She bent low, her face near his and grinned. "It will be soon."

Despite his initial reluctance, Snotty moved quickly, gathering his gear together, eating as he did so. The others were just as organised and before the first rays of the sun had struck them, they were making their way down the ridge on which they had slept.

Two hours later, Sola called back that he could see the top of the cleft. They were almost at the place Cloud had identified as the point of entry from the dunes. Snotty motioned Sola and Situ to wait. Getting down the cleft would be easier if they were all together.

The twins sat and watched Snotty, Biscetti and Cloud slip and slide down the steep slope as they approached.

Situ tilted his head and turned toward the cleft, concentrating. "Listen."

Sola faced the gash in the cliff, straining to hear. "Yeah." A great grin spread across his face. The voices of Tasha and Dram were coming up to him. "Biscetti," he shouted and waved. "We've found them. Tasha and Dram are in the cleft. We can hear them."

As Sola was giving the good news, Situ called to Tasha, wanting her to know that they were coming to her. "Are you okay?"

Dram answered. "Sola, Tasha's hurt. We need help."

He told her to wait where she was. "We won't be long."

In the next few minutes, their shouts echoing up and down the split in the cliff, the group at the top heard of Tasha's injury.

"Have you got the rope?" Snotty was assessing ways of getting her over the great rocks that in places jammed the cleft.

"Yes. It's frayed a bit, but ..." Dram was confident that little harm had been done.

The others close behind, Snotty clambered down. As he placed hands and feet with care, his thoughts were not for how Tasha would be raised. That would be hard, but not impossible. He was thinking about Dram. She had behaved abominably, deceived her friends and hit her Queen. She had taken the magic needle and left the Camarilla, believing that without it they would be doomed and come crawling back to her. What Dram had done was unforgivable. How would he feel when they were face to face?

Similar thoughts were running in Dram's mind. Snotty had trusted her. They had shared great times together; hunting, exploring, racing over the snow for the sheer fun of it. She had junked their friendship, turned her back on him, cut herself from the whole clan and walked away. Facing him, facing Biscetti, facing all of them would be so humiliating. The hot flush of shame swept over her, reddening her cheeks, her ears. She could see Snotty climbing down.

"Tasha, I can't." Dram took a step backward. "What must they think of me?"

Tasha took Dram's hand. "Leave it to me, okay? Leave it to me."

One after the other, with Snotty arriving first, Biscetti, Cloud and the twins reached Tasha and Dram. All greeted Tasha with a hug and then stood looking at Dram as though she were some kind of curiosity, something that shouldn't be touched.

Limping to stand beside Dram, Tasha put her arm around her. "Dram saved my life, not once but twice." And she told the story of Dram's courage when the prehistoric monsters had attacked them.

"Is that real, Tasha?" Biscetti knew a different Dram. She found the tale hard to believe.

"Every word. And listen, Dram made some mistakes in the past. That's where they stay, in the past, forgiven and now forgotten."

Snotty grinned, his problem solved. He put his arms around Dram. "Welcome back."

In turn, Cloud, Sola and Situ shared their happiness with Dram that she had saved Tasha and had returned. Biscetti's memories held her back. She stood looking at Dram, unsure of making the new commitment.

Dram took the initiative. "I really am sorry Biscetti. Sorry for many things. I should've gone into the crevasse for you. I know that, but I was scared. In the hollow mountain, the bridge coming back — I just wish ..." Tears filled Dram's eyes. "And despite all I'd done to you, you packed extra food without telling Tasha. You thought of me."

Biscetti frowned. She hadn't wanted her compassion to be made known. "You had to eat."

"I did. And you had the sense to suspect I had no food. You were kind when I didn't deserve it."

"Hmm." Biscetti cleared her throat. "Were you lost?"

Dram nodded.

"How come? You have the magic needle."

"It doesn't work any more." Dram took the compass from her pocket and held it for Biscetti and the others to see the wild gyrations of the needle. "Devils playing in the rock. That's what you said, Cloud. Were they playing with me? Are they playing with the needle?"

Cloud shrugged. She could give no answer.

Situ opened his pack. To eat was always a good idea. He offered meat. Sitting, resting at the foot of the gash in the cliff they ate as Tasha and Dram retold the story of the crocodiles.

"We better go." Snotty looked at Tasha's leg. The dark stain of bruising had spread to her knee. "Do you think you can make it?"

She nodded. "It's stiff and still hurts, but we can't stay here. I'll be okay."

It was agreed that to be roped together would be the best way to get Tasha to the top of the cleft. Sola would lead, his task to find the best possible way around or over the rocks that barred the narrow upward climb. Behind him would be Situ, then Cloud, then Biscetti. Dram as the strongest would be directly ahead of Tasha. Snotty would be last in line, assisting Tasha, supporting her where necessary and as the backstop should anything go wrong.

Mountain climbers, strung at intervals, they picked their way carefully higher until they stood with the cleft behind them. Tasha said that she was fine. "Let's keep going."

The hardest part of the climb had been accomplished successfully. Nevertheless, many ridges lay ahead and, as they had learned, each presented its challenge. At Snotty's suggestion they remained tied, easing the way for Tasha and a precaution should she slip.

Constant movement, the bending and stretching of climbing proved to be good therapy. Tasha knew that for days to come the bruise would seep its way down her leg, but the forced activity was bringing back flexibility and dulling the pain. As the linked climbers made their way higher, she found that she could move more easily.

Well before sunset, Snotty thought it wise that they call it a day. All of them had been going over hard ground since dawn and exertion had taken its toll. On the relatively flat top of yet another ridge they made camp. Situ got a fire going and sleeping places were prepared. The meal was quickly eaten and as the light began to dwindle, each lay down to sleep. The last thing Tasha saw before she closed her eyes was the distant silhouette of the sleeping hare.

Chapter 33

Dumperty took Mangrove's hand. "Can we climb the bluff and see if Snotty's coming?"

"Why not?" Mangrove doubted that the group would be on their way back, but he could not mention to Dumperty the many unpredictable events that might intervene to slow or even prevent the safe return of Snotty and the others.

Hand in hand, he and the little boy walked up the slope to higher ground and as they did, Mangrove was thinking about the possible fate of his friends. It might be days before Snotty got back and if the worst happened ... Mangrove tried to wipe the thought from his mind, but the reality was that Dram, Tasha, the others, had all ventured into unfamiliar territory. He had in mind the scene that Cloud had described among the spires of the ravines. Anything could have happened.

Dumperty sat on the bluff and patted the ground beside him. "Sit here, Manny."

The country they had crossed a few days earlier, the folds of the range, the ridges and the valleys, spread before their eyes.

"When do you think they'll come, Manny?"

"It could be a while. We'll just sit here and watch out for them."

The two sat quietly, waiting for figures to appear on some far-off ridge. Sunshine bathed them with warmth and sitting, idling the time away, the fears that troubled Mangrove were calmed.

He stretched out, the sun pleasantly pressing upon him and might have slept, but Dumperty's yell, the pulling at his sleeve, brought him fully awake.

"There they are. Manny, they're coming."

Mangrove sat up. With his hand shading his eyes, he saw distant specks. First one and then more appearing. "You're right."

"Can we go to meet them?"

Mangrove didn't answer. He was counting the antlike figures, wanting to assure himself that success, not failure, was bringing his friends home early. He added the numbers and grinned. "That's just what we'll do."

Running down the slope of the bluff, Dumperty shouted the news. The word that the Foragers had been seen whipped through the camp. Zita, Belle, Vellum and Hock joined Mangrove and Dumperty. They would come too. Others had the same idea. The welcoming party swelled, became a streamer tagged to Manny and Dumperty, everyone excited that the expedition had returned, all eager to be the first to hear what had happened. The fact that Dram was one of the party put a keener edge to curiosity.

When the two groups came together, Dram stood apart, self-conscious about her past behaviour. In the hubbub of questions, with so many people talking at once and the happy laughter of friends that were again together, Dram was alone. The reunion at the bottom of the cleft was being repeated. She was the odd girl out, a stranger in a gathering to which she had once belonged. Acceptance of the fact that she had betrayed the trust of her friends seemed to shrink the organs of her body. Dram felt hollow, no longer tall and strong. In her own eyes she had become small, shrunken by remorse. *Is it always going to be like this?* That she would be treated as an outcast was a dismal thought.

Tasha saw Dram standing alone, went to her and taking her hand brought her to the centre of the group. The laughing and loud talking faded to silence.

Looking into every face, Tasha made it clear that without Dram's courage, their Queen would never have returned. She took time to tell the whole story, omitting no detail, wanting full understanding of the role Dram had played. "Without Dram, I would already be lost in Endless Night. She saved me from the monsters and she carried me when I couldn't walk. Dram is with us again, just as she used to be. She is one of the Camarilla, one of the trusted band. There is nothing more to be said."

Dumperty ran to Dram. Lifted in her arms he hugged her and told her how glad he was that she was home. Mangrove waited until Dram had set Dumperty down. He felt relief that Tasha had reinstated Dram. The clan depended on unity. How else would they have survived in a world set against them? To lose both Tasha and Dram would have been a terrible blow. Dram had disappointed him, but she had redeemed herself. With them both back and differences buried, the Camarilla was whole again. Mangrove put his arms around Dram and thanked her for bringing Tasha home safely.

Belle, Zita, all the others took their turn to welcome Dram, enveloping her in warmth. Dram smiled. A new chapter of her life had begun.

Tasha called Sola and Situ to her side and instructed them to run on ahead. Like town criers they were to announce to those who had stayed at the camp the full story of the exploits she had shared with Dram. "There are to be no recriminations. There is no reason for them. Make sure that is understood."

Messengers bearing good news, the twins set off, happy to have the responsibility and glad to run.

Advised in advance, those at the camp prepared their greeting. Jemma took charge. The return of their Queen, the restoration of Dram as a loyal Forager, had to be celebrated with a feast. By the time the cavalcade entered the camp, pots were bubbling, the enticing smells of cooking adding richness to the reception.

For hours after sunset the rejoicing continued. Tasha played her flute and tapped her foot when others made the tunes. Melodies and the words of songs floated across the rust-red range. In the clear night sky the uncountable stars shone diamond-bright upon the festivities and high above the sleeping hare, the jewelled points of the Southern Cross presented their lure to the dancers. A promise gleamed, but a promise of what?

As they both caught their breath from dancing, Mangrove sat by Tasha. "One of us and two of us become one of us." He quoted from Cloud. "It happened as she said it would. The clan was a happy unit, we became divided, but now we are whole again."

"That's true, and death falling from the sky almost took you, but Manny, Cloud said more."

"Yes."

Among the revellers, in the quiet island of thought they shared, Tasha and Mangrove hoped that whatever materialised from Cloud's vision, fate would be kind.

Everyone slept late, rising only when the sun had left mid-morning behind. Throughout the camp, conversations recalled the fun of the previous night. In good humour, people readied to take up the journey again, performing the ritual of packing belongings that had become a familiar part of daily life. Bent over, busy ensuring nothing was left behind, the sound of thunder rolled among them with a force that shook pots and set loose articles to rattle. Those who had stooped to stuff their packs suddenly straightened, searching the faces of neighbours for some explanation of the unexpected sound.

Mangrove looked toward the sleeping hare. Dark cloud was sweeping over it, boiling higher as he watched. Inside the moving mass, lightning flickered in places, momentarily turning purple to yellow that instantly darkened as the lightning played elsewhere.

Fascinated, Mangrove watched the cloud approach, building in volume, barrelling across the sky as though it were alive. He ran to Tasha. Lightning, no longer confined to the sky, struck in brilliant shafts that joined earth with cloud for long quivering, malevolent moments. Each strike was closer, electric prongs jabbing at the rust-red ground, finger-walking toward the Camarilla. All around, sound split the air and hammered at the ears of frightened people.

Tasha watched as a tree was blasted, the power of the bolt cutting it to the ground, leaving it burning. "Lie down, lie down."

She hobbled a few steps and shouted again, using her arms to motion that everyone should drop to the ground. Satisfied that her instruction was obeyed, she lay beside Mangrove.

"This is wild." He spoke looking up at the sky, reminded of storms that he and Snotty had weathered, thinking of the last time he had seen such a sky. "Tasha, I think it's going to snow."

"Is it cold enough?"

"No but —" He felt something strike his face and run wet down his cheek. "Hey, what's this?"

Around them the earth began to erupt in tiny bursts of dust. Mangrove held out his hand. A raindrop slapped against it. Mangrove licked his palm. "It's water. Water is falling from the sky."

Amid the flash of lightning and claps of thunder, the rain became heavier until it fell in a cloudburst upon the camp. The Camarilla were experiencing the first rain of their lives. It wet their heads and faces and trickled inside their clothing, but as the lightning moved on, people stood and stamped in puddles and laughed. Rain; no one could have imagined that water would come from the sky.

Clouds are soft, Mangrove thought. I've seen the wind pushing them as they float. Snow is as soft as the down of tiny birds, but water? How does a cloud hold water? It was a puzzle he could not immediately solve.

The rain passed and with the sun the cavalcade got underway. The ground steamed in the sunlight and all people could talk about was the strange phenomenon that had fallen out of the clouds.

Walking with Tasha, helping her at difficult spots that hurt her leg, Mangrove's mind was occupied. He saw tendrils of steam rise from the damp earth and watched as the vapour thinned and disappeared. Walking automatically, his thoughts elsewhere, he recalled Homecave when cooking pots had boiled and clouds of steam had risen. In his memory there were pictures of the roof of Homecave when sometimes it had become wet and drops had fallen from where steam from cooking had condensed. He wondered if there was a similarity. Shaking his head, still unsure, Mangrove came to the conclusion that the smoky tendrils rising from the wet ground must join the air and invisibly rise to the sky at sometime to form again into cloud. Why it should fall as water remained a mystery. Well, he thought, some things cannot be explained.

For three days they climbed steep ridges, eyes fixed on the sleeping hare. On the fourth day, the sun rose with the band looking up at the heights of the goal. By nightfall the whole group expected to be at the summit of the mountain. What lay beyond would then be revealed to them.

Tasha had the map in her hands looking with some nostalgia at the lines drawn on it. The map had been invaluable. Without it, plotting the easiest passage through the mountains would not have been possible. She spent a moment tracing the path she had taken through the ravines to rescue Dram. That's another thing, she thought, if Dumperty had not brought the picture from that place, we would have lost Dram. Tasha folded the map and put it in her pocket. Its usefulness would end when they all stood at the peak of the sleeping hare, but she would keep it as a memento. She ran her hand over her thigh. A slight soreness remained, but the stiffness had gone. The mountain would not present a problem to her.

At midday, Snotty and Mangrove examined the challenge yet to be climbed. The sleeping hare appeared larger than they had thought and the shape, so easily recognised from a distance, had lost its clear definition. Nevertheless they were content that the summit would be conquered by late afternoon. Their plan was to mount the shoulder of the hare and from there climb to the laid-back ears.

The rain that had fallen a few days before seemed to have washed the sky clean, polished it to peerless blue and given the sunlight an extra brightness. Where in places the red rock of the range had not dried, it had the sheen of fresh paint.

In the sparkle of the perfect day, raptors were circling, searching for the updrafts that would lift them to altitudes where they had an unbroken view of the world below.

Snotty watched the spiralling birds and laughed. "Once on top of the hare, we'll see what they see. To be so high, Manny, we'll be like birds."

"Keep an eye on those raptors. I don't trust them."

"They learned their lesson," Snotty said. He had reason to believe it. The birds of prey had not attempted to attack again.

"Perhaps." Manny was not convinced.

They led the others in the climb.

On the final incline that would take them to the shoulder, Mangrove stopped and cocked his head. "Listen."

"Yeah, what is that?"

Below, the file of climbers halted, their heads tilted upward as they watched and wondered what was going on.

Manny and Snotty were standing quite still, only their heads moving in an effort to locate from where the sound was coming and to identify what they were hearing.

Tasha and Dram clambered up the slope to join them and they heard a subdued growling.

"Is it thunder?" The sound was new to Tasha, yet it had the quality not unlike an approaching storm, the rumbling of gathering clouds.

Snotty shook his head. "This sound is continuous. Listen carefully. It rises and falls, but it's always there."

"Yes. Like water falling into the lagoon." Dram glanced at Tasha, bringing the scene back to mind. There was a resemblance.

Snotty had not seen or heard water falling. To him, the dull roar filling the air could have come from a distant avalanche. "There's only one way to find out," he said. "I'm going up."

Tasha made no comment. Snotty looked at her, waiting for the nod to get on his way. She hesitated. Since they had left Homecave, danger had intruded at almost every turn. Too often their lives had been imperilled by events they could not foresee and over which they had no control. *To have come so far and endured so much ...* She looked down at the upturned faces of the climbers and thought of the ones who had fallen to the wraiths in Kaldor. In her ears the roaring rose and fell but never ceased. *This may be the end for all of us.*

Thoughts that the privations of the exodus had been suffered for no purpose, that flight from the Torterats had only delayed the inevitable, were like sharpened flakes of flint, cutting her with doubt.

"Well?" Snotty was impatient.

"You wait here. This is a risk I must take."

Mangrove argued that he and Snotty had spent years chancing their luck with the unknown. They were experienced, Tasha should send them. "One thing's for sure, no one should go alone." He raised his eyes to the raptors rising in the air currents.

Tasha remembered Avon's counsel that a Queen must seek advice and take it into account when making decisions. Manny's advice had merit. But Avon had also said the Queen's greatest strength lay in having the courage of her conviction.

Sheltered by the rising shoulder of the sleeping hare, standing in sunshine so bright that the land around them gleamed as though newly minted, yet with the air full of sound that they could not explain, Tasha faced again the dilemma she hated. Whatever decision she made would be wrong, or it could be right. *Why must it be this way?*

"Don't leave me out, Tasha." Dram tapped her bow.

Tasha nodded. Manny was right and Dram was the best shot. Perhaps there was safety in numbers and there was no way of telling what they might be up against.

"Okay. The four of us will go."

Tasha called to the line of people below to stay where they were. She and Dram with Snotty and Manny would check out what lay beyond the sleeping hare.

Chapter 34

With every step on the slope that took them toward the shoulder of the mountain, the noise grew louder. It rose and fell, sometimes booming, fading to a growl that rolled on and on before becoming louder again.

The air eddied around them, elevating the sound, depressing it. "There must be a wind at the summit," Mangrove said. "The higher we go the stronger it will be."

Dram began to shake. The sound was low-pitched, but its rising intensity took her back to the monster coming at her. She imagined a pack of the giant animals that perhaps had detected a whiff of human scent to stir them to anger.

Tasha calmed Dram. It couldn't be, but the possibility did exist. The sound was ever louder.

"If you're right Dram ..." Mangrove was listening intently. *We're getting closer.* The air around them had become a cauldron of noise.

From afar, the ears of the hare had appeared smooth. In fact they were not. Exposed rock had weathered to create a thin soil. From it, rough gorse eked a poor existence and in depressions, short trees had taken root. The Foragers stood between the ears, the wind plucking at their clothing. They stood fifty metres below their goal.

"From here I go alone," Tasha said.

The others nodded. That was Forager practice.

Tasha climbed, at times clutching at gorse to pull herself higher, using the rock where it suited her purpose. The breeze was much stronger, the roar louder, riding on the wind. Breathing through open mouth, Tasha felt her heart beating in her throat. In a few metres she would be at the crest. On the plateau swept bare of cover, she would be conspicuous. She looked back at the three watching her and waved. The time had come.

A tiny figure, flat to the ground, she scrabbled upward. All she could hear was the roaring in her ears, no longer rising and falling, but a flat line of immense sound. She raised her head. The plateau was wide. If she wanted to see, she would have to stand.

Tasha rose to her feet and walked across the barren summit of the sleeping hare. As she walked her eyes widened until standing at the far edge she sank to her knees and gave thanks to the stars.

Below, the ocean broke upon yellow sand, wave following wave, lines of breakers curling, smashing down, exploding in white to roll on jumbling to the shore. Tasha stood with her hair flying in the wind and listened to the noise of the surf.

She could see valleys that ran back from scalloped beaches, valleys that were green and welcoming, extending back to hills thick with trees. Way in the distance the perfect cone of a single mountain rose high. From its peak a wisp of white curled into the blue.

Tasha gazed on a place like no other she had ever seen and knew that this was the south they had travelled so far to find.

Running back she shouted for Dram and Mangrove and Snotty to come up. In her excitement, laughing and crying, trying to tell them what they were about to see, lacking words for so many things because they were new to her and to them.

The four stood in wonder and saw paradise.

Mangrove recalled Tasha's words. *I don't know what we're looking for, but when we find it we'll know.* He caught her eye. She smiled widely, knowing what he was thinking. "This is it, Manny."

"I know," he said. "You've found the place we'll call home."

Epilogue

The new land laid out its promise. New lands always do, but promises are not always kept. The valleys that Tasha and Mangrove admired and saw as their new home had also attracted others. Whilst no humans had entered the lovely valleys for millennia, during those thousands of years other beings had fought for territory and survival.

The new land was a place where benefits abounded. It was also a place of ambush, of death that could come without warning. The Camarilla would enter their unnamed paradise, seen by the unseen. Whatever they did would not go unnoticed.

At the very moment of success, standing on the summit of the sleeping hare, the trusted band was, without knowing it, between the hammer and the anvil; Torterats behind, the unknown in front.

Life for the Camarilla was about to become very interesting.

www.ingramcontent.com/pod-product-compliance
Lightning Source LLC
Chambersburg PA
CBHW072206170626
46813CB00003B/813